ROXANE
GAY
BO□KS

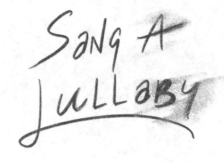

And Then He Sang A Lullaby

Ani Kayode Somtochukwu

ROXANE
GAY
BO□KS

New York

FIRST EDITION

Published simultaneously in Canada
Printed in the United States of America

First Grove Atlantic hardcover edition: June 2023

This book was set in 12 point Bembo MT Pro by
Alpha Design & Composition of Pittsfield, NH

Library of Congress Cataloging-in-Publication data is available for this title.

ISBN 978-0-8021-6075-1
eISBN 978-0-8021-6076-8

Roxane Gay Books
an imprint of Grove Atlantic
154 West 14th Street
New York, NY 10011

Distributed by Publishers Group West

groveatlantic.com

23 24 25 26   10 9 8 7 6 5 4 3 2 1

For my mother, Ifeoma,
whose life and death taught me to never
simply accept this unjust world as it is.

And for Harold,
who will always live on in my heart.

CHAPTER ONE

August's mother refused to name him before his birth. There remained this gentleness still, to the child growing in her womb. A hushed quality that kept her from pinning her hopes on it. She would not name the baby until it was squirming in her arms. Her daughters did not understand this. Or at least Uzoamaka and Chinyere did not. The youngest, Peculiar, was too young to understand or not understand. She simply walked in her sisters' footsteps and repeated the questions they asked. It wasn't something their mother could explain to them. She did not want them to worry. She herself worried sometimes, when her faith faltered. On those occasions, she read herself the letter she'd received from Kaduna, sitting in the darkness of her room. To her right, the curtains were drawn, as though if she let light fall on the brown paper, it would crumble into dust in her shaking hands.

Dearest sister, you will have a son, and it shall not kill you. I dreamt of your blessing. God is always faithful, and His word says, of whose report shall we believe? Have faith.

Her sister's letter did not make her heart impervious to her doctor's warning. She still remembered the way he'd pointed at her.

"Mrs. Akasike, I hope you heard me. *Don't* try again. Don't, at all, at all. You will *not* survive it. Take care of the ones God has given you."

But the letter made her feel as though she had God's very own grace behind her and with that came a sort of courage. A courage that eluded her husband.

"I'm afraid," he told her once, his head resting on the roundness of her stomach.

They were in the living room. She, lying sideways on the couch so that her protruding belly was resting on the cushion. He, sitting on the floor in nothing but shorts, rubbing her stomach gently. The children had already retired to their rooms and an old episode of *Checkmate* was playing on the TV. She loved his belly rubs, and the way his whole face would light up if he felt the baby move.

"It's just pregnancy," she said, laughing.

When he kissed her stomach, rubbed his cheek against the warmth of her belly, she said, "God will make a name for himself. I trust in him."

August grew up thinking his mother brave, though foolish. It was one of those things he never said out loud, a thought he allowed himself only in the privacy of his own mind. He knew how sad it would make his sisters. How they would repeat it to one another, whispering, making sure their whispers were loud enough for him to hear.

"Did you hear what August said? Did you hear?" Their heads would be shaking morosely from side to side.

Sometimes, when August said or did something his sisters thought unacceptable, they told him a story about his mother to make him sufficiently remorseful for what he had done. What she had sacrificed for him to live. August gathered all those stories, nursed them until they were ingrained in him, almost memories of his own. He knew the folds of his mother's skin, the round immunization scar on her right shoulder, the contours and ridges of the stretch marks that danced outward from her navel in slender lines, even the way her voice broke when she cried. He knew his story, too, every bit of it. Every detail of every event. He could trace the defiance in his mother's face as she sat in the car almost two months before her due date, trying to breathe deeply and evenly. The more he ruminated on these memories, the more he was enveloped with pangs of incompleteness, an almost, something he should feel that he never would, someone he knew enough to love but never met.

She would have been alive were it not for you, he sometimes thought to himself.

August was named by the nurse who cared for him the morning he was born. She picked the name for its promising meaning. Awe-inspiring. Majestic. Venerable. But August Akasike, at birth, was none of those things. Knowing that August's mother had no son and had been told by the doctor not to have more children, the nurse saw him in an almost heavenly light. When she held him, his pale-yellow skin thin and scratching, he appeared to her to be the most glorious baby she had ever held in her hands.

As dawn approached, the rain thundering heavily outside, August's father was nowhere to be found. The way August's sisters relayed the story of their father's disappearance, the way Uzoamaka clicked her tongue, and Chinyere sighed, "We waited and waited and waited for him," August could have sworn he knew, even as a baby, that he had been abandoned. Stories had that effect on him. They possessed him over and over, until they stopped being mere stories and his mind drew up urgency and emotions and tears. By the time he was seven, it was almost impossible for August to imagine that he did not bear conscious witness to them. Each time he saw his father, each time the man refused to look him in the face, August remembered that night, that emptiness of space where his father's body should have stood.

The night preceding August's birth, the rain thundered down so heavily on the streets of Enugu that one could barely hear one's self speak. When he was seven, August dreamt each night of rain, hard violent rain, and woke to paralyzing pain in his thighs. Sometimes, on the nights he saw his mother's shadow looming somewhere in the shower of rain, he felt the pain in his arms too. The doctors had no idea what was wrong with him. When he woke up in tears, his sisters would assemble in his room, their voices low, so as not to wake their father. They massaged his aching muscles, and Uzoamaka told him a story from when their mother was alive because she knew how stories of her calmed him. It could be the most mundane of things. An afternoon their mother fed Chinyere ice cream as the hairdresser styled her hair into painful braids. Or the day she lost her footing and fell, just outside their compound. Or the day she drove to Uzoamaka's school to scold the headmistress. August loved that story because of how much it animated his mother. It was the only memory he had of her where she quarreled. He liked to imagine that it was him she defended like that. Because she knew he loved that story, Uzoamaka told it many times.

She was in primary two and her teacher had flogged her for losing her pencil. Their mother was furious. They drove to the school that afternoon and caught the teacher just before she left. The bewildered teacher was sitting at her table, doing up her makeup. She stood to her feet when she apologized, as though that would calm August's mother, but the apologies fell on stubborn ears.

"My sister," the teacher called August's mother. "My sister, you know how careless these children can be."

"Don't sister me," August's mother was shouting.

The headmistress heard the noise and came to intervene. And so, their mother turned her fury on the more authoritative figure.

"How do you flog a six-year-old because she lost a pencil? What is wrong with you people in this school?" their mother asked.

When Uzoamaka shared this detail, she pointed the way their mother had pointed, index finger sticking out straight, the thumb above it pointing up, the three other fingers below it slightly curved. August practiced keeping his hand that way. And when he did, it made him feel as though he was there, standing timidly in the safety of his mother's shadow as she went to war for him.

The stories distracted him from the pain. And even then, his sisters would stay till he fell asleep again. Later, after a doctor at the Teaching Hospital at Ituku-Ozalla laughed at him and said, "It's nothing serious, it's just growing pains.

The pain stops on its own, no?" the dreams stopped and with them, the pain. For a long while after, August felt guilty for keeping his sisters worried all those nights for something that wasn't serious, just his body visiting him with a bit of the pain with which he'd arrived on this earth. August's mother—and August knew this—had screamed and screamed the night before he was born. The furious rain made it hard for her screams to reach far past their car, but her voice reverberated, branding fear in the hearts of everyone inside the car. August knew the pitch of those screams. He knew how scared his sisters were. He remembered his own fear, or something of that nature, which he imagined for himself. He remembered, too, the hardness of his father's face as he made it through the traffic. In August's memories, there was a benevolent Angel of Death whispering in his father's ears, the way benevolent spirits warned bereaved people of their loved ones' deaths, in the face of dire illness or other such insurmountable circumstances. He knew his father had not steeled his heart for this eventuality, and so it broke him when it happened, damaging him as badly as a man could be damaged.

August knew all these things. What he didn't know was *how* he was born. In the matters of August first, Uzoamaka was the central authority—but even she was unsure. All she knew was that their mother went into a curtained room and screamed and screamed and screamed, until her voice died, a whittling fire on a cold harmattan night. And after that, there was only silence—long-pressed silence that stretched and stretched until the Angel of Death came for them too.

"You came in the morning," his sister told him once. "Some hours before Daddy returned, they put you in my hands, just for a few minutes. August, you were so beautiful."

But August knew that part wasn't true. He had read all the medical reports and heard them say it. He was yellow, a sickly kind of yellow. He was tiny and had cracked skin. There were many things he remembered the doctor saying to his father. *Elevated bilirubin. Neonatal jaundice. Malnourished.*

He cherished those reports because they gave him something his sisters didn't have—memories his sisters' stories didn't birth. He sometimes imagined his father ran away after, not before, he saw him, with his skin looking as though it would peel right off his bones. He imagined the man took one look at the sickly baby that killed his wife and ran.

August's birth broke his father. It somehow robbed him of the strength to continue living. The man August grew up knowing to be his father was a ghost for whom life held no more surprises, or disappointments, no pain or happiness. When his sisters discussed this, when they talked of their father way back when he still cared, when he was still the type of man who picked up his children and tickled them, they made sure to absolve August of guilt.

"If only death did not take Mummy," they said. "Death is wicked. So cruel."

But August knew. So versed was he in the art of knowing, in the skill of unwrapping his sisters' words until he discovered the truth they never admitted to themselves. Before his birth, August's father was a happy man who clicked his tongue at the mere suggestion of a second wife.

"O' boy," he would say to his friends when they made the suggestion, "you want to break my home? You want to put me at loggerheads with my God and my wife? Though I'm not even sure what the difference is some days." Then he would laugh, the sound of his laughter saturating the air and squashing all dissent. When his wife told him about the prophecy, he laughed too. His laughter was always his answer, the weapon with which he fought the world.

"Look at the letter my sister sent me from Zaria," she said. She placed the letter on the mattress.

"Are you actually serious?" he asked her.

"You've not even looked at the letter. It's from Amara—"

"I don't care if it's from Abacha. This is foolishness!"

His wife buried her face in her hands and began to cry. He stopped, sat back down on the bed, and put an arm on her back.

"Come on now, it's not a crying matter," he said, rubbing her back gently. He had always felt great powerlessness in the face of her tears.

"Why must my own be different?" she said. "What sin have I done that God would deny me a son?"

August's father wanted to hold his wife, to console her, but he did not want to water the seeds of hope in her mind.

"I don't care what people say," he told her.

He was lying. He remembered the letter his mother sent him telling him how people were calling him a weak man who could not father sons. Why else would an only child not remarry? It had bruised him, especially because he knew his mother could not write. She had dictated that letter to someone else. Still, he spoke the lie because it was a good lie.

"I don't care," he said. "Don't listen to what people say. We have three beautiful girls. You want to die and leave them for who? For what?"

August's mother had a point to prove, a duty to fulfill. And so, August came. The morning of his birth, August's father knew even while running about trying to save his wife that he would never forgive himself if she died. They told him there were too many complications facing both baby and mother. She lost so much blood that the blood the hospital had in its blood bank was insufficient to see her through her surgery.

He called just about everybody he could think of. He drove to Akwuke to pick up a colleague of his whose blood count ended up being too low to donate. Then he continued calling. "We have notified our contacts too. Hopefully we'll find a donor in time," the doctor said.

If he could have given his wife all the blood in him, he would have. But their types did not match. He would have offered his children as donors, too, but he knew their blood types matched his. A positive. Later when he learnt that August was O positive like his mother, he would break down and weep at the irony, the cold cruel irony. He had just arrived with the fourth person who could maybe save his wife's life, his own life—a friend of his wife's who swore to be O positive—when they told him his wife had died, bled out on the table. No one's fault, they swore. The surgery most likely would not have saved her anyway. At first, August's father got in his car to get air, to get away from the stench of disinfectants in the hospital. Then he drove from the hospital down through the landscaped streets of GRA. The rains had stopped and, in its place, was pitch silence, punctuated only by the sound of his own breathing and the car engine. He drove all the way to their home on Zik's Avenue. He turned the engine off and resting his head on his steering wheel, he wept.

He had never known loss like this, loss so encompassing he was fighting the knowledge itself, knowing what it would do to him. He did not immediately return to the hospital; he did not want his children to see him broken like that. It took him long hours sitting alone in the noise of his own tears to gather himself. Yet back at the hospital, when he looked down at August all tiny and shriveled, possessed with such tragic beauty, he bent over the boy and sobbed again. Uzoamaka hugged her father's waist, and it made him more inconsolable to realize how much his children needed him, and how uncertain he was that there was any of him left to give.

August stayed in the hospital for ten weeks before it was safe to take him home. When he was brought home, it seemed as though the stream of visitors would never stop. They brought gifts with condolences. An *ndo* sitting next to a Praise Master Jesus. Sympathies offered with congratulations. August's paternal grandmother danced, quite happily. She never cared for August's mother and was happy her only son now had a son of his own, someone to carry on the family name.

Afamefula, she called August. What sort of name was August anyway? What kind of silly person named a child after a month? Afamefula Akasike! The name never stuck and never made it onto his birth certificate. After August's grandmother died, the name was forgotten but its spirit never left August. He sometimes felt it, heard it in the voice of his mother. *You must bear this name,* the voice seemed to say. *You must carry on the blood of your father and his fathers before him. No one else will do this, if not you.*

Sometimes it made sense. Most times it didn't. But so much had been sacrificed to carry this name, to preserve it for the sons who would follow. Once, when August was barely six, his grandmother told him this. That he had to bear this responsibility as carefully as he bore his own life. "You live not just for yourself, Afam. You live for us all. For Akasike. Always remember," she said. That was a year before she died.

August never liked her much. On the day of her funeral, he did not cry. At first, when he saw the commotion, the old, wrinkled women rolling on the floor until their skin tore, the old men shouting in hoarse voices, he wanted to cry, but his sisters were all stony-faced. They sat next to each other in the first row of the family canopy next to their father. The canopy was beige and brown and tilted left, as though it couldn't make up its mind if it wanted to stand or fall. Everyone expected them to lead the crying, but they were calm, stoic even. August did not know what to read in those faces. Only later in life, after he had been blessed with the gift of a defiant young mind, would he realize what his sisters' faces said, that a woman's children would pay their mother's dues. That night, after the funeral, his sisters traded stories of their grandmother. Those are part of August's memories too. That Thursday in May 1989, his grandmother said something that made his mother bend over the stove and weep—he was in that kitchen. He was sitting on the fridge or standing by the door.

After Peculiar was born, when his grandmother wondered out loud why a woman would only give birth to girls and still refuse to die, or to allow her husband to marry someone else, August was sitting next to his tired mother as she cried onto the baby she cradled in her arms.

He remembered, too, the laugh of triumph that came to his grandmother when she heard that her son's wife had borne a son, and now slept in death.

August grew to resent his grandmother, even in her death. It was one of those things he kept hidden within himself and away from the fussy ears of his sisters. He imagined they would break if they knew there was space in his heart for resentment. They allowed him no vices, not even the ones they allowed themselves. August, always, was the beautiful, pure baby their mother left them. A parting gift, a promise fulfilled, something to nurture. And so, they shielded him as much as they could from things like hate, things that could hinder a beautiful boy from growing into a beautiful man. But there was only so much salvation a boy could suckle at the feet of his sisters . . . only so much. At night when he closed his eyes, August saw his mother's face, heard her voice, looked into her eyes, felt the heaviness of her sacrifice, and woke plagued with feelings of unworthiness. He was not sure he was strong enough to be what he knew everyone expected, a perfect boy who would take the torch that was the family name and run his own race. He was not sure his frail bones were strong enough to bear the burden that was his name.

CHAPTER TWO

August was not very good at school, but he was strong. He knew this—his grades hovered right below average—but he was strong enough to shove whichever of his peers shamed him for it into the dirt and feed them sand. His sisters of course fussed over this, too, the unruliness. They said to him, "August, this is not how a child with your potential should behave."

When he brought home his report cards, they put their hands under their chins and shook their heads from side to side, as the results moved from one disappointed set of hands to the other.

"August, God blessed you with a powerful brain. Why are you not putting it to good use?" Uzoamaka asked him once.

August imagined his mother saying those words. *God blessed you, August. You must reflect God's blessing.*

What he could not make up for in class, he did on the field and the track. He lived to hear the crowd cheering his name, clapping as they watched him zoom past other athletes. He sometimes wondered what he would have done if his PE teacher in primary three had not pulled him aside that afternoon and said, "You like running, right? Yes, you do. See the long legs God blessed you with."

Now it was *the* thing he was known for. He was the boy who could run really fast.

"Quick as lightning, this one. Our very own Jesse Owens," his principal used to say.

Everyone said the same thing about him on the football field. "He's not that good a player, but when he gets the ball, no one can catch him. Quick as lightning."

August loved that they loved him. The afternoons each year when his school held inter-house competitions were his happiest and most memorable, not because of the buckets and bowls he won for finishing first place, but because being cheered on by a crowd was as close as he'd ever come to a surety of self.

Weeks after his fourteenth birthday, by an act of God, or something just as significant, August saw Usain Bolt on television for the first time. It was an instant thing, his worship for the superstar athlete. He was sitting on the floor, his sisters splayed on the seats around him, but he could well have been alone. It felt that way to him, like a personal encounter of existential consequence. The competitors were arranged on the track, bouncing around, warming up, and even then, August knew that Usain Bolt would win. There was just something glorious about him. The dark chocolate hue of his skin. The way his muscled legs poured out from underneath his green track shorts. The protrusion of his crotch. When the camera fixed its gaze on Usain Bolt's face, and he waved, August felt his neck heat up. When Usain Bolt won, beating his chest as he broke through the tape, August jumped with joy. His sisters looked at him, and then at each other, bemused. They would never understand the nature of his obsession with Usain Bolt, or its extent.

In his room, August practiced Usain Bolt's victory stance, wearing his tightest shorts and a gold jersey top. He thought about Usain Bolt's crotch sometimes. In truth, it scared him, how often he thought about it. On certain days he stuffed his own crotch with socks to give it a bulge. He looked down at it in the mirror and separated his legs a few centimeters. He pulled his hand back into Usain's victory stance, the lightning bolt. He could almost hear a crowd shouting his name. He imagined he would one day be a professional athlete, just like Usain Bolt, and hundreds of thousands of people would come out to cheer his name. It would no longer matter that his highest grade was a C in Agriculture.

He did try to improve his grades. Days before his exams, he would sit in his room for hours staring at the words in his notes, trying to absorb the knowledge. But his results always came out the same. August dreaded getting his results. His sisters' disappointment, his father's thinly veiled indifference, it made him shake. August's father did not care what he scored in his exams. August sometimes wondered if the man cared about anything at all. Every term he brought back yet another unsatisfactory result, his sisters would scrutinize it all afternoon, and then nudge him toward their father in the evening.

"Go, show him. He doesn't bite."

They said the same thing when they simply wanted August to sit with him.

"He's your father. Just sit with him, talk to him."

August approached his father always with shaky feet. His father had never given him a reason to be afraid, but something about the man's perpetual disconsolation scared August anyway. His father would take the result sheet and read through it slowly, looking up occasionally to meet August's eyes. Those glances were the closest August came to knowing his father, or at least August thought so.

After reading the results, his father would hand them back. "There's always room for improvement," he would say.

And because August suspected that more should be said— he saw it in those glances his father gave him while reading the results—those looks seemed to be filled with apology. *Sorry, but I can't bring myself to care.*

One year, August got two Bs. One in Agriculture and another in Social Studies, but as though in a trade-off, he'd failed both English and Math. By then, he was nearly thirteen and had just finished his second year of secondary school. Uzoamaka was preparing to take her fifth Medicinae Baccalaureus exams. August knew how stressed and excited she was. He suspected she studied throughout the entire night and all day, every day too.

"Sis, are you even human?" he would ask her before he left for school. The question always made her laugh.

"Soon August," she'd say. "Soon I'll be a doctor."

He knew that the REPEAT written on his result sheet in all caps would create a tear in the harmonious orderliness of everything. When she saw the result, Uzoamaka lay in her bed and cried. August stood in the doorway unsure if he should enter. She ignored his knocks.

"Sis, I'm sorry," he said, deciding to brave it.

"Why are you doing this?" she asked him, sitting up on her bed. "Don't you care? Are you going to school for me? August, why?"

"I don't know how it happened," he said.

"You did not put in enough effort, that's how. Please leave my room."

"Sorry," August said again. "Sis, I'm sorry."

"August, just go, please. I want to be left alone," Uzoamaka said.

He walked slowly to the kitchen, leaving his sister alone in her room. He had an ugly feeling in his stomach, like everything in it was rotting, coming apart. In the kitchen, August realized he was not alone. Standing near the counter was another disappointed sister.

She stared at him and then put an exasperated palm to her forehead.

"I'm sorry," August blurted out, lowering his eyes.

"Your mates are going to leave you behind," Peculiar said. "Just imagine."

Chinyere was away at Ibadan, where she went to university. She too was studying medicine. August wished she were here. She would have said something in his defense. "It happens." Or, "It really isn't the end of the world."

When August's father saw these results, he shook his head with disinterest, almost as though he wished someone else would say something on his behalf. "August, you did not do well. You have to buckle up," he finally said, handing the results back. August had imagined that at least he would get a frown, a small lecture, something, anything to show that his father cared about his success at school, that his father cared about him.

It made August cry. In the darkness of his room, hidden from his sisters' eyes, he wept for those words. It made him realize his father was incapable of loving him.

August's sisters decided among themselves that they would not let him repeat a class. He was to move schools. Like most of the decisions they made for him, they informed him of this decision as a matter of fact. August never even had time to decide if he wanted to stay in his old school and repeat. His father, as usual, had no objections. He let his children do whatever they wanted. Because August was never asked what he thought in matters like this, he crumpled whatever objections he might have and threw them into the furthest reaches of his mind, so that even he forgot what they were.

Obiajulu was the first person August met at his new school. August saw him kneeling defiantly near the administrative quadrangle the day Uzoamaka came to register him.

August and Uzoamaka walked past Obiajulu on their way to the principal's office. August felt sorry for him the way he was kneeling there, baking under the sun, in full view no less. He did not yet know they would be in the same class, nor that they'd end up sharing what they shared. Or rather, what he imagined they shared. Obiajulu was a rash boy who took great pleasure in sweaty brawls. In fact, Obiajulu's recklessness had tamed August in surprising ways. After they separated, August would find himself wishing they had never met, that he'd stayed back in his old school and repeated the class. That first day, August was not sure he liked Obiajulu. In fact, he would not have spoken to him were it not for the way the vice principal shouted at the boy.

"Take him to your class," the vice principal said. "He's your new classmate. Don't even dare try any nonsense, my patience has run out on you."

Obiajulu got up grudgingly and set out towards the class-room. His feet dragged on the gravel as he walked, and August wondered what was wrong with him. *Why couldn't he walk like someone who had life?*

In the class, he folded his hands on his desk and said, "Your mother is young."

"She's my sister," August said, settling into his own seat. He touched the padlock on his desk, pushed it this way and that just to hear how it squeaked.

Obiajulu was smiling ominously. He made August uncomfortable with that smile. Several weeks later, their first fight would be about Uzoamaka too. Obiajulu muttered something lubricious about Uzoamaka and in retaliation, August wondered aloud if his sister was the most attractive person Obiajulu had ever seen, given that none of his own relatives were anywhere near that attractive. The class cheered when Obiajulu tackled him. The other students locked the door and gathered around them to clap and laugh, such was the practice at Immaculate Boys' High.

It was not the first time Obiajulu had tackled August. He did it on the football field, often. He seemed to enjoy such things, throwing himself at people. Bringing them down with the sheer force of his weight. August slammed Obiajulu into the desk and pinned him to it. For the first time, it seemed, Obiajulu had met a challenger. August did not manage to hold Obiajulu like that for long. It was a spectacle, their bodies twisting this way and that, their uniforms wrinkled and stained. He was pinning Obiajulu's arms to his sides when their Intro Tech teacher stepped in to separate them. No one knew who had opened the door to let her in. August and Obiajulu were marched to the vice principal's office and made to kneel on the gravel just outside the building.

For a while, they knelt silently. Then Obiajulu spoke, asked August about an assignment that was due that afternoon. August saw the question for what it was, an apology.

"I did it this morning," he said, eyes trained on the gravel.

"Hmm. Please, I'd copy from it. I forgot to write my own," Obiajulu said.

August began to laugh. It was hilarious, Obiajulu saying he forgot to do his assignment like this was the first time such a thing happened. He never did assignments.

"Fuck off," Obiajulu said, laughing too. "You sef, are you sure of what you wrote?"

Their laughter continued. It was painful laughing while kneeling on gravel, but August couldn't help it.

"Remember the very first day I came to this school, you were kneeling here, at this very spot," August said when their laughter stilled.

"And now you're kneeling with me."

"You're a bad influence," August said.

Obiajulu chuckled, proud of the accusation. They would fight many times after that, sometimes playfully, other times trying to inflict as many injuries on each other as they could.

Sometimes, August wasn't sure which it was, the two easily switched; a playful tussle turning quickly into a dangerous affair; lighthearted jabs turning into serious punches; slight pushes taking on the gravity of war. August thought that friendship was the best thing that had ever happened to him. He thanked the good fortune that had made him fail that class, and his sisters who brought him here. Otherwise, he would never have met Obiajulu.

Soon enough, August's grades improved, inching closer to average with each subsequent examination; his sisters were placated. All was well. Life was good when the sun was up. August would meet Obiajulu near the Paskan Jake bakery or in front of the Anglican church. They were inseparable. After school, they trekked down to the Game House and played *God of War* until dusk. On the days they fought, they simply went their separate ways as though they did not know each other.

August came to school on the first day of the second term of Senior Secondary Class one, but Obiajulu had left. Just picked up and left. No warning, no good-bye. August waited patiently at first, morning after morning, but Obiajulu's desk sat empty. He trudged slowly to Obiajulu's house. Perhaps to ask why. Maybe Obiajulu had fallen ill, or perhaps a relative had died. He knocked, adjusted the strap of his schoolbag, and took a step back. No answer. Nothing. He knocked again, shifting his weight from one foot to another. The gateman came out. He saw August and smiled.

"Obi them don park go Abuja o."

August stared at the man, dumbfounded. "But when are they coming back?"

"They don park go," the man insisted, waving his hand off to the distance. August followed the direction of the stout man's hand with his eyes but said nothing, his expression blank. The gateman limped back into the compound and August stood there awhile, by himself, in the sun. It felt like someone had reached into his chest and squeezed as tightly as possible. For a while, he just stood there and stared at the gate, unsure if he had imagined the whole thing.

"Just like that?" he muttered to himself.

Of all the things he missed about Obiajulu, perhaps August missed their fights the most. The weight of Obiajulu's body on his, holding him, bruising him. The exhilaration of those moments. His sisters noticed his sadness, the way he came home from school each day without that characteristic smirk on his face. The way he slumped his shoulders so that his schoolbag slid off and onto the floor. Peculiar noticed first. Having spent the most time with him, she could read him like a book. And so attuned was she to his peculiarities that it did not take her long to notice that something had happened.

"Something is bothering you," Peculiar said. It was a question.

"No, I'm fine."

"You've been looking glum for days now."

"Ah—I'm fine," August said, staring into his book.

She seemed not to believe him. If she could have forced him to admit he wasn't fine, she would have. August's sisters took it almost like a personal slight when he did not tell them things.

Next was Chinyere. He was sitting at his reading desk staring at his notes. His sisters loved when he did that. Normally, they'd peek in from the hallway, and rather self-satisfied, announce: "Well done. If you want some soya milk, there's some in the fridge."

August found this patronizing, the way they marveled when he did things he knew were mindless tasks to them. He tried not to dwell on it, and to instead enjoy the privileges that came with it.

This time, Chinyere came into his room and leaned on the doorframe, staring at him. At first, he ignored her, waiting for her to say how wonderful it was that they no longer had to beg him to read. But she was silent. August tried to remember if there was anything he should be apologizing for. Did he forget to turn off the washing machine again? Or maybe he left his dishes on the dining after lunch.

"What did I do?" he finally asked, frustration bubbling in his throat.

"Did I say you did anything?"

"You're just standing there."

Chinyere's tone softened instantly. "Since I came back," she said, walking to the table to put her hand on his head, "I've noticed you've been down. *Ogini?* Tell me."

"I'm not down."

"But you've not been yourself lately. What's wrong?"

"Nothing," August said. He could tell that she, too, did not believe him. He did not believe himself. "Maybe it's stress," he said. "We're doing like all sixteen subjects. It's a lot."

Chinyere made a sound. A hmmm. She asked him to take it easy and asked if he wanted her to bring him something to drink.

It was true he had a lot of school to worry about. The SS1 curriculum contained everything from Financial Accounting to Chemistry. August was scared he might not manage to pass all his classes. There were some fairly easy ones, such as Commerce and Agriculture and Civic Education, but there were hard ones too. To his mind, the rigor of his curriculum should have been sufficient enough explanation, but his sisters had a knack for worrying.

He came back from school one day to find Uzoamaka at home, and from the way she hugged him and asked, "How are you? Hope you've been taking care of yourself?" he knew she had come home because of him.

Unlike the others, she did not ask him directly. She talked about her classes and her upcoming final exams. In the evening, with the three of them making food in the kitchen, all he could hear was his name. He lay in his bed and thought about Obiajulu again, what school he must go to now, what friends he must have. He wondered if Obiajulu ever thought of him, if Obiajulu missed him this badly, or at all. August was aware that caring this deeply was unusual. He was ashamed of it even. It was something he would never admit, not even to Obiajulu. Especially, not to Obiajulu. He imagined Obiajulu would laugh at something like this, tell him he was being stupid.

But August felt the way he felt. Uzoamaka started coming back to the house each weekend, and many times, he found his sisters whispering. He tried to appear cheerful. He felt sorry for them. They were way more affected by his gloom than he himself was. They let him watch TV whenever he wanted, for however long he wanted. They made soya bean milk or zobo or stocked the fridge with Chivita and made no fuss, no matter how much of it he drank. They pushed him to talk to his father.

"August," one of them would say, "your father is in the living room. Take some water to him."

When August took the water into the living room, without sitting there for some considerable minutes, they would click their tongues and shake their heads.

"You don't have any other father o. Only this one. And he doesn't have any other son, only you," another sister would say.

August would have to go back to the living room and sit with his father and ask him about work and politics and other things the man would potentially give answers to. His father would, in turn, ask him about school, which subjects he liked, which ones he found difficult, which teachers he preferred. At the end of the term, August passed all his subjects, even getting As in Agriculture and Commerce and Biology. Everyone was overjoyed—and August was unsure how he felt about that. Even his father offered something close to a smile, before saying, "You tried."

Peculiar made him his favorite dish, spaghetti with so much *geisha* that each time he took a spoonful, he got a mouthful of fish. Chinyere bought him a pair of Nike running shoes that felt like they were springing him forward when he ran in them. And Uzoamaka, she bought him a phone—an N70 that could minimize programs and play high-graphic games. It was a curious thing, the way his sisters celebrated his good results. August wondered if his mother would have done the same. If she would not have looked at

his result sheet, and seen it for what it was, a weak attempt
to be as good as everyone wished he was. He had seen his
sisters' results from way back when they were in his class. He
knew how uncommon it was for any of them to get a grade
that *wasn't* an A. So, each time they commended him, it only
reminded him of what he wasn't. He could almost hear his
mother's voice saying, *Look at the grades you're getting. How poor
they are. You're not fulfilling your God-given potential, August.*

He wondered if his sisters did not feel dishonest saying,
"August, you did so well. So well. You just have to keep this
up. More grease to your elbow."

He tried not to think about it. He listened to music on
his phone and played games and did his best not to think of
Obiajulu, where he was and if he was thinking about him
too.

CHAPTER THREE

Segun stopped below the trees to step on the dried grass. He stopped there often on his way from school. The tree branches peeked over the fence, and as he walked the length of the wall, he pressed the soles of his feet slowly into the crackling dead leaves. He found it soothing, the sound of dried leaves being crushed. He liked to watch leaves that were once scrunched up and taut, lay flat against the ground, broken into multitudes of separate and tiny pieces. Sometimes he wondered if that was what his mother meant when she clapped her hands, pressed them between her knees, and said, "How will they not fight? How do you crush people into the earth and expect them to just lie there and take it?"

She spoke of boots a lot, mostly in the evenings when her voice would rise to match that of his father. The television would show different images of men with masked faces and huge guns. Sometimes, the masks were off. These men were not afraid of the government, not the way his mother was.

Every day, she prayed for them. "God, protect your people. God, protect Asari-Dokubo. God bless his family. God, destroy this administration. Destroy this government before Obasanjo kills all your children."

His father watched his wife with interest but he always said, "Amen." Guiltily even, as though remorseful for his support for the Obasanjo administration.

Segun's parents loved to go at it. In the evenings, they would argue and argue and argue and argue. They seemed to disagree on everything, on Obasanjo's decision to concede the Bakassi Peninsula, on how much rigging actually happened in the 2003 elections, on the Paris Club's debt-relief package, on the Niger Delta People's Volunteer Force.

His father always showed more restraint than his mother, making sure to always speak only of Asari-Dokubo, the leader of the Ijaw Youth Council who split from it to create the NDPVF. Everything else was out of bounds.

Segun would sit at the dining table and try to do his assignment as they argued with each other. Now he looked at the broken veins of the leaf and imagined his sandals were state power. *Crushing the people's right to subsistence on their land with state power. Oh, the evils of this administration are endless.*

At home, he took the key out from under the welcome mat and let himself in. His afternoon routine was simple: drop his bag, wash his uniform, take his bath, and then eat the leftovers in the pot, if there were any. In that order. If he did something out of order, his mother would somehow suspect and get it out of him. But that afternoon, he was too tired.

He had cried all afternoon. Crying in school was a regular occurrence. His classmates were not very kind. Sometimes he wished they would ignore him, the way his parents did. He tried everything to make himself unseen, to never speak, to never offer to do anything with them, to never call their attention if, for instance, they stepped on him. And yet, they saw him. And regarded him with nothing but cruelty. Sometimes they just taunted him and did it in a way that could hurt a little boy. Other times, they pushed him to the ground and rubbed his face into the grass. The matter of contention always seemed to spontaneously materialize, perhaps a sign of how adept they were at creating issues with which to take offense. That Wednesday, it had been sports day, and again they took issue with him, this time because of the way he ran during the general exercises. He dreaded this, the way they would taunt him, their voices crowding into his head. That day, Timi grabbed Segun's face with his hand and pressed his fingers into Segun's jaw until it ached.

"Sorry o. I been think say you dey break," Timi said. Timi was usually the ringleader. He cracked the jokes everyone else laughed at, and decided which of the others' jokes were funny and which were not.

That Wednesday, they pushed him down and dragged him by both legs along the grass. His uniform chafed, and so his back was bruised badly. They laughed as they pulled Segun along and then left him there to cry, until he gathered himself together enough to go home. He lay down on the living-room floor, needing the coolness of the tiles on his back. He would do everything else, later. He was glad he had no bruises on his hands. His mother would have been so disappointed if she found out.

When he first told her about the incidents, she dismissed them. "They are just messing with you," she said, but after the bruises began to show, she stood Segun before her in the living room and examined his shirtless body in shock. "Are you seeing this?" she asked his father. "How can primary three children be this wicked?"

The television was on, and President Obasanjo's face appeared on it occasionally and then other faces belonging to men covered in rolls and rolls of cloth. It made him feel like a burden, to deprive his parents of that evening. He wanted to disappear, to just dissipate with the wind and never be seen again.

"What kind of play is this?" She seemed to be asking his father, but Segun felt the need to answer.

"I wasn't playing with them."

"Is this what they've been doing to you? Tell me."

Segun could only nod.

The next morning his parents were at the school. They met everyone. The disciplinarian. His teacher. The vice principal. The principal.

Three of the boys were called out in class and flogged, an exercise they seemed to relish as an opportunity to demonstrate how immune they were to the pains of the cane. Their punishment only made them more cruel.

One night his mother asked him, "Why are you letting them do this to you?"

He had been crying and had a bad case of hiccups. His father was reclining in his seat watching Segun cry with a scrunched face.

"Fight them," his mother said, her voice rising the way it did when she was watching TV. "When they push you, push them back. I can't go to school with you."

His father beckoned to him, sat him on his lap, and wiped his tears. "They are boys like you. They may be barrack boys but they're still boys like you."

It sounded to Segun like they were blaming him, like they thought he was getting attacked because he did not fight back. He had tried to fight the bullies off in the beginning. He had returned each push, but those boys had trouble in their veins. They taught him never to do that, very quickly. So he just cried and cried and cried. Sometimes he heard his parents whispering about transferring him to another school. They only talked in hushed tones for two things. One, for money, because they had so little of it. Two, for him, because he was their only child. He gathered that they did not have the money to transfer him to another school. The military primary school he was currently attending had been the gift at the end of a long battle to get him out of the government school, where according to his mother, he was taught nothing. They got a soldier, a former classmate of his father's, to stand in as his guardian so Segun could pay the military child fees. They could not afford the civilian fees. Every term, they only managed to pay his tuition, on military status, just before the school authorities started caning and sending children home for nonpayment.

Each time there was an incident, it would so upset his mother she would come to his school and shout at his teachers. She was a very quick-tempered woman. The teachers would beg her forgiveness and promise to punish the culprits, but those promises were not enough. For days on end, she would not be herself. She would not shout at the television.

She would not rebuke Obasanjo. She would offer no soliloquies about Atiku's schemes with his American wife. *Schemes.* She used to draw it out as though to milk every last sound in the word. Scheeeeeemesssssss. She would become a shell of herself. If he listened attentively enough, he would hear her saying things like, "My heart is not at rest leaving Abe in that school. Look how thin he is. Every time he's crying. The thing is draining him of blood."

Segun's mother invoked blood a lot. She had seen a lot of it in her life. During the Abacha administration, she came face-to-face with death on many occasions and had the scars to show for it. Having heard so many of those stories, Segun had grown to hold his mother in awe. Because of this, nobody thought it out of place when she spoke of blood. She could say, "This administration is a bloodsucker. Are we really better off than a military regime?" and it would sound like the most natural thing. And so, it scared him to hear her say such things about him. In the morning, he would look at his thin limbs in the mirror, and fear that perhaps he did not have enough blood to carry him through the day.

Now, lying with his back to the cool tiles, he imagined how much trouble he would be in if she saw these bruises. He fell asleep, lying there on the living-room floor. His mother must have put two and two together and understood what happened, because when he woke up, he found his uniform already washed, hanging on the clothing line.

After primary school, Segun left home for boarding school. He was a little apprehensive to be going to an all-boys secondary school. When his mother noticed this hesitation, she did her best to reassure him. "They're very disciplined. Even the rumor that you did something against the rules. Only rumor o, piam, you're out. Expulsion immediately."

"Hmmmmm. I hope they'll not expel me o," he said.

"Hian. It's not possible. My own son. It's not even. I'm not even shaking. I am your mother. I know what you are capable of. This school will just fit you. No wahala school. And I know some of the teachers there."

Segun did not protest too much. He had passed the school's entrance exams with flying colors, and they awarded him a scholarship. That was the biggest reason he was going there, the burden it would lift from his parents' backs.

But, in the new school, his lot wasn't any better. Segun was a boy who naturally attracted attention. The way he walked, the way he talked, his gesticulation. So out of place was he, in a place full of boys trying to establish dominance over their peers, that he immediately became a target. His mother was right about the expulsion though. The school prided itself on its expulsion record. Every day the principal boasted about it during morning assembly. "Zero tolerance," he called it.

Zero tolerance protected Segun, not from the verbal taunts and shaming that immediately followed him wherever he went, but at least from any physical altercation. His peers had to make do with calling him all the names they could think of. He had already learnt to put up a tough demeanor. Only lying in the darkness after lights out did he allow himself to cry, silently, until there were no more tears in his eyes. It became a theatrical experience even, his wallowing in the loneliness he felt, that absence of his parents' steady and constant voices. He found it almost poetic, his holding on to his pillow as he gave up all his tears, as though if he did not do this, he would break in class the next day and demonstrate a weakness his classmates would never forgive him for. When his parents called, he told them everything was fine. No one was attacking him anymore. It was all good. He was making many friends. He was happy. That first term, his grades sank so low the school told him he would need a miracle to keep his scholarship.

"What's happening?" his mother asked, alarmed at his grades. She had come to take him home and did not bother waiting for the both of them to arrive home before asking her questions. Segun struggled to drag his traveling box along as he tried to muster a response.

"This is unlike you. You're a very brilliant boy. Very brilliant. Naturally gifted. You're my son. I carried you inside me. Tell me what's wrong."

But Segun had no explanation to give. He didn't do anything different. He updated his notes, listened in class, and read as much as could. He did not know why his results were so bad. The next term, he fretted over every score, over every test and every assignment, as though his life depended on it. And perhaps it did. A sense of dread shadowed him now, of placing an even bigger burden on his parents if he lost his scholarship. They teased him about this, too, his classmates. They relentlessly mocked him for staying back during recess, to read of all things. That term he passed with extraordinary grades. Everyone was happy. The school was elated they wouldn't have to revoke his scholarship. His mother was especially happy. She teared up and pressed him tightly to herself. This time she took his box from him as they walked to the school gate.

"I knew you would make me proud. I know my son," she said.

The way she said *I know my son* touched Segun. And it must have been true because despite maintaining his grades, she told him one rainy Sunday, on a visiting day, that he would be withdrawing from the school after JSS2.

"I know you don't like it here," she said. "You lie to me, but I know. You will transfer to St. Emmanuel's Boys' College. That way you can go from home. Let's try that one and see how it works."

Segun started at St. Emmanuel's grateful for the chance to start afresh, again. He tried his best to speak as deeply as he could, walked as intentionally as he possibly could, and kept his hands to his sides when he spoke. He wanted, for once, to go to class and not brace himself for biting remarks.

It was at St. Emmanuel's Boys' College that Segun met Tanko. It started as an innocent friendship, while he was preparing for his final Junior Secondary School exams. Tanko was an SS2 student who made it his duty to protect Segun when he could. Each recess, Segun would sit at the steps close to the canteen, away from class, far away from the football field. Sometimes, other junior boys gathered there to draw lines in the soil and chase themselves within the boxes. Tanko would whistle to him from the window of the SS2 class and give Segun money to buy him snacks from the canteen. Sometimes Tanko didn't give Segun money at all. Always, Segun did as he was told, even if it meant no lunch for him.

And from that uneasy coalition, something of a friendship sprouted. The closer Tanko got to graduating, the closer they became. Soon they were speaking to each other late into the night, an SS1 student and his SS3 senior, taking advantage of the midnight call feature of MTN, to talk about mundane things into the early hours of the morning.

Segun suspected that what they had was no longer just a friendship. There was something more in the way Tanko showered him with compliments about his beautiful eyes that sat like stars on his face, or his prominent cheekbones, and the way they perked up when he smiled. It was something he did not question, as though a natural consequence of things. All he knew was that he felt more and more comfortable and at home with Tanko.

The day he visited Tanko at his house, he imagined he could get used to the privacy and the childlike mischievousness they shared, just by being alone there, the two of them. Tanko's house was big. His father had many wives. Most of Tanko's siblings were grown and had gone off to start their own families. Tanko's mother was a wife of old age. Tanko was the only son still in the compound, and so he had his own room in the boys' quarters. He introduced Segun to his sisters. They were polite. He lost count of how many they were, there were so many of them. They went to his room and played games and talked of nothing and everything, lying on the bed, and Segun wondered if this was what it felt like to have a sibling, to not be alone, to have someone with you. It was on the day of Tanko's graduation that Tanko kissed Segun for the first time. They were at the back of the SS1 quadrangle. Everyone else was

in the school hall, where the ceremony was happening, and
they were shielded by trees, but the moment nevertheless
had such a naked, palpable risk to it, that made it seem like
the most honest thing in the world. Tanko said something
cringy and sweet, something along the lines of, "I don't
even want to graduate. I want to stay with you." Something
like that. "I've actually liked you since you entered this
school, but you were just behaving as if you don't know
what's up," Tanko also said.

Segun smiled but said nothing. He felt light-headed and
full of air, like he could float up and join the clouds. Tanko
made him feel special, made him feel important, like a prize
to be won.

"Let's go to my house," Tanko said.

"For what?" Segun asked.

"Ahn-Ahn you know for what nau. Let's go."

"I can't. They'll call me for prizes."

"Okay. After prizes, we'll go."

"I don't think it'll be possible. I'll have to leave with my
mum."

Tanko stared at Segun and then sighed.

"Sorry," Segun said.

His mother was leaving early to get back to work and he
could have gone back with Tanko to his stuffy room, were it
not for his fear that he was not prepared, that if he went with
Tanko, he would end up soiling Tanko's bed with shit and
would never recover from the shame. Nor would whatever it
was they had between them. It would be days later before he
went to meet Tanko. He would spend hours in the bathroom
preparing himself.

The sex was not a pleasurable experience, by any account. Tanko was not a patient boy. They were awkward limbs unable to find any rhythm, and Segun was only aware of the backbreaking pain. Segun kept pulling away before Tanko could fully penetrate him.

"Relax," Tanko kept saying. "Just relax your ass."

But try as much as he did, Segun could not relax. He kept tensing up, and even after Tanko was inside him, he could not relax. They tried so many positions because Segun was not comfortable in any of them. Eventually, they settled on Segun on his back because Tanko could easily hold him in that position and prevent him from moving away.

If Tanko heard the times Segun asked him to stop, he did not show it. It went on in that way for what felt like forever, with Tanko only speaking to tell Segun to be quiet.

"Do you want them to catch us? Okay, you know what? Wait. Let me put on my stereo."

When it eventually ended, Segun was just relieved he did not shit himself.

Tanko held him in an embrace after they were both cleaned up and dressed. He asked Segun, "Did you like it?"

And Segun said yes, with as much fervor as he could muster; so enamored was he with Tanko. So grateful was he that he had someone who wanted him, this way.

CHAPTER FOUR

Segun fell in love the same week Yar'Adua apologized to the country for the 2007 elections. Or perhaps he only realized he was in love on that day. He was in Tanko's room that afternoon. The windows were locked, the curtains were drawn, and the room had that stale, stuffy smell about it. It was a holiday, and occasionally there was the sound of children playing outside. Lying there in Tanko's bed, Segun realized he did not want to be anywhere else. The low light irked him and the way everything was locked made him feel trapped. And yet, he wanted to be nowhere else but there, in Tanko's arms, snuggled against his warm and hairy chest.

It worried Segun. Tanko did not seem the type of guy who had any use for a love like that. More and more, all he did was ignore Segun. He rarely picked up when Segun called, and they only spoke when Tanko wanted to speak. Many times, Segun longed for the Tanko he used to know. The guy who stayed on the phone with him deep into the early hours of the morning, telling him how he was the sun himself. Perhaps it was only part of the chase, saying all those things. And now that Tanko had him, there was no longer use for that type of affection that tingled. All his life, Segun had wanted to find love. To give all of himself to someone who loved him the way his parents loved each other, and that afternoon, lying in bed with Tanko, he realized he had jumped without looking. But wasn't now the best time to risk it all for love, now that he was young? If not now, when?

Tanko said something like that to him once. "You know, we have to enjoy this life now, before we grow old and settle down."

To that Segun said nothing, only made a sound. He did not like how entrapping Tanko made it sound. But it was true, and he had carried that with him ever since, the understanding that eventually, he would have to give in to the beckoning of social comfort that came with doing what society expected of him. But still, it worried Segun that Tanko did not love him with the type of vigor and passion that was electrifying. They were lying on Tanko's bed now and he was engrossed in his phone. After a while, he dropped it.

"Are you ready for another round?" he whispered in Segun's ear. Segun pretended not to hear him. He did not want to have sex with Tanko again. He just wanted both of them to lie there in that comfort. Tanko kissed his ear, then his neck. Segun did not know how to refuse. Tanko turned him around.

"Come on," he whispered to Segun, "my darling."

Segun's parents agreed on President Yar'Adua. It was unusual. They rarely ever agreed on anything political. It was the basis of their relationship, to disagree on everything. They did not agree on Asari-Dokubo. They did not agree on Obasanjo. Not on Bola Tinubu. Not even on Fashola. But for Yar'Adua, the stars aligned. For one, there seemed no one else his mother could support. She had celebrated Atiku losing the presidential nomination of the People's Democratic Party, as if it were a personal victory.

"Yes. Let them fight each other. Let them fight."

And of course, she could never support Buhari. She had flown in and out of prison during his short-lived administration in the eighties for protesting land seizures to make space for even more oil exploration. She had scars and stories from back then, which she fed Segun as a child.

"These people kept arresting me," she told him once. They were cooking and their small kitchen was so hot and humid. Both mother and son were sweating.

"After Major-General Buhari issued decree two, they just began mass arresting people. Especially journalists," Segun's mother said. She untucked an end of her wrapper and wiped the sweat on her face.

"But you were not a journalist," Segun said.

"No, but I was organizing against the many land grabs that were happening. I was linked to many radical formations in Old Rivers State, back before Bayelsa was carved out of Rivers. After Pan Ocean Oil stole land from Oghara in Old Bendel—I think that should be in Delta or Edo State now—to destroy it all in the name of 'indigenous oil company,' and we protested, they arrested us. I was in kirikiri for more than a month."

She turned and checked on the pot. "When I tell people Buhari is evil, I remember it. This one is not just *them say, them say.*"

And so Buhari was just out of the question for her, reformed democrat or not. She fiddled with supporting Ojukwu, but only playfully, the way one would support a passionate friend's business even though they were sure of its imminent failure. When Yar'Adua, the PDP nominee, selected Goodluck Jonathan, it was to her almost like an apology, a renunciation of some sort of everything Obasanjo had done to the people of the Niger Delta. And so really, Yar'Adua was the natural option that came to be.

The day President Yar'Adua apologized on national television, looking genuinely remorseful, as though the multiple rebukes from every election observer who had monitored the elections had hurt him personally, Segun's parents held each other and watched with pride, their aspirations palpable. Between them, there was a sense of hope. For a new Nigeria where life was not so hard. Where soldiers did not march out to meet protesters in the streets. He promised many things, this new president. It was a new era in Nigerian politics, of this Segun's mother was certain. She, who never believed any politician, government or opposition. She, whose natural inclinations were to resist and fight but who now touted Yar'Adua's promises with the rigidity of faith. She invoked his Seven-Point Agenda to anyone who dared question her certainty.

"Yar'Adua will revitalize our roads, rails, the infrastructure we need. Yar'Adua will develop energy. Nigeria will have food security because for the first time, our president will fight for it."

Yar'Adua made her into a believer. But Segun's father was not as sold on Yar'Adua, not the way his mother trusted and loved him. Three years later, when she would hear the news of his death, she would break down and weep. For days, she would trudge around in grief muttering, "They've killed him. They did it. They got rid of him."

She would mourn him, almost like he was her last hope of a better Nigeria.

It was a cold evening in late September the day Segun first spoke to his mother about Tanko. They were making yam and garden egg sauce for dinner. Segun was pounding the garden eggs in the mortar while his mother was at the sink, slicing and peeling the yam.

"Pound that thing like someone who has life," she said. "We don't have fuel o, unless you want to cook this thing yourself, in the dark."

Segun pounded harder. His limbs were weak, heavy. He just wanted to lie down and escape the kitchen's heat. There were vegetables boiling on the stove, and as Segun pounded, he stared at the dancing lid on the pot and at the steam that escaped it. He hated cooking because of the heat. He felt suffocated.

His mother reassured him it was just their kitchen. "It's unfortunate that this is what we have, but the heat is not that bad. I'm here and it hasn't killed me. Besides, you're young. What great harm could some small heat possibly do to you?"

And so Segun had to make do with the breath of cold air that greeted him when eventually he could escape the small space. That evening he longed for it more especially. He quickened the tempo of his pounding, to satisfy his mother. Soon she came over and peered into the mortar. She retied

her wrapper and snatched the pestle from him and proceeded
to grind the garden egg vigorously. Some of it splattered
on his leg. She pounded until she was satisfied. Then she
dropped the pestle.

"Oya you can go," she said.

Segun stood to leave.

"Wait," she said. "Come. Let me ask you, maybe it's just
in my mind." She lifted the pot from the stove and turned
down the fire, then she turned to him with grave seriousness.
The lid stopped rattling and the kitchen became suddenly
silent. "I've noticed since you came back from school today,
you've been sulky. What is it?"

"Nothing," Segun said.

"You know, that's my problem with you. You don't tell
me things. You don't tell anybody anything. I don't know if
you have another mother somewhere else. Aberemangigha!"

"Ma."

"Did anything happen in your school?"

"No."

"Then what's the problem?"

"Mummy, there is no problem." He shifted his weight
from one foot to another. He knew his mother could tell he
was lying, but he also knew she could not force anything
from him.

"Is it that Tanko boy?"

"No," Segun said, and then wondered if his reply had
come too fast.

"By the way, what's your relationship with that boy?"
she asked.

"How?"

"Don't ask me *how*. I know why I'm asking."

"He's my friend."

"I'm not comfortable with your closeness with that boy," she said.

"I cannot have friends again or what?"

She regarded him silently, and Segun tried to keep his eyes steady.

"Abe." This time her voice was lowered.

"Ma."

"How old is that boy?"

"How should I know?"

"That boy is not your mate. I am not comfortable with this your friendship with him. Do you know how much time you spend in their house?"

"What are you even saying?" Now he was annoyed.

"I've said my own o."

His mother returned her attention to the stove and turned up the heat. Segun walked out angrily. Outside the air hit him. There were beads of sweat on his eyelids. He wiped his face and hissed in annoyance. Earlier that day, Tanko told Segun he'd been admitted to study at the University of Lagos. He gave Segun the letter and Segun read the printed words line by line, as though he needed to, as though his mind had not already gone blank after the first words. The University of Lagos. An offer of provisional admission. Biochemistry. He didn't understand why the letter was so long, or why it worried him so much. The university wasn't that far.

Perhaps it was just that he had always imagined both of them, together, here in Tanko's stuffy room. Now Tanko was leaving to go to university, without him. And he did not want to be alone.

"Congrats, congrats," he kept repeating. He did not know what else to say. He wanted to ask Tanko when he was leaving but he also did not want to give the impression he was anything less than enthusiastic about his admission. He should be happy about it. What was this stupid insecurity, that Tanko would get to school and forget him? He went home thinking about it, about what this admission letter meant for them.

As the days dragged by, he steadied himself for the absence that would replace his afternoons. It was only a week before the session was to resume, that Tanko told him he would go from home, instead of staying in a hostel.

"UNILAG is not that far from Iyana-Ipaja. Even with Lagos traffic," he said to Segun.

It fell on Segun to hide his happiness and play devil's advocate. To remind Tanko of the traffic, and the stress of traveling on Lagos roads, let alone doing that journey to Yaba every day.

"I'd rather do it," Tanko said. "I don't want to be somewhere I won't be seeing you. I want to be here, with you. I'm doing this because of you, because I love you."

And Segun's heart warmed with content, the easy sort that came with teenage love. In those moments, it felt like this love of theirs would last an entire lifetime, against all odds.

Tanko's love was the kind that was there and then it all of a sudden wasn't. It took faith to sustain it. There were many times it seemed to Segun like there was nothing there, and through those times, he had to have faith. Sometimes Tanko spoke to Segun as though he were still a mere junior student, whose job it was to do his bidding. Tanko could call Segun on a Saturday, ask him to come over, and it would be left to Segun to find a way to make it happen because he understood how furious Tanko would be if he did not. On an afternoon that Segun could not leave, because his mother would get suspicious, Tanko almost slapped him.

"Go home!" he told Segun. "Just go home before I wound you."

And in that moment, as Tanko stood over him, Segun had been genuinely afraid of him. Not just that Tanko might hit him, but that Tanko might injure him so badly he would need an explanation for his bruises. But when the love was there, when Tanko held him close and kissed his neck and the tip of his nose, when they lay in his tiny, poorly ventilated room, their legs entangled, when Tanko spent entire afternoons promising him everything that could be promised, it made Segun into a man for whom faith was easy, a man who could easily persevere through whatever words Tanko said in the midst of a mood. Many times he thought back to how their relationship began, how their friendship was so much a product of chance. And he wondered what his life would be like without it. Perhaps it was part of what kept him with Tanko, until the very horrible end. If he left Tanko, where would he go? Even after Tanko started seeing other people, Segun would cry until his eyes were bloodshot, and still, he answered when Tanko called. It began as a mere suspicion, something of a premonition. Tanko's increased secrecy only served to fuel it. Once Segun saw a text. Once he saw a picture. Once he saw condoms. Tanko never used them with Segun because they started without condoms, and later, Segun had not known how to ask Tanko to start using them. He made a weak attempt once. He said, "Don't you think we should be using condoms?"

Tanko waved him away. "Why? I don't like those things. Besides, I'm clean. Do you have anything?"

Segun shook his head. "No."

"Ehe," Tanko said, and they never spoke about it after that.

And so, when Segun saw those condoms, he knew Tanko was having sex with other people. He cried and cried, not knowing how to confront Tanko about it. What would he say? For weeks he said nothing. It was his fear that he would contract an STI that eventually forced it out of him. They were in Tanko's room, on a weekday. Segun, having come from school, was in his uniform, his shirt unbuttoned. He was sitting on the bed, a pillow in his lap. Tanko was sitting on the edge of the bed, sorting through his uni documents.

"Are you seeing other guys?" Segun blurted out. Tanko turned to look at him in shock before answering.

"What?"

"Are you cheating on me?" It sounded so hysterical, this question. Segun felt so exposed, naked, as though someone had ripped his clothes from his body in public.

"What would even make you think that?" Tanko asked.

"Just tell me the truth."

"Why would you accuse me like this without facts?" Tanko's voice was rising.

"I saw the condoms, Tanko."

"What? Those . . . they don't mean anything."

"What do you mean they don't mean anything?"

"They give them out to us at school. Is that it? That is what you're clutching on to accuse me?"

Segun was quiet. "I just thought . . ."

"You thought what? That I would do something like that to you?"

"I'm sorry," Segun said.

"Sorry for yourself."

Segun went over to where he was sitting and hugged his back. "I said I'm sorry nau."

Only a few weeks later, when Segun found out his suspicions were correct, Tanko did not offer any apologies.

"You did not tell me you were coming," was what Tanko told Segun.

Segun knocked and stood at the door for minutes while they scrambled around inside the locked room, Tanko and whoever was in there with him. The man who walked out of the door when Tanko opened it had a perfectly groomed beard. The first thing Segun thought was that the man looked very much like a university student.

"You lied," he said. "I asked you and you lied to my face."

Tanko let Segun speak. He simply stood there, his eyes lowered as Segun spoke. At a point, Segun's voice cracked, and he began to cry. He believed it was his fault, what Tanko did, and he would believe it for a while. They remained together, but Tanko did not stop seeing other people.

"We're gay," he said. "What are you, my wife or what, that I can't fuck other guys?"

"I don't like your tone," Segun said.

Tanko sighed. "I'm sorry . . . but you can't expect us to be husband and wife. Everyone does this thing. Me fucking other men doesn't change how much I love you."

The condom issue resurrected, again. This time it caused an argument because Segun's fear would not let his mind rest.

"I told you I don't like that thing," Tanko said.

"But you use it with other people."

"To protect me from them, mumu. To protect myself because I don't trust them. What is wrong with you?"

"I'm going home," Segun said, standing from the bed. Tanko pulled him back with so much force he struggled to maintain his balance.

"You're testing my patience," Tanko said. Segun snatched his hand from Tanko's grip and stormed off, fighting his tears.

For days they did not talk. Many times Segun thought of apologizing so that everything could go back to the way it was. But for what? What would he be apologizing for? He was ashamed of how helpless he felt each time Tanko threatened to hit him. On some level, he didn't believe Tanko would ever actually do it, but he wielded the power, threatening it like a knife. Tanko eventually came to apologize. It had been so long since Tanko visited Segun at his house. When Tanko came inside, Segun's mother grunted a reply to his greeting. Her face was visibly hostile. She had decided, very early and very easily, that she did not like Tanko.

"I should not have handled it like that. You know I get angry easily," Tanko said when they were alone. It was the closest Segun ever got to an actual apology. They began to use condoms after that, but even then, Segun did not trust Tanko. Too many times more than Segun cared for, Tanko would get rid of the condom before he was able to see it. So whenever they had sex, Segun would reach back to guide Tanko's penis into himself, so he could feel with his own hands the latex of the condom. And even that did little to assuage his fear.

CHAPTER FIVE

And then misfortune befell them. When Segun heard of the incident, he knew almost immediately that their relationship would not survive. There was a moment, a fleeting moment, when he almost found consolation in knowing it was payback. Karma for Tanko's cruelty to him. Or something of that sort, because of the way it happened. This worried him. How could he ever think *that* about a man he loved? Segun never got the full story of what happened on that day, because Tanko never told him. Segun didn't know how to even begin prying. All he knew, he learnt from rumors on the street, piecing them together one by one, removing the details he knew couldn't be true. How much of it his mother heard, Segun did not know. But she bristled more loudly whenever Segun left home, and there was more venom in the way she said, "That Tanko boy."

Every version of the story had Tanko's unscrupulous and vindictive classmates in it, eager to teach him a lesson. Segun could not imagine what Tanko's wrong could have been. But there was hardly any wrong that could have matched what they did do to Tanko. For a long time, everyone talked about it, almost as though they were grateful something this interesting had happened in their lives, the type of things they only saw on TV or read in tabloids. It was from their gossip that Segun pieced together his version of the story.

These classmates of Tanko's had arranged to set him up, to prove his homosexuality, and then to expose it. One of them had approached Tanko, and they began to talk. He saved their chat history on every platform. On Twitter, on Facebook, on 2go. Text messages too. They were patient. They took their time. The classmates were heartlessly cruel people, the type Segun had before only learnt about in the stories his mother told him. Sani Abacha or Obasanjo or General Buhari, people who could kill entire families and had many times broken his mother's bones. Segun wished he knew what exactly Tanko said in those messages. Tanko, the man who promised him love. It all ended in Tanko's room. Segun imagined Tanko, in just his boxers, surprised by five men storming into his room. He could almost see how scared Tanko must have been. How the room, with all its closed shutters and drawn blinds, would have morphed from a familiar place in which he was sheltered, into a corner in which he was trapped. They took everything while he knelt there begging them not to ruin his life like this. Tanko was a very proud man. Segun imagined it must have been spirit shattering to be reduced to that. And yet his pleas fell on deaf ears. When they tried to drag him out of the room, he resisted, holding the doorframe while he begged. So they beat him. They beat him until his limbs were too battered to hold on to doorframes. They took his underwear too and then marched him outside naked. A crowd materialized from thin air, as they are wont to do in Lagos. Tanko's sisters were drawn out by the commotion, and they all burst into tears. They joined the crowd, pleading for their brother. They followed the violence all through the streets, the way Jesus's apostles followed him. And after Tanko was handed over to the police, it was his sisters' scarves that covered his naked, bleeding body.

On his way from school that day, Segun had seen a smudge of blood on the road, somewhere near New Era Street. When he heard what happened, he wondered if he had just walked past Tanko's blood smeared into the asphalt and not felt, somehow, who it had spilt from. He was overwhelmed by fear, confusion, anger. And then it occurred to him that Tanko might no longer be alive. This crushed him, broke something in him. There was a swelling pain in his chest, a pain so visceral, so physical, he imagined this was what a heart attack must feel like. He wanted to call Tanko's phone, but how could he? Perhaps the police had it. There was nothing Segun could do but cry. He wept and wept and wept. When he heard his mother return, he locked his door. She must have heard him lock it; she came over and knocked.

"Good evening, Ma," he said, trying to keep his voice as unshaken and emotionless as possible.

"Evening. What are you doing in there that you're locking your door?"

Segun did not reply.

"I know I'm talking to a human being," she said.

"I'm not doing anything," Segun responded.

"Are you crying?"

"No."

"Hei God. What happened this time?"

"I'm not crying. I just want to be left alone."

And so she left him. He sat there, in his room for hours, wondering how long it would take the police to come and arrest him too. He was turning over in his mind all the texts he had sent Tanko, and how he could possibly deny their meanings. He wished he could only worry about Tanko, but as he sat there, consumed by his fear, he could not help but think of himself too. It was sleep that eventually relieved his worry and even that did not last very long. He woke up a short while later to a knock on his door. He jumped.

"Abe, what is this rubbish nau? Open this door."

It was only his mother. He opened the door.

"What kind of oyibo sleep are you sleeping? Your father is back."

Segun followed her to the living room to greet his father and then to the kitchen to help her make dinner. Then he swept the living room and the passage, then the kitchen. As his body performed this routine, he wondered how his parents would ever overcome the humiliation when eventually the police came for him too.

Segun wished Tanko would speak to him about the incident. He wanted to be there for him. But the attack had shut down something in Tanko, broken his spirit fundamentally, so that all that was left was a shell. The day Segun finally saw him after the incident, Tanko was hardly the same person.

"Honestly, I'm so sorry," Segun said, "I can't even imagine."

"It's fine. I survived."

They sat in awkward silence, Tanko finding something, anything, to busy himself with, almost as though Segun were not even in the room.

"How is the situation in school?" Segun asked.

"School dey."

"They're not harassing you anything?"

"All these your questions, what is it sef?" Tanko snapped.

"I'm just worried about you," Segun said.

"Eh thank you very much."

Segun sensed that Tanko did not even want him there. He stayed for a short while longer before leaving. He had hoped that at least he could be there for Tanko, that they could be there for each other. He was not there when it happened but every night they came for him too, in his dreams. Some nights he dreamt of his classmates from primary school. They come in the evening. His mother fights them. She tries to protect him, but there are too many of them. Eventually, they push past her and get to him. At that point, he would wake up out of breath, his shirt matted to his chest by sweat. He would quickly switch on the light, or on the nights when there was no electricity, reach for his rechargeable reading lamp. After he woke up, every object in his room would look like a menacing figure in the dark. Only light—so he could see with his eyes that he was safe—calmed him.

For weeks, his heart skipped each time someone said his name. Even in school. They won't come to a secondary school, he told himself. How could they even know this place? It was not in any text message, and Tanko would never betray him, not like that. But that assurance did little to calm his nerves. In every wall, in every corner, he heard his name. And at night, those fears manifested in all sorts of nightmares. He wished Tanko would at least speak to him. Perhaps that would have made it better, bearable. He knew how selfish this was. Tanko was, after all, the one who really suffered, not him. But the more the silence between them grew, the more it seemed inevitable that this tragedy would take whatever remained of them and tear it to pieces.

All Segun could do was hope. Regularly, he would stop by Tanko's house and ask after him. Tanko's sisters would be the ones to give him answers. If they tried to veil their hostility, they did not succeed. They blamed him for what happened to Tanko. Finally, one afternoon they told him not to bother coming by anymore.

"Tanko now lives in school. If you want to see him, go to Yaba. Go to UNILAG," they said.

It did not so much surprise Segun that Tanko had left—he too would not have been able to stay here if he suffered what Tanko suffered—as it shocked him that Tanko did not give him the courtesy of telling Segun he was leaving. It hurt, the way Tanko just wholly recoiled from him. It made him wonder if Tanko ever actually loved him. Perhaps love was simply something Tanko professed, out of courtesy, because he too did not want to be alone.

Tanko's attack changed Segun. It surprised him, the way a single day thoroughly disrupted the semblance of normalcy of his life and reshaped it. It taught him that there was so much evil in the world, so much violence, so much cruelty, more than he previously thought possible.

His mother used to say, "This world is rotten, Abe. To better it, we must fight it. We must resist its violence or it will crush us."

And now he understood. Aberemangigha. That was, after all, the name she gave him. He who fights his battles. Such a peculiar name. He sometimes wondered what she thought of herself now. When he was little, he used to blame himself for stealing her joy. Always, she was angry at something and hers was the embittered type of rage. But in her pictures, holding her placards and cardboard sheets, she seemed at ease, at home. Before him, she was a free spirit, drawn toward all the injustices of this world. She wanted to wipe them off with her thumb. Even when she was up against insurmountable odds, she stood firm. There were newspaper cutouts of columns dedicated to the protests and riots she organized and marched in.

One of them, from the 1980s, had a picture of her standing with a sign whose message Segun could not make out. Behind her, a thicket of mangrove, marked out for destruction and pipelines. The newspaper column caption read

OBASANJO, LET THIS LAND BREATH.

Now, she was his mother. Every day, she went to the Mushin Ajina market and sold her eggs and then she came back and worried over him. To his young mind, he was a leech. He tethered her. But now, older, he came to understand she had made that choice. She chose him, and he often wondered if she regretted it. He thought, too, of how much more he would love himself if she had given him some of that courage that fueled her through her youth.

It was Tanko's attack that told him what he already knew: just how much the world did not love him, and how far it would go to hurt him. And so the next time a classmate mocked him for his way of gesticulating, Segun responded with as much bile as he could muster. Every day, walking home from school, he would look at that spot where he had seen Tanko's blood and feel a raw wave of anger course through him. Tanko had made him imagine safety, because Tanko was the type of boy who never roused suspicion, who so easily blended in, who passed. When Tanko was in school, no one ever called him anything. He commanded reverence from everyone. And because he had a room that afforded him privacy, Segun imagined that was safety. Surely, it was the safest boys like them could ever be. Yet, they found him, the evil in this world.

When another classmate, Echezona, a boy who had a stutter and was famous for his temper, called him woman wrapper, Segun replied with venom. Everyone was surprised. So rarely did Segun use his voice in retaliation. Echezona pushed him. Segun staggered backward, almost fell. Surprise gave him the advantage, no one would have guessed that he would drag Echezona by the collar and yank him so hard that he lost his footing. But he did. And it worked. Echezona lost his balance and the fighting commenced. It took a while for Echezona to get the better of him, enough time for Segun to get a few good punches in. Segun still ended up pretty bruised and beaten. Echezona was, after all, older and stronger, and Segun's limbs were not accustomed to fighting. But after they were separated, Segun looked at the injuries on Echezona's face and felt a strange sense of pride swell in his heart. He would get better with each fight. More attentive to weak spots, faster, more ruthless. If he wasn't already in the second term of his final year, he might have been expelled. Always the vice principal would make him bring his mother and only for this did he feel remorse. She did not like to miss her morning sales. Each time, she refused to apologize for his actions. The first time she came she asked the vice principal, "What is the problem here exactly? I don't see why you called me. Where are the other boy's parents? They should be the ones here."

"Madam, you don't understand. Your son threw the first punch."

"But he was pushed."

"Madam, a push and a punch are not even nearly the same thing. We take cases like this very seriously. Your son could be expelled."

"For what? He defended himself."

Later that evening she made Segun stand before her and his father and narrate the events exactly as they happened. He told it from the beginning, the years of taunts and name-calling and mockery, so eager to have her on his side. But when he got to the part where he answered a push with a punch, he couldn't tell from her facial expression if she approved. She did not say anything, simply let his father give him a warning.

"Just find a way to avoid these children," his father said. "I don't have money to enroll in another school if they expel you now. Avoid them and jejely write your WAEC."

She sat there until Segun's father was done admonishing him, then stood up and went to her bedroom.

Each time she was called to the school, she took his side.

"Can't you see they're bullying him? What other option does he have?" his mother asked.

"He can report. We have a zero-tolerance policy against bullying."

"Well, your zero-tolerance policy is failing. This boy has been in this school for nearly four years now. And your zero-tolerance policy has never protected him. And I still want to know why you don't call these other boys' parents to come and answer for the bullies they have as children."

The vice principal sighed. "Madam, you don't know that. We speak to the parents of all the boys involved, of which your son is one."

"Well, the easiest solution I see is they should stop bullying my son," Segun's mother said.

As his classmates came to realize provoking Segun was not something they wished for, the fighting subsided. They still called him every hurtful word they could imagine, but for the first time, Segun could respond with as much venom as he wanted and not feel fear. When they called him woman wrapper, he told them their parents must be so ashamed to have children who barely passed their exams but had all the free time to call someone else who did names. When they called him a faggot, he dared them to spell it or told them to find new words to add to their very limited vocabulary. And when they called him *homo*, he called them *hetero*. It did not have the same taint, it did not even sound derogatory. But Segun felt that if he embraced that word, *homo*, fully enough, if he understood the word not as a dagger but, simply, a descriptive term, it would no longer hurt him.

Their senior certificate exams commenced. First WAEC, then NECO. During each paper, Segun sat and wrote alone. The other boys put money together to pay the external invigilator, so he wouldn't monitor them. Everyone but Segun paid; still, they drew up a list of everyone who paid so they could exclude his name. Segun had no problems with this. His parents did not have that kind of money, and he could never ask them for such a thing. The exams gave him the serenity to mourn the loss of his love. Sometimes he thought of calling Tanko, just to ask how he was doing, to hear his voice. But each time he did, there was no answer. Segun buried his grief in his books. One Thursday he bought a new SIM card, just to see if Tanko would pick up. Tanko did. As he listened to Tanko say "hello" repeatedly, tears welled in Segun's eyes.

"Tanko, it's me. It's Segun," he finally said. Tanko immediately hung up. Segun doubled over in pain. It felt so surreal, how something so encompassing, that burnt so brightly only months ago now simply no longer existed. How a man who used to be his entire world now didn't even talk to him, didn't even take his calls.

The exams gave him time, finally, to confront the emptiness he felt. He wrote well in his exams, of that he was sure. He was almost grateful for the isolation. It allowed him to finish early, revise his work, and hand it in before time was up. On some days, during those papers whose answers were not leaked on mobile phones, the invigilator would take Segun's paper and call out his answers for the other boys to write down. It did not matter to Segun. Very little still mattered to him.

After the examinations were over, some of the boys in his class decided they owed him a debt. They found him under the tree next to the science lab. They did not say anything to him before they started to kick him. It felt like they were stabbing him from many angles. He had never been attacked like that before. He did not know how to even begin fighting back. He simply held his head and curled into his body. As they kicked him, they called him all the names they wanted, as though they had been saving their hatred for this moment when Segun would not be able to speak back. He could feel his body absorbing the damage, absorbing the words. He would have stayed there like that, until they left him alone. But they weren't stopping. He could taste blood in his mouth now. A lot of blood. It spilt out and onto his shirt. He began to shout.

"Aunty! Aunty! Uncle! Uncle! Uncle!"

All he could do was hope a teacher would hear and come to save him. No one did. Their last paper had been an evening paper and all the teachers had left. When the boys were done, they left Segun lying on the ground and ran off. It was after they had run off that the tears came. He lay there and wept. He lay there for long minutes that felt like forever. Then he tried, at first without success, to stand up. Eventually, he found his balance and began to make his way home.

"Jesus!" his mother shouted when she saw him. "Jesus Christ. Abe! What happened?"

"Nothing," Segun said. "Just some of my class boys."

"Which class boys? What did you do to them that the fight would get to this extent?" his father asked.

"Are you okay?" his mother asked. "Oh Jesus, do these people want to kill you? Do they want to kill you for me? Is this all your blood? How can children be this wicked?"

His father, who had nothing on but a towel around his waist, rushed into his room and came back wearing a polo shirt and shorts.

"Let me at least take him to a clinic, to be on the safe side," his father said.

"Daddy, I'm fine. I just need to rest," Segun said.

"There's blood all over your shirt," his father said.

"I'm fine. The wounds are not deep. Once I take a bath, I'll be okay."

"Don't listen to this boy o. Take him o. Go, go, go. Hei. They want to kill my son. Let me come along."

They left for the clinic, the three of them. That night, Segun was admitted to the hospital, given a blood transfusion and more stitches than he could count on one hand.

"It's a very good thing you brought him in," the doctor said. "This boy could have died."

It was then that his mother began to cry.

CHAPTER SIX

Segun and his mother disagreed on which university he should apply to. She wanted him to apply to the University of Lagos, but he could never go there, not while knowing Tanko was there. His father wanted him to go to Lagos State University, but Segun knew they could not afford LASU, not after the fee hikes Governor Fashola had introduced.

"Ah!" his father shouted. "I paid two hundred and fifty naira when I went to school there."

"*Then*," Segun reminded him.

"But this is too much. Where are people supposed to get almost two hundred and fifty thousand for one year? One year o."

"Per child," his mother added. "So you can imagine if you have more than one child. Just tell your son to apply to UNILAG, like I suggested. He doesn't listen to me."

But Segun had already made up his mind to go to the University of Nigeria. Far away from Lagos, from Tanko—but not too far. His parents vehemently refused to even consider this. Enugu, as far as they were concerned, was too far, and UNN was too selective, the quota system would work against him. The road between Lagos and Enugu was bad, perilous. So many accidents, so much banditry.

"Stay here where we can know you're close," his mother told him.

But Segun filled it into his JAMB registration form, despite their protestations. In the space for the course of choice, he wrote Law. He too had heard the rumors about how high the cutoff marks were and how impossible it was to be admitted if you did not make the first list, the merit list, but it was still, after all, human beings who made that list. When the JAMB results were released, his score was good, just not good enough for Law. He told his mother, when she returned from the market, that he needed money to apply for a change of course.

"I'm not even sure I like Law that much," he said.

"So what course do you like?"

"Maybe Literature or Political Science."

"So it's now Literature you like?"

"It's a good course," Segun said.

"Why not change your institution instead? Put LASU. I'm sure they'll give you Law."

"Mummy, two hundred and fifty thousand? Every year? That's more than one million. Only on tuition o. I heard their acceptance fee is twenty thousand. Where are you going to get that kind of money?"

"Do you go hungry in this house? Or are you now the parent? I have only one child in this world. If I have to sell my wrapper so you can study what you want to study, I would do it happily."

His father said the same thing. "PHCN will soon promote me. We will find a way to make it work."

But even if all that was certain, even if the national electricity company did promote his father, Segun still did not want to put them through the extra financial strain. Even the school fees at UNN would be a hassle. He insisted, and changed his course to English and Literary Studies. His name was on the first list.

Adeniran, Oluwasegun Aberemangigha—English and Literary Studies.

His parents worried that this course he chose was not professional enough to guarantee him financial security. They celebrated with him nonetheless, but it was a muted celebration. His fees were paid. They helped him pack his bags, accompanied him to the bus park, and watched him get on a bus headed for Enugu. As it left Lagos, Segun promised himself to only come back as frequently as was needed to keep his mother satisfied.

Nsukka was a fresh start, a new beginning. It was beautiful, in the way ancient things were beautiful. Segun quickly learnt to navigate the campus, its huge buildings dated, as though they had always stood in those very spots. The food stands and cafeteria, with food that was sometimes delicious and other times bland. Department social activities that happened all at once within the space of a few weeks. All his roommates, Uchenna and Ifeanyi and Francis, were Igbo. They loathed him and made their animosity clear. The petty torments started almost immediately.

"I thought it was a girl speaking at the door," Uchenna, the fair, pimpled one, said. Segun smiled but said nothing. He greeted them and went around shaking everybody's hand. Normally he didn't bother with handshakes, but he wanted to make a good impression.

"Are you sure you didn't mean to go to the female hostel?" Francis said, and they all laughed.

Segun dragged his bag to his corner and began to unpack. He decided he did not like any of them and would make no further attempts to win them over. He was here for himself, to center himself, aggressively so. He would speak to them only when necessary and mind his business otherwise.

In class, things were a bit different. His classmates were friendly, in an effusive way that made it clear that the friend-liness was deliberate and impersonal. When one classmate did make fun of him, a girl who sat in front of the class, Julia, immediately turned around and shouted the offender down. The whole thing happened in moments. He commented on Segun's thin long arms, on how elegantly he moved. "Like woman own," the classmate said with disgust.

"And what is your problem with that?" Julia asked, turning back to face him. "You don't know how to mind your own business, or you hate women so much, that it pours over the rim unto effeminate men?"

She was the first one to call him that: effeminate. It didn't sound crude, the way terms the others used on him did. It sounded neutral, academic even, a word without intent.

"What's your own?" the boy asked her. His name was David, or Daniel, something like that.

"Say that again, to yourself."

"Ah Julia, calm down," someone said.

"I should calm down? Me? So this is okay?"

"It was just a harmless joke."

"I don't know what her problem is," Daniel said. "I wasn't even talking to her."

"Joke my foot," Julia said, hissing.

She was one of the people who made Segun's days bearable. Her company, her wit, her anger, the way she always defended him, the way she lifted some of the attention away from him, and pulled it to herself. For all this, Segun was grateful. That same semester he took a job at the business center, typing, printing, photocopying documents, selling snacks and other groceries. He needed the money, but also the routine to take his mind off everything else. To fill his time, so he did not have to dwell on how empty he felt. How angry and empty. Not because he wasn't used to the taunts and jeers but because for so long Tanko had been a central part of his life. Larger than life, around which his life fitted itself. Now, all that remained was empty space. He didn't know how to accustom himself to this feeling, this gaping feeling that he had lost something and that he would always feel that loss, that grief.

He went out with people, visited their rooms in this or that lodge, and had sex with them. The old Segun would never have found the temerity to meet up with the strangers he met on 2go or Facebook, but this one did not care. He knew how dangerous it was, and yet he did it. At times he asked for their pictures, to convince himself he was being careful.

Once a boy who stayed in Hilltop Lodge sent him a fake picture, but Segun didn't say anything when he arrived and found out the boy had sent him the picture of someone else.

"I thought you'd be angry," the boy said after they had sex. "Sorry. It's just . . . I don't give guys my picture in this Nsukka. This place is a jungle, very dangerous. Guys in the community would set you up with their full chest."

Segun nodded. "It's fine," he said. "I don't care."

The boy laughed. "It's because I'm cute. If I was ugly, you'd be raking."

Segun rolled his eyes. "Don't flatter yourself," he said. He hated how happy the boy was.

"Lighten up," the boy said.

His name was Trevor. This fascinated Segun. The name sounded so novel that at first, Segun thought it was something else he'd lied about. Later Trevor would show Segun his book and his school fees receipt, to prove his name was indeed Trevor.

"You could have just told me you weren't comfortable sending people your picture."

"Would you still have come to see me?"

"Yes," Segun said.

"Ha. Are you not afraid?"

Segun exhaled. He laced his shoes and stood to go. Trevor pressed two folded thousand-naira notes into his palm. Segun opened them, flattened out the notes, and gave them back to him.

"Just manage it for transport. I don't have more," Trevor said.

"I don't need this. I have transport money."

Trevor took the money back, his face glazed with confusion.

"When will we see again?" he asked.

"I don't know," Segun said.

That night he called his mother to hear her voice. He missed her, missed their conversations as they prepared dinner in their small kitchen, missed the way her voice rose at the television. He told her about his classes, about his lecturer who had been Achebe's student, about Julia, about how sunny Nsukka was, and he listened to her talk about her business and the class action suit they were pursuing to stop the Mushin Local Government from demolishing Mushin Ajina.

"This market has been standing here for a hundred years," she said. "They say they want to demolish it to make it better. Nonsense. Fashola must think we're children. Babies. Without brains. He's a very stupid man. So they cannot renovate it without demolishing it? He just wants to sell Mushin Ajina to TVIS. He will not succeed."

Segun enjoyed his mother's anger. How much he had missed that too. He reassured her and asked her to extend his greetings to his father. Then he called Trevor to ask if he would be free the next day. Trevor sounded surprised, but he said yes. They met in the evening and this time Segun slept over. It had been so long since anyone held him, so long since he let anyone hold him. Normally, he was on his feet and out as soon as the sex was over. But there was something about Trevor he found comfortable, trustworthy. Trevor would be the first person he told about what happened with Tanko. Trevor reminded him of his mother, the way he was eternally preoccupied with oppression. His was an academic preoccupation. He did not have bitterness in his tone when he spoke, did not invoke death and blood, the way Segun's mother did. There were always books by Ake and Okwudiba Nnoli and Bade Onimode. Segun would listen to Trevor talk for hours, fascinated with the way he knew a bit about everything, how easily he could recall the names of countries in Eastern Europe, or lay out the timeline of a war.

Trevor gave Segun books. *The Communist Manifesto. How Europe Underdeveloped Africa. Handbook of Revolutionary Warfare.* He taught Segun how to say Nyerere, so that the name rolled easily off his tongue. If Segun's mother gave him righteous anger and moral clarity, Trevor's books gave him the language with which to articulate that anger, and in doing so, understand it. Trevor also found it amusing, Segun's anger. *Angst*, he called it. Proletarian angst.

"You will grow tired of this eventually, this anger," he said. "Because how long can one person realistically expect to sustain anger?"

"For as long as there is something to be angry about," Segun said.

"Do you know anyone who has done that? Look at the older generation, haven't they all resigned themselves? Why do you think yours will be different?"

"My mother shows me every day that it is possible."

"Your mother?"

"Yes."

Trevor thought to himself for a bit and then asked, "But is that even a good thing? Do you think rage like that can coexist with happiness?"

"Rage like that is the result of the deprivation of happiness. Don't put the cart before the horse here."

"No, get me. If you have this much rage, it commits you religiously to a desire for revolutionary change. And when that never comes, I think it's so demoralizing. You know, as opposed to not feeling this strongly about it even though you know that things are bad."

But if there was anything Segun's mother's life had taught him, it was that Nigeria had a way of crushing its children. He already knew how impervious it was to change. His commitment was to himself. He would fight because it was the only way he knew how to convince himself of his value. Once, during a blackout that lasted for weeks, his mother told him, "None of this is normal, Abe. We are so used to it because it is the only reality we know. But none of this is normal. Do you think Fashola's children are in darkness? Do you think they sit under streetlights just to do their assignments? This country is evil to its core and there has never been a time when it wasn't so. Maybe that's why we are so used to it, so complacent. If people get light, they relish it. If not, they stay in darkness, or they use their generator if they have money for fuel. But no one questions the legitimacy of a state that gives its peoples' land to oil companies to destroy, and yet cannot provide electricity. Who will think it? Light is just a trivial thing. To us, it's no big deal. It's just light. And that is what we do to ourselves, we devalue ourselves. Strip ourselves of entitlement because otherwise, it will be obvious how little power we wield over our own lives. We tell ourselves we're not entitled to light, to food, to houses we can afford. To doctors, unless we have money. Only by rejecting this logic can we retain our God-given value as dignified human beings."

And so Segun came to hold on to that rage. Because then he could look at his life, look at everything that had happened to him, and take solace in the conviction that it was all of that, and not him, that was out of place, abnormal. In that way, his rage brought him comfort.

The day Mushin Ajina was demolished, Segun's mother was not in the market. She had gone to meet one of the poultry farms that supplied her with eggs. The bulldozers tore through the market, razing everything in its path. Segun's mother heard of it by phone. She immediately got on a Keke Napep and made her way to the market. There was nothing left of her stall but wood and zinc and smashed eggs and crates. Her heart could not bear the loss, it gave out, and she collapsed on the dirty market floor. Everything she had, it was in that shop, it was those eggs. She would not be the only one to faint. Seven people died that day. High blood pressure. Heart attacks. Injuries from the bulldozers themselves as the vendors tried to save what they could of their wares. Segun's mother had a heart attack.

When his father called to tell him, Segun felt his own heart stop too. "I don't want you to panic," his father said. "But Fashola has demolished Mushin Ajina. Your mother is in the hospital right now." Perhaps Segun would have had a heart attack too, were it not for his father's steady voice.

"What? What happened? What happened to her?" He was sitting on the edge of his bed. His mosquito net, which he folded up each morning, had come undone and was now resting on his back.

"Segun, calm down. Your mother collapsed. Her eggs were all destroyed."

"Is she okay?"

"The doctors are trying their best to save her."

Segun eyes welled with tears. His roommates gathered around him. They were looking at him as he ended the call.

"It's my mother," he told them. He felt ashamed that they were seeing his tears. "She had a heart attack. She's in the hospital."

They sympathized, patted his shoulders. It was unexpected, their sudden kindness.

"Nothing will happen to her," they said. "I'm so sorry. Don't worry, she'll be fine."

He began to throw some clothes into his schoolbag.

"Guy, are you going now? It's already evening."

"Will he even get bus to Lagos at this time?" Ifeanyi asked.

"Let me just try nau," Segun said. If he did not find any bus to Lagos, he would take one going into Enugu and take a night bus from there. He did not care what time it was.

He was fortunate. The last Peace Mass Transit bus hadn't left. He boarded. It was the first time he was traveling to Lagos at night. He was restless. His mind drifted in and out of sleep. All around them, the darkness pressed into the windows. There was the outline of trees standing ominously at both sides of the road. Segun thought of the bulldozers, crawling all over the market. One hundred years, his mother used to emphasize. He thought of his mother's stall. A stall so small she had to sit outside on a plastic armchair. She used to be able to get to whichever part of the stall she wanted to just by climbing over the crates. Segun remembered watching her do this; climb and walk on crates of eggs, without breaking them.

"How?" he asked her.

"Abe, I've been in the egg business for over fifteen years. It's a matter of experience."

Sometimes she sat on the eggs. There was a picture of her sitting on the crates in an album in his parent's bedroom. And now Fashola had destroyed it, a market that had stood for a century. The bus reached Lagos in the early hours of the morning. When he arrived at the hospital, his mother was still unconscious, but the doctors were sure she would wake.

His father hugged him. "You're here already? You did well, my son. You did well. It will be good for her to see you as soon as she wakes up."

His father left for work and Segun sat with his mother. He called Julia and told her what happened. Knowing Julia, she would cover for him. Sign attendance, take quizzes, if an impromptu one was given.

"Just don't worry," she told him. "Your mother will be fine."

Trevor said the same thing. "I'm sure she will wake up soon. Just be strong, for her."

But Segun's mother did not wake up that day, nor the day after that, nor the one after that. The doctors became worried. No one knew why she wasn't waking up or for how long she would continue to sleep. Segun could see it slowly take its toll on his father. With each day that passed, his own faith waned. Segun did not know how to process such a fear.

He had never imagined the possibility of his mother dying, not because he thought her immortal, but because he had simply never held her and death in the same thought before. Growing up, he thought her invincible. Now, he looked at her, at the tubes and wires, and his tears choked him.

His father was so focused on finding money for the hospital bills. "Today, I will meet Chief Francis," he would say. Or, "Tomorrow, I will ask the bank for a loan." Things like that. Responsibility shielded his father, Segun imagined. It gave him something to focus on so he did not have to confront his wife's mortality.

But even he could not avoid it forever. One day as they were having dinner in the hospital, Segun's father broke down, his plate of rice resting on his lap. "Segun . . . I don't know what I'm going to do. I just don't know."

His father's tears embarrassed Segun because he had never seen them before but also because they were in a public ward. All that separated them from other beds was a thin curtain drawn around them.

"I've spent all I have on oxygen. I've borrowed and borrowed and borrowed. Money I don't even know when I'll finish paying back. What will happen when I cannot find more people to borrow from? Tell me what then? What?" his father asked.

"Daddy, nothing will happen to her," Segun said.

The rice on his father's lap looked as though it would fall over, but his father picked the plate up and dropped it on the floor.

"How do you know?" he asked Segun. "Segun, even the doctors don't know."

Segun did not know. He stayed up at night thinking of this, willing his mother awake. His father continued to borrow, and it was good that he did because, on a Sunday afternoon, five weeks after she was hospitalized, his mother opened her eyes. She started to choke, to convulse, and for a terrifying moment, Segun thought maybe she only woke up to die.

The nurse rushed over. She pulled out the tube that went into Segun's mother's stomach for feeding. Slowly, his mother calmed. Her shoulders were still shaking. Tears streamed down her face. She let out a shrill scream. "I've lost everything. Everything. Fashola destroyed everything," she said.

"Madam, take it easy," the nurse said. "Haba. You're still alive. Your son is here, you still have him."

His mother turned to Segun, slowly. Her eyes were blood-shot. Slowly, she turned away without saying a word to him. The nurse put the tubes in a big stainless-steel pan and left. Segun went to his mother's side; she was crying audibly now.

"Abe, they destroyed everything," she said, hoarsely. "Everything."

She hugged him and buried her face in his shirt. Segun held her while she wept.

CHAPTER SEVEN

August met June in 2009, just as 2go was taking off as the social media app to be on. Everyone would gather in class to compare star levels and exchange usernames. The school chaplain gave many sermons denouncing the app, but it only made everyone want to be on it even more. August and June were first friends on 2go, before realizing they went to the same school. When they met, August had recently joined the platform and was making his way through the groups there, adding strangers and accepting friend requests. At night he stayed up for hours chatting in those groups to boost his level. He mused over those things like they were achievements. Professional. Leader. Master. Ultimate. It was in one of those groups that he met June.

"You know I've been noticing you in school, even before you added me on 2go. We call you the *quiet senior*. I saw your picture, and I knew it was you," June would later say to him. But August had no idea who June was when they met.

August's profile had a picture of him standing in front of their gate. Peculiar took that picture.

When June told him they went to the same school, August said, "Oh you go to Immaculate Boys'?"

"Yes," June said.

"Nice."

"Is it?"

"Lol," August replied. He was not laughing but it amused him the way June said it.

"Lol," June wrote back. "So what's your name? No one knows. We legit just call you the quiet one."

"August."

"Seriously? Like your real name?"

"Yes," August said. It brought a smile to his face.

"That's so cool. You can call me June. I mean my actual name is Chukwudi but June is a cool name too, right? I've always wanted a month name."

August laughed. They met at the canteen the next day and talked. August found June intriguing. How he was cynical, the way he said lol when he was amused.

"You think the Nigerian government cares about transparency? Lol."

August wanted to say that it didn't really work in face-to-face conversations because it was obvious he wasn't laughing out loud, but June made him shy. And this shyness was a curious thing because June was a class below him.

If June asked for abacha, August bought him abacha. If June asked for Zobo, August bought him Zobo. The dynamics of what they had seemed sometimes to consist solely of August being perpetually trapped in the effort to impress June. Many times he said things specifically because he hoped it would be the sort of thing June would say.

The days he ran, before the student athletes took their position at the white line, August would look through the small group of spectators and try to find June's face. Zipping through the breeze, he would imagine he could hear June's voice cheering him on. Saying, "Run, August, run. Yes," and each time he won he would look at the stands to see if June was clapping for him.

The first time June came to watch him run, as they walked to class together, June told him, "You run funny."

August looked at him and smiled. "But I won," he said.

"Yes, but others, they look like they're running to the finish line, but you, you look like you're running from something. Why are you looking back?"

"That makes no sense," August said, laughing uncomfortably.

"I think it does make sense," June said.

August did think of it later, the way he ran. It wasn't even about getting somewhere, or away from something. It was about the power he had over himself in those moments. The power to whip himself into a frenzy of accelerating muscles, to feel himself cutting through the air. He told June this because it sounded like the sort of thing June would like to hear.

On a rainy Tuesday, when June came to borrow movies from August, the issue of August's mother came up. June wanted to know what happened to her.

"She died doing something stupid," August said. June shook his head sadly, almost the way August's sisters did.

It was the first time August was saying something like this out loud. He wouldn't dare say it to his sisters. And he never said it to any of his friends, either. Obiajulu would have laughed and made fun of him, and his mother. And

August was not sure he could tolerate anyone making fun of his mother. Somehow, he trusted that June wouldn't do that. August did not expect that June would just sit on his bed staring at him and shaking his head.

"She wanted to have a son, real bad, and it didn't end well. For her. I survived." August chuckled lightly.

June was completely silent; perhaps he regretted asking the question, which was good because August normally got anxious whenever he had to talk about his mother.

Eventually, when he found his voice, June said, "Well, I'm sure there's a different view of things from her perspective."

"She wanted to have a son. She died. Not much else."

"Well, I don't know. You didn't live her life."

August made a sound but continued sorting the stack of DVDs on the floor.

"Also," June continued, "it brought about you, so it wasn't all tragedy, I guess."

"She should have just stayed alive instead," August said. He could feel June's eyes boring into him, so he didn't look up. Not once did June offer condolences. They just left it at that and August wondered if it was because June pitied him too much to say anything else.

August's sisters liked June. When June visited, they enjoyed entertaining him, serving him juice, and chatting with him as though he were their friend too. If August was out, his sisters would let June wait in August's room.

"He's so polite," they said. It was all they ever said about June. "That your friend Chuks is so polite. His parents must be so pleased."

August knew June was not really polite. He was chilly, almost vindictive, and it intrigued August. But June knew how to put on an act. Or perhaps his sisters were just pleased August had a friend.

On Saturdays, August and June would go for morning runs together. June didn't like running, so mostly, they walked the long distance to their school. It gave them time to talk. It didn't matter what it was they talked about. They talked about everything, and of nothing. Other times, they simply walked in comfortable silence. It mattered very little to August what they did. At the school, some men would be using the football field for a match. August and June would sit on the concrete slabs and watch the men play for a while, imagining what their lives and jobs were like, devoid of parental interference.

"This one works at the bank. He looks like a bank person. He's not a teller though. That one, the one with the beard, a doctor."

"I don't think he's a doctor."

"He looks like a doctor."

"I think he works at the State Secretariat or something." They laughed.

"What about the other one in tight shorts?" June asked.

"Hmmm . . . I'm not sure," August said, squinting his eyes in the man's direction.

"He's probably a banker," June said.

"Mumu, all of them are bankers."

"It's not impossible for all of them to be bankers," June said. "This could be their office sports thing."

"How big is this bank?"

"Big enough."

They would sit there for a while and then August would ask, "Do you want to run?"

Always, June said no.

"I'll let you win o," August would say, and June would laugh but remain seated.

August would pat the ground with his palms and rub them together, do a small countdown in his head, before taking off. He would run back and forth, back and forth while June sat there watching him. And then, when he was exhausted, they would leave. They repeated this routine often, almost every Saturday, coming back to watch the men play, and hypothesize on what their lives were like. Then August would run the tracks until he was exhausted and sweating and they would walk back to his house together. June would stay in the living room chatting with Chinyere or Peculiar, or at August's desk, going through his books while August had his bath and changed his clothes. August cherished those Saturdays. June made him feel understood, made him feel like a person in his own right.

One afternoon, as they took turns playing *Tomb Raider* on August's phone, June told August he liked him. That day, June was quiet. Unusually quiet, and August was afraid to ask why. For him, quiet meant he had done something wrong, disappointed his sisters again. But June's silence was unnerving.

"What?" August asked eventually.

"Nothing," June said.

August looked up from the phone to look at June. June stared back.

"You know I like you right?" he said.

August coughed. He had no idea what to say. As his coughing subsided, a silence filled the room. Even the noise from the game stopped.

"I don't know." June chuckled. "Maybe it's because of the way you just . . . I don't know. You're just this really nice sort of person."

No one had ever told August they liked him before. He didn't know where to look, how to keep his hands, what to say.

"You're really handsome," June continued.

"We're both guys." August finally managed to find his voice.

"I know. Look, I know you may not like me back. I get it."

The silence returned. August was irritated at his own lack of words. "I-I don't know what to say," he eventually said.

"You don't have to say anything. It's cool."

"Why did you even tell me? I could tell people at school. I could even get you expelled."

June smiled sadly. "You would never do that to me," he said.

"You don't know that."

"August, I know what you can do. I'm not afraid of you."

August did not know what to feel about this. A part of him felt unworthy of that amount of trust. When June reached out to touch him, August recoiled. He cleared his throat and repositioned himself on the bed.

"Jeez. I just wanted to collect the phone," June said.

August handed it to him.

"I'm sorry. Maybe I shouldn't have told you. I don't want you to start treating me differently. I like us like this."

As June spoke, he did not raise his face from the phone. He wasn't playing. He was just staring at the screen.

August wanted to say something, to tell June that he did not feel that way at all, to tell him never to bring up something like that again. But all he could think of was how on top of the world he felt when, after winning a race, he would come back to see June smiling so proudly at him.

"Sorry. I'm not like that," he said in the end.

At first, all August could think about was how proud his mother would have been to hear him say that. I'm not like that. A renunciation, a testament to knowing who he was. And who he wasn't. He could almost hear her voice saying, *Good, August, good.*

June stopped coming to the house. August's sisters began to ask after him. "Whatever happened to Chuks?" they asked. "Did you two quarrel?"

August shrugged, as though he did not understand why June's absence would be noticed. Other times he pretended not to hear the question.

When they ran into each other at the school canteen, they exchanged pleasantries but there was a coldness now. June never stayed long.

One afternoon August asked him, "What happened?"

"What do you mean what happened?"

"You've been behaving strangely, somehow. Are you avoiding me?" August felt embarrassed asking these questions. For a moment, he was afraid June would laugh at him.

"Avoiding you? No. What? Of course not."

Someone, a classmate, called to June, and June excused himself. August was left standing there in the middle of the canteen unsure what to do with himself. That afternoon when Peculiar asked him about June again, August said, "I've told you nothing happened. I don't know why you can't just leave me alone and mind your business."

Even he was surprised at how angrily he said those words. Peculiar stood there shocked, her mouth hanging slightly open. She looked like she would say something, or cry, but she left him alone. He later apologized for his outburst. Peculiar waved his apology away saying she wasn't even angry, even though August knew she was. He knew too that June meant way more to him than he cared to admit. On the days he ran, his wins felt routine because there was no June in the cluster of students that came out to watch. June did not really like track sports. He told August this before, that he only came because he knew someone who was also running. Some days August tried to imagine that June was there, clapping, calling out his name. But even on those days, after winning and getting pats on the back from the coach and other boys he ran with, he walked back to class alone.

August fantasized about redeeming the whole situation. He stayed up at night imagining it. He would stop June and apologize—for whatever it was he did wrong—and they would stay in his room after school and take turns playing

Tomb Raider or *Asphalt 6.* They would walk to school on Saturdays and sit on the grass and watch the men play football once more. They would point out who was a doctor, a bank teller, or a sales rep. He would point out that June thought everyone was a banker and June would smile softly and deny it. They would run. Maybe then he would get June to race him. August had always wondered what it would take to get June to let loose enough to allow himself one race. August imagined that June would be laughing as the wind blew in his face. They would run and at the end, he would let June win. Many times, he started to convince himself that he would indeed go through with it, apologize to June, or tell him the truth, that he felt something for him too. Something that made his insides tingle, that made him smile to himself at the most random moments, that made him look forward to each new morning. Something he was ashamed of.

CHAPTER EIGHT

August did not like his birthday. Every year his sisters made a big celebration of it, with music and balloons and food and colorful ribbons crisscrossing the living-room ceiling. No one said anything about his mother, and this was something else for which August felt guilt. Because of him, no one was allowed to mourn her on the day she died. Even his father lost his characteristic glumness for days, so that looking at him, one would not be able to guess that he had resigned himself to nothingness.

August wrote to his mother—poems, snippets of a letter, an entire eulogy. In some of them, he forgave her for dying. In others, he mused how better off he was not to have witnessed the death so directly, the way his sisters did. He watched them as they ran about planning for a party August did not want. He had held that position for many years. Still, each year he played along out of fear that his not wanting a party would perturb his sisters. The party happened in the afternoon. Because his birthday coincided with the long vacation the party was always packed. Friends, cousins, people he did not know. August dressed up and lived the life that was assigned to him. Smiling, making polite conversation, thanking people for coming to his party, praising God for everything. He knew his sisters were watching him and he knew they would be proud.

August's mother threw parties like these when she was alive. There was always something to celebrate. Birthdays, promotions, the day Moshood Abiola won the 1993 elections. August liked to imagine her parties were just like the ones his sisters threw him. That way, he could tell himself that he would not have enjoyed them. He had memories of them; his mother in a sequined dress smiling at everyone, being pleasant. After his birthday parties, August would hide in his room and cry because there was this emptiness in him that those parties widened, this inadequacy they left festering in him, a scratching yearning to win his mother's love. He wanted so much to live a life she would be proud of.

Most of the guests for his seventeenth birthday were people from his school and people his age who lived in their neighborhood, people his sisters imagined were his friends. Most of them attended all his parties. Most of them he grew up playing football or racing down the street with. Perhaps they were, indeed, his friends. He never felt like he belonged. They carried themselves with a confidence he envied, a surety he wished he had. He tried to cultivate it by focusing on their admiration for him. He was the one everyone wanted on their team. And sometimes he believed that if only he was within those circles, where he was wanted so much, it would give him that surety he never seemed to be able to find. They were talking to him now, Jude and Nonso and Esteem. Jude was making a joke about drinking beer when the party was over and the real party began. For the big guys. August laughed, perhaps a little louder than he should have.

"My sisters are dulling," he said.

August had never spoken to his sisters about alcohol, but blaming them seemed like the obvious thing to do. The guys nodded. It was easy, standing there as they traded random stories, holding his Coke and smiling when necessary. Sometimes he told a story of his own or made one up if he didn't have any relevant anecdotes. For a second he thought he caught a glimpse of June. The figure was standing so far away and the music was so loud that he couldn't decide if it was him or not. He let Nonso finish his story before he excused himself. The closer he came, the more obvious it became that it was June. August wasn't even sure why for a moment he doubted that it was June. The living room was not that big and no matter how loud the music was, what had sound got to do with anything?

When August invited June, he told August he couldn't come.

"I have a boring family thing," was his excuse. Even then, August knew he was lying.

"You can come late. You don't have to come early."

"Sorry," June said.

Yet here he was, standing next to Peculiar. She saw August first. "Oh, there he is," she said to June. June turned around. He stared at August and it made him feel self-conscious.

"Hey," August muttered. "You came."

Peculiar wandered off and June inched closer to August.

"Yeah, I decided to ditch my family thing. Happy birthday."

"Thanks."

For a while after that, all that existed between them was the sound of music and indistinct chatter. August didn't know what to say. They walked to the edge of the room where the music wasn't so loud. June plopped down on the seat and August perched next to him. He wondered what June thought of his party, the banal balloons hanging from the blue and yellow ribbons.

"When did you arrive?" he asked June.

"Oh, not so long ago. You said I could be late though."

August gave a small smile.

"How did you get out of your family thing?"

June shrugged. "Sorry," he said.

"Yeah, I guessed as much," August said. He had tried many times to convince himself that June wasn't manufacturing an excuse not to attend his party.

"In my defense," June said, "I do hate parties."

August laughed. June chuckled along.

"How can you hate parties?" August asked, even though he himself could not remember any party he'd attended that he did not regret, including his own.

"I just hate them. The noise, people going around forcing themselves and each other to be nice. Urgh!" June shuddered and it made August laugh again and fill with gratitude that June was there.

"We could go inside. The noise isn't so loud there." He drank the last of his Coke. They walked to his room, June dodging anyone he knew well enough to talk to, August greeting everyone and asking if they had eaten or had drinks. Something about leaving his own party felt sneaky and exciting. He opened his room and stepped aside to let June in, looking around to see if any of his sisters saw him. When he stepped into the room and closed the door behind him, the sounds of the music became muffled, so faint it could have been coming from the next compound. Only then did August realize that his room was untidy. The bed was unmade and some of his clothes were on the floor next to the bed. His underwear was on top of the reading table. He went about quickly collecting everything and flinging them into his wardrobe.

"So, did you hear that the vice principal died?" he asked. He needed something to say and there was nothing as generic as repeating the story going around.

"Yeah, I heard. You think it's true?"

August shrugged. "Immaculate boys at our lesson center were talking about it. I don't know sha, everyone was always saying she was sick."

"Oh, you go to lesson?" June asked, and it shocked August because it was such a thing that June would have known.

"You stopped talking to me," August said. It was an accusation, one that was almost painful. He kept replaying that afternoon in his head, wondering how he would have done things differently. He dreamt about it, frequently, himself, June, and his mother in his room, their conversation playing out while his mother watched on.

"What are you talking about?" June said, but his voice gave him away. August could tell that even June did not find those words convincing. The room became silent for a while before June shrugged.

"Sorry," he said simply.

"But why? What did I do?" August asked. He eyed the
door, overcome with a strange suspicion that his sisters were
standing on the other side with their ears pressed against it.

"You didn't do anything. I just didn't want things to get
weird."

"So you started avoiding me?"

"Look, I really like you, and the way you freaked out, I
didn't want you to treat me differently, like I was this dirty,
worldly thing."

"June," August began, but June waved his hand in the air
frantically.

"Let's not talk about this . . . thing," he said, drawing out
the word till it took on a life of its own: *thing*.

August could almost feel it as a presence in the room, and
with it, the fear that if he did not say the right things, he
would never get another chance.

"What if I feel the same way?"

"Don't mock me," June said. August shook his head. He
came and sat next to June on the bed. He wanted to take
June's hand in his but he was afraid June would laugh.

"I don't know. Maybe. It's possible." June's hand was warm
when August took it in his. He brought his face next to June's
and pressed his lips to June's. August could feel his heart
beating hard in his throat. June put his hand on August's
head and pulled him closer. August could feel June's tongue
everywhere in his mouth. At first, August felt repulsed, but
soon the repulsion faded into nothingness and he became
aware instead that his penis was straining painfully against
his jeans. It felt like it would break in two from the sheer
pressure.

Earlier that day, Uzoamaka had asked him if they weren't too tight and now, August wished he had changed them for one of his more loosely fitting chinos. They stayed locked like that, tilting toward each other. It felt like June was sucking out all the oxygen in him. The kiss seemed to last forever, and when someone knocked on the door, it forced them to quickly disentangle, August felt relieved. He reached for a pillow behind him and placed it on his thighs before saying, "Come in." Uzoamaka poked her head into the room.

"What are you doing hiding here? People are beginning to leave, you have to thank them before they go." She seemed to notice June only after speaking.

"Good evening," June said.

"Chuks! I didn't even know you came. Hope you're enjoying the party?"

"Yes, thank you," June said.

"Have you had something to drink?"

"I'm fine."

"Nonsense," Uzoamaka said, throwing the door wide open. She shot August a disapproving glare. "I have cold Chivita in the kitchen. You can take it home if you don't want to drink it here."

June stood and left the room.

"What are you doing sitting there? Come on before your guests leave without seeing you."

Your guests. August had always wondered how they were his guests when it wasn't him who threw the party. Long ago, when he was still little and could ask them things without worry, he had asked her this. Why were they *his guests* even though it was she who invited them?

"They're here for you, August, not me. They're here to celebrate with you," she said, and it terrified him, made him dwell on how much there was to celebrate, how unremarkable his life was.

Now she was standing there at his door looking at him, but August couldn't stand up without exposing the protrusion in his jeans.

"I'll be right there," he said and sat there. When she left, closing the door behind her, he threw the pillow at the door and buried his face in his hands.

He felt tainted, defiled even, and guilt began to bloom unfettered, somewhere in his chest. He could almost hear his mother saying, *Oh August. What a shame.*

His sisters had always assured him that she was in heaven and that she watched over him from there. It was one of those things he accepted without question. Now, the more he thought about it, the more it disturbed him. He knew that were his mother able to speak to him, she would be disgusted at this thing he had allowed himself. June's words came back to him, ringing loudly in his mind, and he wondered if he had been afraid of the same thing: becoming a dirty, worldly thing.

For weeks after that, August was plagued with fear that now that he had let this part of himself escape, he would have no way of reining it back in. It would simply roam until it subsumed him completely. He tried to see it as something completely external to himself. It was the only way he could make any sense of it, seeing it as separate, a foreign feeling in a boy's chest. He battled with the fear that now he would not be able to absolve himself of the stain that came with it. In school, with June, he tried to behave like everything was the same.

They started walking to the tracks again to watch the men play football. And he still tried to get June to run with him. But the truth was that now he felt different about June. He wasn't sure exactly what it was. Perhaps some of it was anger and some of it was disgust and some of it was envy. He reminded himself that it was *he* who had kissed June, but it didn't abate the anger he felt. That kiss would, for a long time, signify the day he lost control of himself, gave in to the one thing he feared the most about himself.

August and June would end as abruptly as a speeding car smashing into a sturdy tree, its bonnet crunching up at the impact, and the windows shattering with the sheer force. It was a few weeks before August's WAEC exams. It started, like many things in his life, with the word of God.

August's sisters were not fervent worshippers; his father did not attend church services at all. He spent Sunday mornings sitting in front of the television in boxer shorts and a faded polo. Some days he left the TV tuned to a worship channel, and on others, he turned it to a movie channel. Once August saw him muttering along with the sound from the TV. He never saw his father in a church service. The story goes that before August was born, his father attended Sunday Mass with the rest of the family. But after August came, he slackened. Not even Uzoamaka could say with certainty that he had received Communion since then. However, August and June's end did not happen with a Catholic Church. It began at Immaculate Boys', during prayer service, in preparation for their forthcoming final exams. Spiritual preparation was what the chaplain called the prayers. But the pastor who gave the sermon spent all his time shouting about sin. There was something about his tone and the manner of his voice that was frightening.

When he said, "Homosexuals, God knows. Even if you hide from the world, God knows," it struck something in August. God became for him, not an abstract omnipotent force, but a personal one, hoping on him to do the right thing.

Thinking of God like this made him afraid of himself, of June.

When the pastor said, "Some of you are here looking at me thinking God doesn't know about the evil you do in secret," August realized this thing he felt wasn't something that could exist independently of him, it wasn't a skin he could wear or shirk. It was him, or it was not. But it could only be one. He had to decide.

When the pastor walked past him, August's heart beat faster, such was his fear that the man would drag him out and shout, "God can see you!"

August's friendship with June died in that place. He left it overwhelmed with shame, and determined to overcome his shame by conquering himself.

Now it was his turn to avoid June. At first, June seemed not to notice that August no longer wanted to associate with him. He would stick around during recess and make conversation no matter how monologic they were. One Friday he asked August to buy him Zobo. They were walking to the canteen from the senior's quadrangle.

"Buy your own Zobo," August said.

June stopped walking, but August continued on his way. In all this, August's anger toward June did not wane. If anything, it grew stronger. And he needed that anger to prove to himself that he was redeemable. He did not see June again that day, or for weeks after that. The next time he saw June was at home. He heard the gate and looked through his window to see who it was. Somehow he knew it was June, even before he looked. Peculiar welcomed him and the sound of their voices exchanging pleasantries carried all the way into his room. He could hear them saying his name. He sat at his reading table and arranged the books there. He opened his Commerce textbook to a random page.

When Peculiar knocked, he kept his eyes on the page as she opened the door.

"Chuks is here," she said.

"I'm busy," August replied.

"What do you mean you're busy? You have a visitor and I've already told him you're around."

"Tell him to go away."

August didn't raise his eyes from his textbook, but he thought he heard her gasp.

"August," she began.

"Just tell him to go. I'm trying to read, please."

"Did anything happen?"

"I don't want to see him. I'm busy."

Peculiar stood there for a few seconds more before she left. He strained his ears, but all he could hear was silence, then there was the sound of the front door opening and closing. He rushed to his window to watch June leave, his head facing the ground. He looked ashamed, and August felt a perverse pleasure at this. It was almost as though August had transferred some of his shame to June. That night, as August sat at the dining table eating his supper, he could hear Peculiar and Chinyere talking. He could hear the sound of their voices but he couldn't make out any words. He knew they were talking about him. He imagined they were shaking their heads and clicking their tongues, and that when they called to tell Uzoamaka, she too would shake her head. They were so afraid of any blemish on his character, anything that would point to mistakes they had made in raising him. And it saddened him because he wanted so badly to be the man they wanted him to be.

CHAPTER NINE

The dreams started after that. August would wake from them drenched in sweat. In those dreams, his mother's teary face would be staring on as he tumbled around in the sand with June. It would start with June agreeing to race him, and no matter how fast he ran, he would always arrive at the finish line to see June's smiling face waiting. They would then replicate that kiss from his room, this time with a team of bankers playing football in the background.

They would end up on the ground, their bodies, now naked, matted with sweat and sand. Sometime in June's place, there would be a man whose face was familiar, but whose name August could not remember.

August would wake in the middle of the night and falling back asleep would be impossible. Instead, he would stay up thinking of his mother, and how much he must be over-thinking it all. She was, after all, an excessively good woman, kindhearted to a fault. Surely some of that kindness still existed, even now. Surely she could see how much he did not want this, how much he loathed this, of himself.

There was this memory he had of her. He remembered first hearing it from his father, but this was unlikely. His father never spoke to him of his mother, so perhaps it came from Uzoamaka or Chinyere. It was about Uzoamaka's primary school books. A woman living down the street had come to return a textbook that her daughter had stolen from Uzoamaka. Between exorbitant fees to keep her in a good school, her parents couldn't afford the textbooks, so the girl decided to steal one. August's mother decided to buy her textbooks. It seemed to August such a banal gesture, but he liked to think it must have required some empathy for his mother to think of the girl, not as the girl who stole her daughter's textbooks, but as the girl whose parents could not afford the books she needed. He imagined she could see him like that too, not as a broken thing but as a son trying to earn his dead mother's love. He knew, too, how foolish it was, trying to earn the love of someone dead. But he felt it as a duty to prove, even if just to himself, that he was worth her sacrifice.

August's exams began on a rainy Tuesday. And with it came an intense fear of failing. In the months leading up to it, August agonized on what to fill out in his JAMB forms. The University of Nigeria, definitely (his sisters could not bear to see him go to school somewhere far away). But what would he study? There was a huge prospectus in the school library with all the courses and the O level subjects needed for them. August was hard-pressed to find something he liked. He even temporarily entertained the thought that university was not for him. Temporarily, because he knew he did not have the heart to say such a thing to his sisters. Eventually, he decided to apply for History, not because he had a sustained interest in History but because it was the most obvious option, considering the subjects he was sitting for in his WASSCE.

"Why History?" his sisters asked.

"Why not," August replied, and then realizing that this was not a suitable answer added, "I will be what I know will make me happy. Being a historian is what I want to do. I could further in Archaeology. A lot of our history is shrouded in time."

His sisters stared at him as one would stare at a naïve sheep straying into the forest unaware of the existence of wolves. But they held their peace. The truth was, August did not really believe his own words. What did it really entail to be a historian? August did not know. All he wanted was to give his sisters the satisfaction of believing he was doing what he loved because otherwise, they would worry.

Reading became harder and harder as the exams drew closer. The more he read, the more frightened he became that nothing he was reading would stick long enough to help him pass. Each day, before he went to the venue of his exams, Chinyere would slip some money into his hands.

"Uzoamaka said you should have this," she would say, "just in case."

August never used any of that money. He never needed to. The prefect always wrote his name on the list of students who paid, and no other student ever complained. It was, after all, August.

He pushed through the exams, forgetting each experience immediately after. By the end of the monthlong examinations, he had not had one bad paper, but he still felt like he would fail.

August had his first lapse only a week after his exams. The second and third ones would come months after but as follow-ups to the first. Then they would get more frequent, sometimes daily. Seeing them as lapses helped him convince himself they were mistakes, momentary slip-ups, brief moments of weakness.

It began on the football field at Immaculate Boys' and swept out of his control before he could stop himself. He had come alone and sat for some moments to watch the men playing football. He ran a few laps and then sat back down to catch his breath and continue watching the men play. Eventually, the match ended, and the men dispersed. One of the men walked up to where he was seated. His skin was a rich dark brown and he had a goatee that made him look rugged. He sat next to August and nodded a quiet greeting. August mumbled something under his breath. The man reclined, back on the grass, knees raised. His jersey shorts rode down his thighs. August could see the soft hairs on his thighs and it made something inside him tingle. He stood up and began running quick laps along the track, trying as much as he could to keep his eyes straight in front of him. Later that day, he would berate himself for not running all the way home. Certainly, with the pace with which he ran those laps, he would have had no problem running home. But he did not go home. He exhausted himself and went to sit back down. The man's eyes were closed now and August wondered if he was asleep. What kind of madman slept on a field? He was a bit startled when the man spoke.

"What about your friend? He didn't come today?"

August turned to look at him and then mumbled something nonsensical under his breath.

"He did not want to come and join you and point?" he asked, and then laughed.

August said nothing, simply looked ahead. From the side of his eyes, he saw the man stand and walk toward him. He stood towering in front of August. August averted his gaze.

"You go to this school, eh?" the man asked.

August nodded. He stood up and dusted off his shorts.

"I'm Timothy," the man said, stretching out his hand. "Your friend, Chuks, is actually my very good friend."

"August."

When he shook hands with Timothy, the older man tickled his palm with his index finger. For some reason this alarmed August. It was at this point that all the bells in his head went off. There seemed suddenly to be something dangerous about Timothy.

"August. Beautiful name."

"I have to go now," August said, nodding.

"Yes, yes. Me too. I'm getting very hungry. Come, I'll drive you. Which direction are you going?"

"Oh, no need," August said.

"Nwoke m, come let's go. I don't bite," Timothy said.

There were more protests in August but they refused to rise from his chest. In the car he said nothing, only gave directions. Timothy on the other hand talked and talked and talked. About June mostly but about everything else too. August wanted him to shut up.

"Do you want to see it?" Timothy asked.

"Huh?"

"Do you want to see it?" Timothy asked again.

August stared at him blankly. *See what?* he thought.

"The *PES 3.*"

"Oh. Yes . . ." August said. It came out sounding more like a question. Yes?

"Okay, let's just hope that these people brought light."

"Wait. Now?"

"My house is really not that far," Timothy said.

Again the protests in August's throat remained there. In the days after this, he would berate himself for this, for somehow knowing what was happening, but not pushing back enough. Timothy lived in a three-story building in New Heaven. The compound was so small the cars had to be parked in a narrow line. His flat was on the third floor. He left August in the living room, in front of the home theater, and went inside. August sat there looking at the game console. He didn't even know how to play it. He fiddled uncomfortably with the controls till Timothy came back out to show him how to use it. They played game after game, till the electricity went out.

"Oh well, they tried," Timothy said. "There has been light since yesterday."

He left the room again and came back with small bottles of stout. He handed August one. August had never drunk beer before, but he did not protest. He took the bottle and mumbled his thanks.

"You drink stout, right? I don't know which one you small boys are drinking these days."

"It's fine. Stout is fine." He took a sip from the bottle. It was bitter but he pushed it down his throat.

"Thank God. Your friend Chuks doesn't like it much. He doesn't have the stomach. Can't down even one bottle," Timothy said and laughed. August forced a laugh. He took another swig of his beer. "I've not been seeing Chuks around sef. Hope he's doing well. Nice boy. But not to worry since you're here."

August looked at Timothy and their eyes held. It was clear to him the kind of man Timothy was.

"I'm not like that. I'm not like him," August said.

"I know. I've seen you running. You're a really fast one, eh?"

August said nothing. He looked away and took another sip from his bottle. Timothy stood and came to sit next to him. August felt himself getting hard. It made a tent in his jersey shorts. And as it rose, shame rose with it. Timothy touched him.

"You have a big one," Timothy said, smiling. August looked away. Timothy's hands on his thighs were warm. When he kissed August, August felt a scratchy uneasiness at the prickliness of Timothy's beard. He turned his face away.

"I don't want this," he said. "I don't want to do this."

"We're not even doing anything," Timothy said. He dragged his lips along August's neck. It tickled.

"No. Stop," August said.

"What wrong?" Timothy asked, peering at him.

His lips were wet. He was a very handsome man, and it was a strange thing that this was only just occurring to August.

"Don't you like it?" he asked, sliding his hand through the waistband of August's jersey shorts. August said nothing. Slowly, Timothy pulled down August's shorts. The leather seat was cold. Timothy's mouth was surprisingly warm. August subconsciously sucked in his cheeks to see if his own mouth was that warm. He really couldn't tell. He closed his eyes.

He could not believe what was happening. His heart was racing. Maybe it was just a dream. Maybe if he opened his eyes, there would be nothing, just the emptiness of his thoughts, and he would be back at the field. It was not a dream. He closed his eyes again. He did not want to watch. Soon he felt the rush, a little tightness in the peak of his stomach, the release, and then that almost painful pleasure when Timothy didn't stop slurping on him. Timothy laughed. When he sat back up to smile at August, August's shame began to turn to anger.

"Now do me. Come on," Timothy urged, taking August's hand and putting it down his shorts. August took back his hand.

"Please," Timothy said.

"I want to go home," August said.

"Please nau."

August shook his head.

"Oh, you're gonna be like that?" Timothy said sadly. "I guess I'll just finish myself off then."

August sat there. Soon he had another erection but he did not touch it. Timothy came, splattering everywhere. He handed August a towel to clean himself up and they went downstairs. In the car, August tried hard to contain himself. Each time he spoke to tell Timothy where to turn, he felt tears at the base of his throat. When Timothy parked in front of August's house, August pulled frantically at the door until it opened. Timothy was saying something but it did not register. All August could think of was how he needed to get as far away from him as possible.

He hated Timothy. He left the car burdened by this disgust for himself. Inside, Peculiar and Chinyere were sitting in the living room, watching a movie.

"You stayed out long," Peculiar said. He ignored her.

"August," she called.

"Yes, I stayed out. So?"

"It's almost six. You've been gone since morning."

"Can't I go out and stay until six?"

They turned to look at him and he feared that if he stood there, he would burst into tears. He stormed off to his room. And sat on his bed, confused and ashamed and afraid. He started to cry. And realizing how stupid his tears were, he wiped them away. But no sooner had he wiped them, then they returned. He slid slowly to the ground, and holding his head between his knees, allowed himself those tears. Each drop symbolizing the things he knew he should be, the thing he promised himself he could be. Something worthy of love, something worthy of his mother's affection.

There was the burning urge to go into the shower and wash the saliva off, but his bones were weak. The tears washed over him as he went through all the things he could have done differently. He should have simply said no. He should have said he didn't want to see the stupid *PES 3*. He could have insisted on finding his own way home. He thought of his sisters. What would they think of him if they knew what he was? A damaged boy, unworthy of his mother's sacrifice. It would have been easy to just say no. But he wanted this. In that room, he wanted to experience Timothy. He wanted to see what it was. He sat there and cried until there were no tears left in him. Then he spent moments more convincing himself that it was one slip. One. Singular. Slip. It would never happen again. He would *never* let himself be that weak again. In the shower, he tried to wash away the smell that seemed now to cling to his skin.

He never knew he could hate someone as passionately as he hated Timothy. That was why it surprised him when it happened again, and again. It was a betrayal of himself, the way it happened again even though for many nights he dreamt of killing Timothy and somehow stuffing his body in the game console. In lapses that came after, there would be less and less conviction, and grief. His mother's words would be the only constant.

They sometimes came like whispers, as though she were there with him, speaking in a tone so lowered that only he could hear.

August, this is not you. This is not my son.

Other times, they came in God's voice booming down on him. Those words never left him. Even when he zoomed through finish lines or ran with the ball, even as everyone cheered, it stayed. He always felt like a fraud, hearing them cheer his name. And no matter how long he spent consoling himself, telling himself God at least loved him and that his love was eternal, always waiting to offer him redemption, he couldn't get himself to believe it. Even God's love felt like something he needed to earn, something he needed to prove himself worthy of. He was repulsed by himself, and how could God ever love something like that? Something this vile. How could God behold sin this grave?

His sisters, as always, watched him with great suspicion. They urged him to visit his classmates. "Staying indoors this much, it's not good for you," they said.

August could tell how worried they were and all that did was amplify his fear of being discovered. They were the only ones to ever love him, and August was not sure they would still love him if they knew what he was.

CHAPTER TEN

August found out he failed his WAEC exams on the day of his second lapse. He had not expected to fail that badly, especially since he passed his JAMB exams. The first thing that crossed his mind as he looked through his grades was how he was going to tell his sisters. There were so many Ds. The computer operator was looking at him with curious eyes.

"They did not mercy you at all," she said. August looked at her but said nothing. He folded the sheet before going to the counter to pay.

Until him, the day WAEC results were brought home came with a celebration in the Akasike house. None of his sisters ever failed even one paper. During Uzoamaka's time, he was too young to actually understand what was happening. All he knew was that everyone was saying she aced her exams. For some days, they all called her Madam Flying Colors. It amused August, made him imagine colors in flight. He wanted that. Even without knowing what it meant, he wanted it. Chinyere's celebration was even bigger because she got distinctions in every paper she sat for. Peculiar came close to that too. And so each time he didn't pass, no matter how much his sisters crooned about how much of an improvement he recorded, he simply found it impossible to believe.

August, he would say to himself, *something is fundamentally wrong with you.*

And now he stood staring at those abysmal grades. He made his way out of the cybercafé and started the slow walk home. Everything around him maintained its normalcy with an almost aggressive certainty. At the Eso bus stop, a middle-aged woman and a bus conductor were quarreling. The sound of car horns rent the air. Because of it, when a honk was meant to get his attention, August did not notice. Only when he heard his name did he turn, and even then, it took him awhile to realize who it was.

August had put some effort into avoiding Timothy. He avoided New Heaven like it was the plague, refused to take any of his calls, and when Timothy called with an unfamiliar phone number, August pretended not to be able to hear anything he was saying and then ended the call. He was almost certain Timothy knew August was trying to avoid him. And yet, here they were, face-to-face in Achara Layout.

"Long time," Timothy said.

"Timothy. Did not know it was you," August replied.

Timothy nodded. "Where are you going?" he asked.

"Nowhere," August said. "Just going home."

"Come on. Let me buy you lunch."

"Oh no, I need to get home. I got my WAEC results," he said, and because Timothy kept nodding as though he did not believe him, August added, "I kind of failed. I'm in trouble. I really need to get home."

"Okay, drinks then?" Timothy said. He was leaning over across the passenger side so he could see August's face more clearly. August turned to look at the road.

"Come on, it's just drinks. We could talk about your WAEC," he said, smiling.

"I . . . I can't. You got me all wrong. I'm not . . . I'm not . . . I'm not like that. Really."

"You can't take drinks?" Timothy asked, smiling mischievously. August turned to the road again. This time he took a step away from the curb.

"It's only drinks," Timothy said again. "I promise."

When August entered the car, he knew it would not be *just* drinks. This time, he stayed out until darkness took over from the day, and the stars spotted the sky.

When August got the results of his JAMB exams, his sisters were so sure it was a sign.

"See? You'll be a lion. You won't even have to spend any year at home," they said. "We are so proud of you, August. So proud."

And after seeing his WAEC results, they maintained their enthusiasm.

"This wouldn't keep you at home. You will pass your NECO. You will soon be a lion. Don't let this get you down."

Even his father, with his characteristic glumness, seemed to believe it. That August's admission was already set in concrete. "Just focus on your screening exams," he told August. "Your NECO might still bail you."

It was almost as though August was the only one who remembered that NECO exams were harder to pass than the

WAEC. All his sisters performed less well on their NECO exams. Perhaps they were coddling him or speaking the way forward into existence, or both. It was all so patronizing. But August was grateful for it. He needed the hope that his NECO results would rescue him. It seemed it was the only way for him to save himself. A new start, in a new place. There, he could be the man he had always wanted to be, a man his mother could smile at, a man worthy of her sacrifice, a man worthy of bearing the Akasike name.

August could almost imagine his life there, midnight parties, award nights, girlfriends, good results. He was so very close to having everything all at once. He began to stay awake into the night, to read. None of it seemed like knowledge he would retain. But he read anyway. And then again and again and again. Sometimes, in moments of fatigue, he would think of Timothy's sturdy hands, the way they wrapped around him like they were meant solely for that purpose. He would think of Timothy's lips and his baritone voice that sounded like a growl when he whispered in August's ear. It never failed to rouse him. And so strongly was August disgusted by his arousal, that he pushed himself to read an extra hour, then another, then yet another. He needed to save himself from his own weakness. Sometimes, his desires manifested in dreams: Himself. Timothy. Some bottles of Smirnoff Ice. Then, Timothy's weight over him, holding him down. On many mornings he woke up to his own semen all over his thighs. University would be a renewal, a recourse, a redemption.

The hour-long bus ride to Nsukka was slow and laborious. It was still early morning when August left. The school was

crowded, and prospective students were loitering outside
the halls where they were supposed to sit for their exams.
Former friends and classmates reunited, friends greeted
each other, new acquaintances were made. August tried
to read amid the noise, a last-ditch effort to push himself
over that finish line. His sisters assured him not to worry.
It was, after all, History.

"They actually want as many people as possible to apply
for History and get in. It wouldn't be that hard."

But August knew himself. The exams weren't difficult, but
August could not say he found the questions easy, either. He
could only say he tried his best. On the bus ride home that
day, he had the premonition of failure, not because he didn't
trust his answers but because it seemed so unlike him to pass,
just like that. When he arrived home, he told his sisters he
wasn't sure he would pass the exams. Peculiar hugged him.
"You will pass, joor," she said.

When he finally saw his screening results after weeks of
waiting, he was surprised. It was the same feeling he got
when he saw his NECO results, the nagging suspicion that
it was a scam, a cruel joke, and that the moment he allowed
himself an iota of celebration, someone would tell him it
was all a lie. That he had failed. That he was unworthy of
anything other than failure.

August's sisters gathered to plan his life as they had always
done. Uzoamaka came back for the weekend. He sat in the
living room and pretended to be watching the football match
going on but all he could concentrate on was their voices.
When they called him, he knew they had made up their

minds on everything and only needed his approval, to give him the semblance of choice.

He tested the water, to know where he could put his foot down.

"Maybe it's better to live in the hostel," he said.

"August, have you seen UNN hostels? They are disgusting hellscapes," Chinyere said.

"And you'll probably have to move room every session. Is that what you want?" Uzoamaka asked.

"Other students do it," August said.

"Other students also live in lodges. Don't tell me you prefer scrambling for a shared room with a bunch of strangers when you can have your own, and a bathroom, and water coming to your sink," Chinyere said.

"There's this lodge I heard of when I was in Nsukka. Divine Lodge," Peculiar said. She touched her fingers to her lips and made a big kissing sound. "It's like the best. It's tiled and everything."

"I think I know that lodge," Uzoamaka said.

"What if I want to live in the hostel?" August said. He could tell they didn't really need him there.

"August, why would you want to live in a hostel? Have you seen UNN hostels? I don't think you understand how horrible they are. It's actually not even safe for living. You will stay in a lodge." There was a finality to her words, this time, and August wanted to feel angry. Maybe if he was he would have pushed back more. But instead he felt nothing. Whether he had his own room in a lodge or he shared a room with other students in one of the university's hostels, what did it matter? He would be in university, straight out of secondary school, no years spent at home resitting JAMB. A new opportunity to be exactly who he wanted to be, with new people who knew nothing about him.

He got to do his own shopping, but they all came with him nevertheless, walking slowly behind him and branching off to get him gifts. Curtains, a rack, a bowl, a tray, a sieve—the things they knew would not occur to him to buy. He didn't protest. It seemed to matter way more to them than it did to him.

He moved to school in mid-October. And before they let him go, they took turns hugging him, clutching him tightly, and saying prayers for him.

"Please don't associate with the wrong people."

"Please be safe."

"Concentrate. You're intelligent. See, you entered uni on your first try. All you need is to focus."

"We love you, August. We love you so much."

August almost cried but he knew that if he did that, they would cry too, and he didn't want that. Besides, crying over leaving for university was not something a man would do.

Nsukka seemed to August like an endless stretch of land with buildings far flung all around it. The day he moved in, he saw it with renewed eyes. It was like he was coming here for the first time. The flame trees blooming on both sides of the tarmac seemed new. The flowers seemed new, and the distance was new, the sort of thing you moaned about even though you didn't mind. Divine Lodge was among a cluster of other lodges. It was everything his sisters described.

As his first semester got on, August breezed through classes with a sort of suspicious pride. He was not sure why he was at university, but he was almost proud of himself for it. He imagined if his mother were alive, she would boast about it to her friends. Perhaps, she would leave out the part about him studying History, or perhaps she wouldn't, but he suspected she would have been proud. And for that, the mere hope of his mother's pride, he came to love the university. It was the first thing he had accomplished for which he knew, with full certainty, his mother would have adored him. His family had a legacy here. Uzoamaka got her degree here, and Peculiar was at the university teaching hospital finishing hers, but above all, his mother got her own degree here. August felt small knowing he was walking in her footsteps. There was that nagging voice, still, assuring him of his eventual failure, and he knew that if the worst happened, he would never be able to forgive himself. During his first week of school, he walked around his faculty building wondering if his mother ever walked there. Was the building even standing in her time? The memories he had of those days had no buildings in them. His mother never mentioned buildings, only her exploits.

"I reigned. My sister and I, we reigned. We weren't party lovers that much but everyone had to get us to their parties. Everyone."

For all the animation his sisters put into stories they told him of their mother, they left many spots blank. Sometimes August was resentful of this. Resentful that his sisters had the chance but did not ask their mother important questions. Like how she got around a school as big as Nsukka. Did she take the school shuttle? Did she drive one of her father's many cars? What type of clothes did she wear to school? Shoes? Did she wear metallic lipstick even back then or did it become fashionable much later on? The deficiencies of his sisters' stories left his memories patchy. Sometimes August found it hard to imagine the expression his mother had on her face as she spoke of her reign. Other times he could see it clearly, her lips drawn into a thin smile, her eyes looking up in happy recollection, the wrinkles on her face holding the weight of nostalgia. Nsukka meant so much to August because of this. He wanted to see what she saw, to walk the grounds she walked, and to be a lion. But with every step he took, a part of him—too much of him—worried that all this could never be his.

August's days were mostly the same—attending classes, taking his meals in the cafeteria, studying in his room. He thought his classes, still comprising mostly of general faculty-wide courses, to be uninteresting. Even his department courses did not interest him. He tried to be interested in them, the way other freshers were interested in their classes, but he felt mostly nothing. It scared him. University was the one thing August thought he would care about and his disinterest made him wonder if he was not damaged in the same way his father was, unable to feel, unable to care about the very things that were supposed to bring him joy.

August's classmates were splendid, always eager to offer their assistance. Yes, they could help him get that textbook. Yes, they could lend him their notes. Of course, they could get him copies of the handouts. They hailed him in the cafeteria because he always paid for their food and their drinks if they asked.

"Odogwu," they would say raising both hands in the air. "I dey hail."

It made August smile. And yet, he did not feel he belonged with those people.

It was this way, until he met Dike, and then, finally, he found something to hold on to, to try to make his.

When they first met, because of how they met, August was suspicious of Dike, in the way he was suspicious of all men who showed him kindness. It was near the Education building. He noticed Dike running behind him way earlier, but by the time they reached the Education building, they were running next to each other. When August turned to look at him, Dike nodded. August nodded back but increased his pace. He wanted to put some distance between them. Dike increased his pace to keep up. August ran even faster. Soon they were hurtling through the Saturday morning as fast as their bodies would allow. August was sure he could outlast Dike, but their race continued until August stopped at Nkrumah Hostel, to catch his breath and buy water from one of the kiosks nearby. He bent over, his hands on his knees as he tried to breathe. Dike sat on the ground, his sweaty jersey shirt clinging to his body. At that point, they still had not said a word to each other.

"You are fast," Dike said between ragged breaths.

"Yeah, you too," August said. Dike laughed. August couldn't tell what was funny. He went into a kiosk and bought bottles of water and sat near the big GP tank near the hostel. Dike stood up.

"You run track?" he asked.

August nodded.

"I've not been seeing you. Year one?"

"Yes."

"I'm Dike. Two hundred level. Economics."

August stared at the outstretched hand for some hesitant seconds before taking it.

"August. History."

"August. Wait. Like . . . your real name is August?"

"Yes," August said, now on edge. He could feel that small beat in his chest, that tingling on the bridge of his nose, the alarms in his head.

"As in, your parents named you August?" Dike said more as a statement than a question, and started laughing. "Sorry. I'm sorry, man," he said, as he tried to compose himself, "I shouldn't be laughing but it's so fucking funny."

August drank his water and stood up to go. He wanted to say something back, maybe ask who the fuck still names their children Dike anyway. It sounded like a name that only still existed in Igbo short-story collections that junior secondary students were forced to buy. But he wanted to get as far away from Dike as he could.

"You should come and train with us sometimes. When we start. We've not started training sha but when we do, I'll tell you. You stay here at Nkrumah, right?"

"No," August said, "Divine Lodge."

"Wow. really?"

"Yeah."

"Man . . . na una dey enjoy. I heard Divine Lodge babes don't do shakara like other UNN babes. They just invite you in."

August chuckled and shrugged. Hearing that put him at ease.

"Is it true?" Dike asked.

"Maybe," August said, smiling.

"Man," Dike said. "Broke guy like me. I'm staying in Njoku."

"I'll be heading out," August said.

"Okay, later then, bro."

They shook hands again and August jogged away. His thighs ached but he moved through it. On Tuesday the following week, he went to the stadium after classes. It was a large pitch surrounded by tracks. He could feel the heat from the concrete through the soles of his shoes. The white lines that curved around the bend looked beautiful. He pushed himself up on his toes, then swayed back until he was standing on his heels, and then he swayed forward once more. He took his bag and made his way up to the bleachers. The concrete seats were covered with a film of dust. He cleaned off a space and sat. There was a warm feeling in his chest. Anticipation. He had never trained on a track before. His secondary school's track was just a stretch of dust with white lines drawn with sodium hydroxide. As a child he had thought what if? What if he could in fact be a Jesse Owens? What if he could run all the way into international medal tables, but it seemed like an excessively optimistic dream to have and so he let it go. But this here, the knowledge that he could train with other athletes, on actual tracks, that he could go places, national outings even if he never became a pro athlete, it just warmed his heart as he sat there staring out at the stadium. He could see himself running here, with people sitting and standing all around him, urging him on. He could almost hear them cheering his name.

CHAPTER ELEVEN

August woke with a start. At first, he couldn't tell what woke him. He looked around. He had been here for a whole semester, but on some days, it still took him moments to remember where he was when he woke up. There was no one in the room and his door was locked. He lay back down, closed his eyes, the weariness in his muscles beckoning him back to sleep. Every day by three in the afternoon he was at the track to train. The Student Union games were coming up soon and August was already sure he would be running for his department. And although it was unheard of for the university to send a fresher to compete at the Nigerian university games, August had his mind set on getting a spot for the NUGA games as well. Each time he ran, he tried to show he could do this, easily. They clapped his back. Earlier that day, at practice, the track coach had pulled him aside.

"How are you feeling?" he asked August.

"Good," August said.

"Okay," he said. "You're doing well. You're doing well."

The man had a penchant for repeating himself. "Okay. Okay." Or, "That's good. That's good."

"You are definitely going to be running for your faculty in the SUG games. NUGA is coming up. Who knows, I think you have what it takes."

"Oh. You think so? I hope o. Thank you, sir," August said, trying not to seem too cocky, desperately hoping the man was right.

He came home each day too tired to do anything else but sleep. He was halfway back to sleep when his phone began to ring again.

"It sounds like you just woke from sleep." It was Uzoamaka.

"Yeah. Training," August said.

"Well, I don't know if you have met Chime," Uzoamaka said. "He has come around to the house a couple of times but I don't think you two ever really met."

"No, we never did."

August had heard of Chime, he just had never seen the man.

"Well, we decided to have the marriage introduction next two weeks. On the twenty-sixth."

"Really? I didn't know things were that serious."

"Me too," Uzoamaka said and laughed. "You have to be home at least the day before, okay?"

"Sure, sure. Of course," August said, suddenly feeling a tinge of loss. An understated loss. The type that came when things you always knew would happen finally happened, the end of an unconscious expectation.

Two weeks later August sat next to his father and his father's cousin and watched the older men talk. Earlier he helped Chime and other men carry crates of Heineken and Gulder beer, as well as tubers and tubers of yam. They arranged the items in the center of the living room and now, August stared at the stacked crates and tubers as the men spoke. Their laughter thundered in his ears and he wanted nothing more than to stand and walk away.

The day before, he had told his sisters he would feel crudely out of place among those men. "What I'm even supposed to say?" August asked.

"You don't have to say anything, August," Uzoamaka said, giving him a funny look, like he had asked a silly question. "Just listen. Listen and learn."

They were in her room and Chime was going through the list of items to be presented. Yams, crates of beer, and cartons of spirits. The palm wine was to arrive on the day of the introduction. Chime was in the living room laughing on the phone with someone. August thought he was handsome. He called Uzoamaka "Darling" a lot. *Darling*, did you call the printer? *Darling*, remember we still have to go see the venue. *Darling*, this. *Darling*, that. Next to him, Uzoamaka seemed to lose all her need for control. She became the type of woman to shrug at things or say a simple "okay." Never before had August seen her leave details to someone else. Chinyere didn't come home for the introduction, but she was home for the traditional wedding. There too, August had to sit in the very front with his father. As his father stood, making a speech in Igbo before pouring some wine for Uzoamaka to carry through the crowd, August thought how ridiculous it all was. How downright ridiculous, this extravagant ceremony. Of course, he would never say this out loud to his sisters.

If she knew how August felt about the absurdity of rituals, perhaps Chinyere would laugh and say, "I know, right? I thought I was the only one that saw through all the bullshit."

But Uzoamaka would be very perturbed. Once, when he was ten, he asked her, "Why do we waste so much money burying people who are already dead? It's so wasteful and pointless." Uzoamaka's eyes nearly popped out of her head.

"You mustn't say things like that, August!" she said, and the volume of her voice frightened August. "You have to realize that there is more to this life than what we can see. Every culture has different ways of expressing these complexities. You must be proud of yours. Ours is a beautiful culture. And you know you are the only son. You have to appreciate things like this."

Back then, August thought how much like their grandmother she sounded. Now he watched her snake through the crowd, making a spectacle of searching for Chime. Men were calling to her, asking to be given the drink. She simply smiled past them and only made her way to Chime after dancing all around the canopy. The crowd laughed. August had no idea what was funny. They danced around to the table to be blessed. August imagined himself dancing in front of all those people, performing some ancient script for them. The very thought exhausted him. The sun went down slowly and the crowd thinned. In their place was an expanse of scattered chairs and bottles and white plastic bags. Some children were combing through the mess collecting corks. August watched them scramble, fighting and pushing each other to collect as many as possible. Soon he drifted, staring first into nothingness and then at his mother's grave at the edge of the compound, near the palm trees. All day he had avoided looking at it, and now that he was staring at it, he felt alone. He always felt alone but today especially, he felt the nagging void in him widen. It was a feeling he was already used to, but today he wanted to feel happy for Uzoamaka. He wanted to share the joy that had possessed all his sisters, but all he felt was a vast nothingness that worried him. It made him wonder if he was capable of happiness.

August had his next lapse when he returned to Nsukka, on the day he went to check his first semester results. He had known they were available for weeks but was too scared to do anything about it. That Thursday, Dike had to take him to the cybercafé.

"You better check this thing and rest abeg. It's not going to change the longer you avoid it."

August bought a scratch card but then held on to it, instead of scratching off the blot covering the code.

"You have to scratch the card," the computer operator said, smiling softly. His cheekbones rose gloriously with his smile.

"Yes, sorry," August said.

"Let me," the boy said, and gently slid the card from him. He carefully scratched the blot away. August marveled at how neat his nails were, how elegantly they stretched. The boy looked at August's details.

"August Akasike? Is that short for something?"

"No, no. Just August."

"What a nice name," he said.

Later that night, those words would ring in August's ears and make his whole body tingle. *What a nice name.* It was the first time he had ever heard that about his name instead of the usual amusement and questions about why he was named after a month of the year.

"You actually did very well," the boy said. "No need to worry at all."

The printer began to hum and August's result crawled slowly through it. The boy handed the paper to August; it was warm, pleasantly so. August folded it and turned to go.

"Congrats," he heard the boy say. But August didn't turn back around. He worried what would happen if he did. If he stayed even a second more and listened to his voice, stared at his face.

August tried to think of other things all day long. Still, in the shower, the boy's beautiful cheekbones appeared to August and his beautiful words for some reason came back and rained over him with the spray of the water. He began, slowly at first, as though simply washing the length of his penis, until he was leaning on the tiled wall, his hand pumping, his breath coming in short spurts.

They would run into each other again, weeks later, at the onset of the SUG games. August pretended not to remember his face. Even when he came over to where August stood and said, "Hey, I thought it was you, Mr. Nice As."

August feigned surprise.

"We met at the cyber," the boy said, and reached for August's hand. "It's August, right? I remember you have a nice name."

"Yes, it is."

"I'm Segun."

When their hands met, August thought how soft Segun's were, almost as if his hands had no bones. Segun's eyes had that same quality, like something August could lose himself in.

The day of the SUG games started exactly the way August expected it to. There weren't as many people in the stands as he would have liked. Dike had warned him that football and women's volleyball were the competitions that commanded crowds, but August was a little bit disappointed. Nevertheless, it was fine. Nothing could dampen his spirits. He could perform no matter how small the crowd was. He felt electrified as they took their places for the 400-meter race. When the go went off, August could as well have leapt into flight. The noise of the stand faded away, the thud of feet around him thinned until it was just him, flying, flying till he tore through the finish tape.

August thrived at the games. He won a medal in every individual category he competed in. In the 100 meter and 400 meter, he got first place.

But August was outshone by a young woman named Betty. Hers was a clean sweep, getting gold in every race. August first saw her in the relay and knew at once that she was a phenom. Her team was behind; she received the baton after the rest of the runners in the last lap had gone off. It was magic, the way she shrank the distance with each elegant stride. August was mesmerized. He nudged Dike. "Who's she?"

"You don't know her? The Cheetah."

"The name makes sense," August said. "She is really fast."

"They say if she ran with the men, she would probably win a medal." Dike laughed. "Nonsense obviously, but she's fast, yes."

After the medals were handed out, August and Betty somehow found each other.

"Hi," August said, feeling a weakness in his knees. "You were amazing."

Betty turned to him and smiled. "Thank you," she said. All around them, athletes were putting their medals in bags, but they held theirs, standing awkwardly there smiling at each other.

"I'm Betty," she said.

"August." He held her hand in his.

"August, like Augustus or something?"

"No. Just August," he said and chuckled.

"Wow, that's a first. Like, your parents gave you that name?"

August nodded.

"You were quite impressive too," Betty said.

"Thank you."

Dike arrived then and gave August a handshake hug.

"Guy, you know you won more medals than any other guy?" Dike said.

"Really?" August asked, feigning surprise, as though he had not been counting.

"I'm serious. You'll be picked for NUGA for sure. For sure, for sure." Dike threw Betty a nod of acknowledgment. And then turning to August said, "I think you should meet the coach. He might want to talk to us before we leave."

August waved goodbye to Betty but as soon as they were out of earshot, Dike hissed disapprovingly.

"Avoid her," he said.

"Why?" August asked, turning back to glance at Betty, who was now bent over her bag, her medals dangling from her neck. "What's the P?"

"She's loose," Dike said. "Like literally, every guy has smashed."

August laughed. "Come on. No need to be dramatic. I'm not even sure I like her like that."

"Man, I'm not joking."

August would soon learn that it was pretty much common knowledge—Betty's promiscuity. Even Betty herself spoke of it, seemed to have no shame about it, which made August uncomfortable and turned him on in equal measure.

"You know how you guys are," Betty said. "Most of you are garbage, no offense. A girl has to go through a lot of you to find the perfect man."

There was a confidence with which she said things that August could otherwise not imagine being said. The closer they became, the more strongly Dike pushed against it.

"Man, I told you that chick is bad news. You don't even know how many guys she has been with. Even me sef, I've smashed. Sorry to burst your bubble. You can ask her."

But August did not care. Betty fascinated him. He envied what she had, the way she saw herself, the way other people saw her.

The first time he tried to kiss her, she stopped him. "August, I really like you. You have to know it wouldn't just be sex. You're not just another fuck for me."

It was the first time she had visited his room, and those words warmed something in him, made him feel a kind of certainty of self. He, too, did not want "just sex." He wanted to fall head over heels in love with her, to love without reservation. He wanted her to look at him and see a man she could spend the rest of her life with, a man she could love without fear of disappointment. He wanted to be that man, her man. And when they walked through school, hand in hand, all eyes following them, August felt a sort of pride.

When August got the call about his father, it was a good thing he wasn't alone. After hearing the news, it felt like he would slowly fade away, if Dike was not sitting next to him. It was Peculiar who called, but after he ended the call, he couldn't remember who called him, whose frantic voice had been muffled in tears.

"It was my sister," he said to Dike.

"What happened?"

August was silent. It felt like the contents of his skull had been put in a container and shaken.

He considered his sister's words until Dike touched his shoulder and asked again. "I think my father died," he said.

"Ah. I'm so sorry, bro. What happened?"

"I don't know. She said they're at the hospital," August said, trying to collect himself.

Dike went with August to the hospital. On the bus ride to Enugu, all he could think of was Peculiar's words. The sound of her voice. The way they jumped through the phone so that it seemed like she was shouting into his ears.

"August, it's Daddy. I don't know what's happening. You have to come now now."

She was crying uncontrollably, August thought he heard death. Sitting in the bus, after he'd had time to reconsider her words carefully, he realized perhaps his father was still alive. He did not know what he felt. He wasn't sure he felt anything at all. No desperation, no panic, no fear. No one's calls were going through and even this did not make him afraid. August felt like he should be afraid for his father's life, but he simply wasn't. Perhaps he hadn't learnt to love his father. Perhaps love was something that needed cultivation; his father never did that with him. And August never tried to do that with his father.

"Don't worry, man. Hopefully, everything is okay," Dike said. But August wasn't worried for his father, and it was *this*—a son unperturbed by his own father's death—that worried him. His phone rang before they arrived at the hospital, but it wasn't any of his sisters. Before he picked up, he imagined it was a doctor calling to give him the news, like doctors did in foreign movies. It took him some seconds to recognize the voice at the other end of the line as Chime's.

"Where are you?" Chime asked.

"I'm on my way."

When he arrived at the hospital, it was Chime who was waiting for him, near the entrance of the emergency building.

August marveled at how defined Chime's jaw was, how everything about him looked finished and brute, almost virile. And it made him ashamed that he would notice such things. That he enjoyed noticing them.

Your father might have died, August. He's Uzoamaka's husband. And he's a man.

As they walked, August turned to Dike and said, "I was actually born in this hospital."

Dike simply nodded. They got to Chime and exchanged handshakes, somber greetings.

"Your sister has been trying to reach you," Chime said.

"I've been trying to reach her. Where is she?"

"She's not in town. They went for a conference in Abuja, but she'll be back tomorrow."

August didn't know if he should feel relieved or disappointed. Things like these weighed so heavily on Uzoamaka. She carried them because no one else could, or even knew how to.

"What happened? Is my dad okay?"

"Your father's blood-sugar level was over the roof. They say he almost died but he's fine now."

August nodded, wondering if the soft exhale he felt in his body qualified as relief. He walked behind Chime, silently, making sure his eyes were pinned to the ground or at the sick patients lying in their beds or on the walls or anywhere that wasn't Chime. When he stepped inside his father's room and saw the man lying so helplessly on the bed, he stopped, stilled. And only then did it all hit him, the fear, the worry, the relief, all at once, and it robbed him completely of air. Peculiar looked up from where she was seated. She stood and walked to him, her hands outstretched.

"August. Oh August," she said, still crying. She pulled him into an embrace, hugged him so tightly that August began to feel the sting of tears in his own eyes.

"Nothing will happen to him," Peculiar said. "Nothing! The devil is a liar."

Uzoamaka said the same thing the next day. "The devil is a liar."

She, too, held August. "He will live long for all of us, to enjoy the fruits of his labor in us. Don't worry," she said.

August wanted to say something, but he couldn't remember what it was he was supposed to say. He just stayed there in her arms, afraid that she was saying it because she did not believe it and needed to convince herself.

Later, after Chinyere came home, they did a prayer for their father in his hospital room.

"The devil lies. He steals. He cheats. He destroys. But he is powerless. God is watching over this family. He protects his children."

August and his sisters hugged their father, and the old man took all the affection in with smiles. It was the most August had ever seen his father smile. Even their prayers and multiple rebukes of the devils made August's father smile. Later, they would gather and talk about their father's sugar levels and RBS values and insulin, things that August heard but his mind refused to retain.

"But why would he not take his drugs?" Chinyere asked, almost to herself. "I don't understand how an adult would forget to take drugs that sustain him, for Christ's sake."

"It's a good thing nothing bad happened," Uzoamaka said.

"A good thing," Peculiar echoed.

"I just don't get it," Chinyere said, again. "Doesn't he know how important these drugs are? Doesn't he want to live?"

"Come on, don't think that," Uzoamaka said.

Chinyere buried her face in her hands. "I just don't know what to think. He could have died."

That night, in his bedroom, August stayed awake, troubled by this, that perhaps his father was tired of living or just indifferent, an acute indifference that made him yearn for everything to stop. August suspected his sisters also entertained these thoughts, what with the way they denounced the devil as though the devil had anything to do with diabetic men not taking their medications.

Back in school, as he told Dike, as he worded those thoughts, it took on an even larger seriousness. Had his father wanted to die? Was that how unhappy he was?

"Just don't think about it, man," Dike told him. "You can't understand it. Maybe, maybe not. It serves nothing to think about it unless you want to confront your old man about it, *na you know.*"

August did intend to ask his father why. He even practiced exactly how he would pose the question.

"What happened, sir? Why weren't you taking your medication?" or "I know this life is tiresome, sir, but I'd really like to know. Did you stop taking your drugs on purpose? Did you want to die?"

But he never asked his father. Even while rehearsing those questions he knew somewhere deep down that he would never ask them, could never ask them. They seemed too much like something only a loving son could ask a loving father.

CHAPTER TWELVE

Segun cried for weeks after Trevor graduated. Their relationship never had an officiality behind it because Segun was afraid of jinxing what they had. The easiness of it, the comfort of lying in Trevor's bed, his head in Trevor's lap, eyes closed while Trevor read him passages of his favorite books. Some of it, Segun understood. The rest was so shrouded in academic jargon that, in the beginning, Segun simply enjoyed the sound of the passages and the poetry of it, enjoyed the warmth of Trevor's body, enjoyed the idle hand stroking his forehead or his moustache, or playing with his hair. But with each book, he understood more and more. He began to borrow them. First, a collection of Sankara's speeches. Then a brown paper copy of Nkrumah's *Africa Must Unite*. And after that, Claude Ake's *Social Science as Imperialism*. So much of what Segun had with Trevor had its roots in those books, in how happily Trevor gifted Segun books he only asked to borrow. Segun knew it couldn't last, this thing they had. Trevor would soon graduate and he would have to readjust to Nsukka all over again. But he let himself enjoy Trevor, enjoy his tenderness and his books. After he read them, Segun arranged the books on the cupboard next to his bed, one atop the other, where he could always see them. Some days, he came back and noticed them lying askew, not the way he had carefully arranged them, and it made him angry. It felt like a desecration, his roommates touching books Trevor had gifted him.

"Whoever is touching my books I don't know what you are looking for in my corner when I'm not around," he said aloud once when everyone was in the room. "That thing that brings you into my corner you better tell me so I can help you find it."

"What is this one making noise about?" Uchenna asked.

"If you want to borrow one of my books, tell me. Don't be snooping in my corner."

"Oh, your name is now Trevor Amadi? You did not inform us," Francis said. Segun had earlier suspected he was the culprit. Of all his roommates, Francis lacked a respect for boundaries the most. Segun had to start locking his bathing soap in his cupboard because Francis was in the habit of using it, without asking.

"Thank you so much for exposing yourself. Stop coming to this corner to go through my things. Let me just warn you now because the day anything gets missing here, you will pay me for it. You will o."

"Look at this guy o. So because I touched your books is why you are talking as if heaven fell?"

"Simple instruction, stop coming to this corner when I'm not around. What is so hard in it?"

"Sorry I touched the book your homo lover gave you o," Francis said, and Uchenna and Ifeanyi laughed.

"Guy, why you going below the belt?" Ifeanyi asked.

"No, he should deny it if I'm lying. Bring that your State and Revolution book and explain why a Trevor is writing 'To my favorite Marxist-Leninist' to you, fucking faggot. That's why he's so angry. He knows what he's hiding."

"Do you know you don't have sense?" Segun said, emerging from his corner to go and stand next to Ifeanyi's bed.

"It's you that don't have sense. Your mates dey use homo collect money but na English dem dey take destroy your ass. Mumu."

"You don't have sense at all. Your parents did not bother telling you. Let me look for anything in this corner," Segun said, pointing toward his bed, "you will pay for it."

"Commot here joor, useless fag like you."

"Yes, I know you added that word to your vocabulary. What else?" Segun asked. "Only fag? Nothing else in your empty homophobic skull?"

"Fuck out of here."

"Both of you should fight and shame the devil," Uchenna said.

"Me I've said my own. You will know I am a faggot when I look for something here and don't find it. Don't stop o, continue!"

And with that, Segun plugged his ears with earphones and buried his head in a book. Many times, he felt like this room was suffocating, choking him of breath, and even when he was not in the room, that feeling followed him. It was why he loved those books so much. They showed him that a world where he could breathe was possible, was inevitable. The more he studied, the more certain he became.

When he saw a flier of the Socialist Students' Forum, Segun was skeptical. He was accustomed to being unwelcome, to being mocked just for being present. And so, joining the SSF was something he agonized over for weeks before deciding to attend a meeting. He did not want to give homophobes the opportunity to reject him ever again. But on this he had to close his eyes and leap. Segun did not want just to believe in revolution, he wanted to participate in building it. And what better place to start than something like the SSF. They met on Saturday afternoons, in the old Sociology final-year classroom. The first meeting Segun attended, there were about twenty people in attendance, most of them men. And this made Segun very uncomfortable. Why were there only six girls, out of twenty-one people? Before the discussions began, they moved the chairs around so that they formed a semicircle. Segun stood aside and let them do it, then he sat down.

"Comrade, what's your name?" the facilitator asked him. She was wearing a Miriam Makeba shirt, and her hair was shaved low and dyed an unusual shade of orange.

"Segun," he replied.

"Comrades, let's all welcome Comrade Segun," she said, smiling, and a chorus of welcomes greeted him.

She turned to the board and wrote, *Liberal Democracy vs The Bolivarian Revolution.*

"Comrades, what do we think of term limits?" she asked. Hands shot up. "Term limits, are they good or bad?" she asked again before pointing at someone to signal them to speak.

Listening to them, Segun felt at home, like this was somewhere he could get comfortable in, somewhere he could learn to feel at home. He loved how they all spoke like there was no shame in wrong answers, the way they gave their thoughts even as they formed in their heads, the way they said Commander Chavez like they were lieutenants in the Bolivarian Armed Forces. The class went on for almost an hour and a half. When it got rowdy, the facilitator, Ngozi, shouted *Amandla!* and all the different voices converged in *Awethu!* fists going up around the room.

"*Amandla!*" Ngozi shouted again.

"*Awethu!*" came the response, and the class was quiet. It felt ungainly at first, but Segun got used to this, the chanting. Soon, when he heard the call, it did not feel ridiculous to raise his right hand in a fist and respond.

"Comrades," Ngozi said. "We've used up our time for today. Obviously, we cannot learn all the lessons of the Bolivarian revolution in one session. Let's summarize our insights."

After the discussion ended, they stood up and sang "The Internationale." Segun did not know the words so he simply stood with them, his hands raised, his mouth trying to move to the tune as best he could.

"Comrade Segun," someone sitting a few seats away called. When Segun looked, the guy stretched his hand forward, offering Segun his phone. The person next to him took the phone and passed it on. Hand by hand, the phone traveled till it reached Segun. The lyrics were on the screen.

"Comrades, I think Segun isn't familiar with 'The Internationale,'" the guy said. "Let's start again so he can sing along."

And so, they began afresh, the beautiful words of the anthem etching itself into Segun's mind.

Away with all your superstitions. Servile masses, arise! Arise! We'll change henceforth the old traditions.

Segun wrote the lyrics down in an exercise book and underlined those words. Joining the SSF opened him to so much he did not know he was ignorant of, songs that lifted his spirits, histories he was shocked he was not taught in school, books that felt like they were written for him, to answer all his questions, to fan the whittling fire in his heart. And he soaked it all in, the despair that weighed on him lessening and lessening, hope blooming and blooming.

The first time Segun saw Betty was at the 2013 SUG games finals. Before then, he had only heard of her prowess. She was the stuff of legends. His first year, he had spent the SUG week holed up in Trevor's room. They had so much sex, the room smelled of it. And the following year, with Trevor gone, Segun decided he would simply stay in his room and read. It was Julia who convinced him to come to the finals.

"Don't you want to see Betty?" Julia asked. "She'll be there."

And so Segun gave in. Like most things about UNN, the games did not begin on time. The stands were mostly empty. They would fill up later when the football match began. The men's track races went first. They strolled out and took their marks. The referee gave the signal and the runners took off, a stretch of sweaty straining muscles. Segun recognized one of them, this fresher whom he had helped check his results. He was in History or Theater Arts, one of those. He had a bad start but soon overtook his competitors. Segun found himself wishing the boy would trip and fall. There was just an unfairness to a fresher competing in the SUG games and winning it on his first try. His name was August, Segun remembered because he had been charmed by the name. It had to be very interesting parents who gave him that name. A nice name, he had called it.

"Thank you. Thank you very much," the boy had said. He hadn't read his result slip, simply folded it up and slipped it into his pocket.

He did not trip and fall and kept his lead till he crossed the finish line. There was clapping. The clapping would intensify as he won category after category. When he came second in the 200 meter, Segun was strangely pleased. Soon the men's categories were over, and it was time for the women's. He had heard so much about Betty, from Julia, from Trevor, from his roommates, and yet somehow when she walked onto the track, his breath caught in his chest. He knew at once that it was her. Her bronze skin shone, as though it caught the light and reflected it. Her legs seemed to stretch forever.

"That girl, what she has walked, the guys she's spread her legs for." Segun could no longer remember which of his roommates said this. Many times they all sounded the same.

"Guy . . ." another said.

"I swear down. I dey hear her scores."

Now, all Segun could think of was how beautiful her legs were. She ran so gracefully, like each movement was a majestic leap. Shouts of *The Cheetah* rent the air, and when she zoomed past the finish line, there was thunderous applause. Watching her run, it was impossible not to love her, not to root for her, not to be entertained. Julia was beside herself with euphoria. After the events, he and Julia stood up and made their way down. Julia didn't want to stay for the football match and neither did Segun. He did not find football entertaining. They agreed to meet back later in the evening for the javelin events. Strolling around, he ran into August. First, when their eyes crossed, Segun looked away. August was sitting on the platform changing his shoes. Something about the way he stood made Segun feel pity for him, and as a result, guilt for wishing him failure. He walked up to him, straightening his back. Before he spoke, he cleared his throat.

"Hey, I thought it was you, Mr. Nice As," he said, and felt ridiculous as soon as he said it. If there was a way to take back words, he would have taken them back and gone off somewhere to go mind his own business. August looked up at him and said nothing. He didn't seem to remember who Segun was.

"We met at the cyber," Segun said. This time he stretched out his hand. August looked at the hand before taking it. He still hadn't said a word. What was he feeling like?

"It's August, right? I remember you have a nice name."

"Yes. It is."

Finally. Segun was beginning to think he was a snob and that this entire introduction was a bad idea.

"I'm Segun."

He saw August's brow arch in question, or was it surprise? And it made him smile. Strangely, it made him miss Trevor. He hadn't seen Trevor since he left for Jalingo to complete his NYSC. Sometimes, when he was sufficiently lonely, he would call Trevor and they would talk for hours. When his airtime was exhausted, Trevor would call back. It warmed him, the phone pressed to the side of his face. August was nothing like Trevor. Trevor talked. He liked people and wanted them to like him back and so he talked. If they were in a bus headed to Enugu to spend the weekend, Trevor talked to the driver for the entire ride, all two hours of it. He started conversations and sustained them, even when he did not have to. Back when they were out together, this habit annoyed Segun. Now, he found it endearing. And all it took to remind him was August's brow raised, as though saying, *I'm curious but not curious enough to ask about it.* Segun congratulated August and took his leave. What he needed was sleep. He texted Julia to tell her he was going back to his room. But when he lay down, sleep refused to come. All he could do was think of Trevor, and how perhaps under other circumstances, what they had could have lasted. Perhaps if they were not so far apart, Trevor being in his final year, he being in his first. Perhaps if they had more time. But this was a muted reminiscence, something he could do only because Trevor was gone now. When he had him, a man so eager to please, so eager to love him, he hadn't allowed himself that freedom. What happened with Tanko had scarred him too badly, left him broken.

Ifeanyi came back into the room and took something and then left. His roommates no longer spoke to him now. Sometimes they spoke about him, but rarely ever to him. His phone began to vibrate in his back pocket. He let it vibrate and vibrate before deciding that whoever was calling must have something important, as they kept calling. It was his mother. He sighed. He knew she would berate him endlessly for letting his phone ring without answering.

"Why do you even have a phone if you won't even pick it?" she would ask him. It was not always like that. There was a time the ring of his phone excited him. But so much had happened since then. Every bad thing that had happened to him, he had learnt of through the phone. And so many times when his phone rang, he would set it to silent mode. Sometimes he listened to the ringtone, or hummed along to it, till the phone ceased to ring. Julia had learnt to simply text him. But his mother would call and call till he picked up.

"I know you don't have two mothers in this world. It's just me. You can't ignore my calls forever. After ignoring you'll still pick."

This time she didn't berate him. Her voice was scratchy and tired.

"Oh, Abe. I don't know what our own special sin is. It's just one problem after the other," she said. "Have us in your prayers. These people are on their privatization bloodlust again and this Electricity they're eyeing, we don't know anybody. People will lose their jobs and we don't know anybody."

Segun had to temper his own rage. She needed him to reassure her, and so he did. He told her that interparty disagreements would grind the privatization deals to a halt. That the unions would stop the privatization and that he would pray for them. And, because he knew how anxious they were about his schooling, he told her he applied for some scholarships and that his results were good enough to get them.

"Aberemangigha," his mother said, "what would I do without you. I thank God for the day he blessed me with a son like you."

CHAPTER THIRTEEN

August's palms were sweaty as he sat in his father's car. Occasionally he would turn to his father and nod or murmur in agreement to show he was listening. His father was talking slowly as he drove. They started in Achara and made their way down Agbani Road, and then they turned around, back through Independence Layout and the suburbs of New Haven. August listened. If for nothing but the static silence that existed between the words.

"Your mother built this one in eighty-four," his father was saying as they pulled up to a brown two-story apartment building. As they made their way into the compound to greet the tenants, August's father seemed even less at ease than normal. The tenants clustered close, shaking his father's hands and then August's.

"Is this your son? He's so grown. Look how big he is," they said, shaking August's hand and fussing over him much like his sisters did, wide smiles plastered on their faces.

"Do you remember me?" some of them asked.

"No," he said each time, wishing they wouldn't stand so close.

"Oh, but how would you? You were so little the last time I saw you." This they said while gesturing, so August would understand just how little, knee-level, calf-level. "Welcome, our son. Welcome," they said.

"I just wanted to show him around," August's father said. "*O di mkpa*. Very important."

August tried to memorize the addresses of the houses, not of need but of a desire to be somehow competent. He imagined that knowing the addresses of all his father's properties was a competent thing to do. He could already imagine doing this later in life, owning those buildings, and it made him feel nothing. He wished he felt something, excitement or pride perhaps, for what his parents had achieved, but it was like everything else, a vast expanse of nothing. He listened to his father's voice and noted the names his father mentioned and chided himself silently for not caring.

At the house on Agbani Road, he thought he saw Segun. He wanted to call Segun's name even, but shouting names wasn't something he felt comfortable doing. He simply stared, hoping Segun would turn and see him. And it was a good thing he did because it wasn't Segun. The boy had an uncanny resemblance to Segun though, the same hair, the same slender frame with arms that stretched out forever, the same fair skin the tone of light honey. He even thought he heard Segun's laugh. He was being asinine, August decided. For the rest of the day, he tried not to think about Segun.

"That's it," his father said. "We've gone to all of them." They drove back in silence and August wondered how Uzoamaka had convinced their father to do this, if she had begged their father, just like she'd begged August to spend time with their father.

"It would help lighten him up, to spend time with you," she said. "It will help him recover. We all have to be here for him."

He did not feel like he was a son being there for his father. August felt like he and his father were two different shapes sitting awkwardly in a box that was too small and too airless for both of them. August had since come to terms with who his father was, and what his father could give. He understood his father, and it felt like that was as close as they would ever get. There was the nagging void of what could have been, but it was simply one of the unfortunate facts of August's life, something to be acknowledged, nothing more. They arrived home, and August got out to open the gate. Later, he sat outside for a while and tried to refocus his mind on things, other than what he wanted to do with Segun. He was afraid that if he went straight to his room, he would crawl slowly down a spiral to somewhere he wouldn't recognize himself but where he was, maybe, the truest version of himself. And that terrified him.

Having those thoughts about Segun, it made him feel foreign in his skin. Weeks after the first lapse Segun had caused, August had fallen sick. It was only days after the SUG games and whatever plagued him weakened every muscle in his body. Peculiar visited him. She said it was stress. All that nonstop training, it was simply too much for such an inexperienced body. August knew it wasn't stress. His body was fighting his desires, he knew. Later, as his condition worsened, he began to fear he might die. He had made God a lot of promises to pass his NECO and be offered admission, and he'd broken them and now he was paying the price.

Of course, he tried to keep those promises. He was nurturing what he had with Betty. They would spend their evenings together talking about school or athletes or some movie that was just released. Other evenings they would kiss each other until they were breathless. One Thursday evening, they went beyond kissing. She pulled him close. He tried to comport himself like someone who knew what he was doing and perhaps Betty bought it, or perhaps she didn't care. They sweated so much August had to stop and reach for his shirt to wipe the sweat trickling down his forehead and into his eyes. After it ended, August felt accomplished. The sex had not felt amazing, his body did not shake with exhilaration, his insides did not knot up and untangle, but it did not feel horrible either. It just was, and August thought there was something beautiful about that, about having average sex with a woman, with Betty.

"That was great," he whispered in Betty's ear. "You are amazing."

"Yes, it was nice," Betty giggled. She nestled closer into his arms and he held her.

And maybe that was part of the problem, part of the burden that rested on his bones and drained them of strength, like a cursed talisman. He felt trusted, and trust was not something August knew how to hold.

He dragged himself to church and to fellowship services and prayed for forgiveness.

"I'm weak," he prayed. "You know I am weak."

It was more of a surrender than it was an excuse: *You know how weak I am. You know.*

After that evening with Betty, August felt at peace. Safe from himself. He felt invincible, even. He had been fighting his guilt since the day he met Segun at the cybercafé and being with Betty felt like a recantation. But it lasted only so long. Only days later, he dreamt of Segun. In his dream, Segun was smiling into his computer screen as his long, slender fingers pushed the keys of the keyboard. August watched him, that stretch of his arms, his cheekbones standing so high up his cheeks, like angels holding the dark depths of his eyes. August went closer and touched those cheeks, cupped them in his palms before lowering his face to them. He knew even before escaping that groggy realm between dream and wake that it was a wet dream. Awake, he sat in the dark looking at the fabric of his underwear glued to his left thigh. The next day, it happened again, but this time he was fully awake and in the shower. Watching the white clumps flowing slowly to the drain, he felt the sickness coming. Sometimes he went to the cybercafé to make a photocopy of his school fees receipt, or his department levies, just so he could talk to Segun and hear his voice, the way he spoke.

"It's our Usain Bolt," Segun would say. "August, you know you should really bring everything at once so you don't keep stressing yourself." But there was a twinkle in his eye and that soft smile of his that made August think maybe Segun liked that he was coming by so often.

"I know. I know. I keep forgetting. I don't know what I'm thinking."

Sometimes he went with Betty, and after they went to the student union building and ate chicken suya and drank Fanta.

August felt himself slowly coming apart and becoming something he had for a long time feared becoming.

On the days he went with Betty, they left as soon as the copies were made.

On a day he came without Betty, Segun asked after her. "How about your friend? She didn't come with you today?"

"She had something she was doing," August said.

"You guys hang out together, a *lot*," Segun said. August shrugged. He and Betty did hang out a lot. He still did not know what he was to her. He asked her to be his girlfriend and she laughed. She laughed and laughed and laughed but offered no reply. August felt a mixture of embarrassment and relief. But he planned again.

Now that the school games were over, he had to take on a lot of schoolwork he hadn't been paying attention to. Betty too, and August liked to think that was why she laughed. It could have been the way he asked her. The way he said, "Go out with me, like for real, like boyfriend and girlfriend, not just sex." And so each time people called them *friends*, with that implied question, he simply shrugged.

Segun made a face and flipped and then reached for a drawer for plain sheets of A4 paper. "You guys seem quite close," he said.

"Yes, we actually are, I think. She's an amazing friend, and you know, the running thing, we train together a lot."

Segun nodded and turned back to his screen.

"I was just wondering, you know. Thought maybe you guys were dating."

"Oh no. At least, not yet," August said, laughing.

Segun continued looking at him. It made August uncomfortable. A customer walked in and upon seeing August came up to shake him.

"You're good, man," he told August. "You can maybe do all these world competitions one day."

August liked the way people were astonished by his speed. When he was with Betty he enjoyed even more attention, and reveled in how they admired Betty and her physical prowess. "The Cheetah," they would salute. She commanded awe and attention and it was one of the things August loved about her. It made him feel like maybe, just maybe, she made him better, got him closer to the man he was supposed to be.

Toward the end of June, they attended Uzoamaka's wedding together. He had not even planned to invite her. It just happened that he found out the date when they were together. He asked her if she would like to come and she said yes. The idea of introducing Betty to his sisters excited August, as did the thought of having a date to a wedding.

They met at the wedding because he had to go home earlier to help out with the preparations. He didn't actually do anything, just sat back and watched everyone run around making sure everything was perfect. He had a suit made to match the colors of the groomsmen. The morning of the wedding, Uzoamaka asked him to go to Chime's house. The best man had problems with his suit and if he didn't make it, August would have to fill in for him.

"What of his other friends?" August protested.

"August, just go. Please. You're all coming to the church together, anyway," Uzoamaka said.

"What am I even supposed to do?"

"August, there is no time for me to explain. You can figure this out. Now, go."

August had no idea what he was supposed to do as a best man. What were best men supposed to do? Chime was already ready when August arrived. August went around the crowded house greeting Chime's relatives, his parents, his sisters, his brothers, the other groomsmen. They were hurrying Chime along, adjusting his tie, telling him how dashing he looked, and Chime nodded to everything. When it was time, they drove to the service in a caravan of cars snaking through the streets. It was a group wedding—there were three other couples also getting married. At the church, August met up with Betty. Her off-shoulder burgundy dress flowed all the way to her ankles and was slit up the middle so that the straps of her heels peeked through when she walked.

"You look really nice," she said, kissing his cheek softly and resting a hand on his arm. "It's the first time I'm seeing you in corporate attire. You should do corporate more often."

August smiled and scratched his head. "Thanks," he said. "You look wonderful yourself."

They sat down, and the ceremony began, everyone rising when they were told to, kneeling when it was time to kneel. The priest went to each couple to officiate their exchange of vows, with an altar boy standing close to hold a microphone to their mouths. Uzoamaka was radiant. Looking at her, August felt something close to pride. This would later morph into loss, a sheathed sense of loss. All his life it had been him and his three sisters and now that was ending, now Uzoamaka was committing to someone else.

The priest soon came to his sister and her betrothed. Chime went first. "Babe," he began. August watched his mouth move. Chime wasn't overly handsome but his groomed face, the way his puckered lips and his defined jaw gave him this aura of charm, made August feel uncomfortable around him. The priest concluded the rites and the couples kissed and then walked outside, hand in hand, to sign the marriage register.

"I'm never doing this," Betty said as they walked out. "I fucking hate weddings."

"You sound just like my elder sister, Chinyere," August chuckled. "Our second born, she thinks marriage is a curse."

"I mean, don't get me wrong. I'm not writing marriage off or anything but this is really like pointless," she said, gesturing toward the altar. "I don't need some deity to approve my marriage."

August laughed. Peculiar came to tell him he was needed for the pictures. August stood in different shots, smiling wildly, holding Uzoamaka, or any of his sisters, closest to him. He took some with Chime, who now relaxed his tie and undid the first buttons of his shirt. At the reception, August danced while Betty recorded it on her phone, laughing. He danced with Betty too, then with his sisters. Everyone seemed so happy, so overwhelmed with bliss.

But August saw extra meaning in Uzoamaka's marriage. She was the first to go. No more an Akasike but now an Obaji. Next, Chinyere and Peculiar would follow. The more he thought of it, the more it felt like a burden, this name he had to keep alive, this name he had to live for. He thought how stupid it was that such primacy was bestowed on names and blood, something he knew no one else cared for. And it seemed the weight of it, of keeping something aflame when the rest of the world didn't, made it an even heavier burden. August sometimes fantasized about his own death, perhaps a car accident or a stray bullet. He could fall asleep and not wake up again, and everything would have been in vain. He remembered his grandmother's words: *You do not live for you alone.* He did not want any of it. He wanted to be free, to live just for himself, to be his own person.

Betty had to leave the reception early; it was a long bus ride back to Nsukka. He saw her to the road and stood with her until a cab came to pick her up.

"Thanks for coming," August said, standing close enough to Betty that their arms were touching.

"Oh stop it. It was my pleasure. Your people are really nice. Also, I got cake," Betty said, waving the foil-wrapped parcel in her hand. When the cab pulled up, Betty hugged him briefly before getting in the car. He waved as the car drove away, watching it glide down the empty road until it took the turn at the end of the street.

August knew Dike would not like Segun. He himself was uneasy around Segun's explosive and flamboyant personality. When August watched Segun walk, it brought to mind flamingos leaping into flight, or something just as delicate. August normally could not stand people like Segun. They irked him. Made him conscious of himself, made him scared that people could see him, could see through him. But Segun was different. He was Segun. All those things, the way he walked and talked—the things August found embarrassing in other men—he found tolerable, charming even, in Segun.

He and Dike met at the Social Science building, late in the evening. The exam timetables had been released and the building was teeming with students studying. August was on his laptop, catching up on his assignments and projects, and Dike was solving some past questions.

"Our Usain Bolt," a voice said.

Before August looked, his chest tightened. He knew who it was.

"Segun," he said. "This is where you come for night class?"

"Yeah, I normally sit up there." Segun pointed to the distance. "My friend didn't come today. Thank God I saw you. Otherwise, it would take me only like this long to fall asleep," Segun said, holding his thumb and index finger close to his face to demonstrate.

August didn't want Segun to sit with them, he wanted Segun to go away. Dike was watching Segun with a scrunched face.

"Is this your friend?" Segun asked, waving at Dike. "Hey."

Dike looked on, unmoving.

"Yes, yes," August said. "This is Dike. Dike, Segun."

They exchanged handshakes and Segun sat down.

"What are you reading?" he asked August.

"I'm not actually reading, I have a lot of reports to write. I wish I could type as fast as you."

"Ha, what's your report on?"

"The Benin Kingdom," August said. Dike stirred in his seat. Segun opened a textbook and placed it in front of himself. There wasn't much talking after that.

It would be days before Dike would say something about Segun, and he said it with disgust. "He does too much," Dike said, his face scrunched up.

August laughed uncomfortably. "Too much?"

"Yes nau. I mean, just look at the way he carries himself. You could mistake him for a girl if you saw him walking. I don't know why he walks like that sha, like he's breakable."

August wanted to tell Dike that Segun typed with power. That if he watched Segun's fingers float over the keyboard he wouldn't think Segun looked so breakable, but he didn't. Instead, he shook his head slowly.

"I pity his parents sha," Dike said.

"Ahn-Ahn! For what?" August asked.

"Just looking at that guy, he probably a gay and his parent will be at home thinking they have a son."

"You don't know. You can't tell people are gay just from the way they walk."

"Man, I'm more than ninety-nine-point-nine-nine-nine-nine percent sure that guy is gay."

"Just say you suspect. You can't be sure."

"Haven't you seen him smile? It's like bewitching or something. I know his type. It's too bad, honestly."

August said nothing else. Just made a sound. He would later go think through all the different things he could have said, ways he would have defended Segun. But he was afraid.

CHAPTER FOURTEEN

That class, that spot, became their special place. They would meet there each evening and talk about things. Random things. One day, Segun told August of how he wanted to apply to the University of Ibadan but everyone in his class was applying to Ibadan, or FUTA, and he wanted to escape everyone that knew him. August thought of asking Segun what he was escaping, but he had a feeling the answer would unnerve him.

"My sister goes to Ibadan," he said instead. "She's studying medicine."

"Lucky for her," Segun said. "It's a very good school."

August nodded and Segun chewed his cheek for a while before he said something else and their conversation drifted. They would talk for an hour, sometimes two, before turning to their studies. August sometimes talked about his books. The wars—there were so many of them, the oral traditions of documentation, ancient and tainted by their age-long transition. Segun would listen, looking thoughtful. August loved the way he kept his face, furrowed, attentive.

"Your friend does not come to night class?" Segun asked once. August thought he was referring to Dike. "He comes sometimes," August said.

"Not him. Who's talking about that one? Your girlfriend that runs."

"Oh, Betty doesn't go to night class. And she's not my girlfriend."

"Oh, but both of you are so cute together."

"She's not my girlfriend," August repeated.

Segun looked up from his book at August.

"Okay," August said. "It's been awhile since I saw her though."

They stared at each other for a while and then Segun smiled. "What?"

"Nothing." August shook his head, smiling too. Segun spoke too of his roommates. Uchenna and Ifeanyi and Francis. They were horrible, he said, shaking his head, a small smile on his lips. August didn't know what to make of that. He sometimes found it hard to understand Segun—the way he laughed even when saying things that should not evoke laughter.

"This one that does not know that the world does not belong to him will be snooping through my things when I'm not around," he said, with a laugh. "What he's looking for, I don't know. He is yet to tell me."

Hearing Segun speak, August felt grateful he had no roommates. The day he visited Segun in his room, he felt even more grateful. Segun's roommates were friendly. They shook hands with him and seemed to care how Segun's day went. Ifeanyi had the bed opposite Segun, and in between, bags were leaning on the wall. August sat on Segun's bed—it felt hard, as hard as wood.

"Are you guys in the same department?" Francis asked from his side of the room.

August thought Segun would answer but when he didn't, August said, "No, History."

"Oh," Francis said. "Sorry o. I'm just asking because you're the first person coming to visit him."

"Shut up," Segun said.

Francis began to laugh. "No seriously o. This one? I don't know if he's human sef. He too like alien behavior, I swear. I'm not sure anyone else in this Nsukka knows him."

"Even his class rep doesn't know who he is," Ifeanyi quipped, beside himself with laughter. August chuckled.

"Don't mind them," Segun said.

"It's just to sleep at the cyber," Uchenna said.

"Or to hole up in his bed reading all these his communist books."

Segun found the book he was searching for and handed it to August. "Let's go. Let them be saying what no one asked them."

As they made their way down, August worried they would run into Dike, even though he knew Dike's hostel was Njoku, not Alvan Ikoku.

"Your roommates seem nice," he said to Segun.

"Of course they do," Segun said. August thought he would say something else but he didn't.

"You know I initially wanted to live in the hostel."

"Thank your stars you changed your mind. Thank them well. If I had money sef, I'd live in the lodge. UNN hostels are dehumanizing, a gross violation of dignity."

He always teased August about his housing. "Rich boy living in this rich lodge." The first time Segun visited he bounced around on August's bed, grinning. "You are living the home life o," he said.

"Well, at least your roommates seemed like nice people," August said. They were now outside Njoku.

"They are a bunch of bullies. Sometimes, they speak about me but in Igbo because they don't know I can understand Igbo a bit. This jovial thing is just how they behave, like their hearts are not black with wickedness."

August laughed.

"It's fine sha. I'm used to it. My own is, if you look for my trouble, you will definitely find it. Because I know they're only going through them because of the notes my friend that bought me the books, Trevor, used to write me in them."

"Why would they even touch your books without your permission?"

"Oh, my God, thank you. Like, it's not yours. Don't touch it. They always make it like it's somehow my fault that they are homophobic assholes with no sense of personal boundaries."

"Wow, you really don't like them."

"You wouldn't like them if you were in my shoes. But I guess it could be worse sha. My secondary-school classmates, I used to fight them on a daily basis. Like, I come to school in the morning and start fighting from the door."

They stopped to buy sachets of water. Segun looked past him and waved to someone. The guy walked up to greet them. There was something about his walk, too. When the guy hugged Segun, a full hug right there in front of the shop, August felt his neck heat up with embarrassment. As Segun introduced them, August stretched out his hand, afraid the guy would hug him.

"I actually thought you would be through with your exams by now," he was saying to Segun.

"You know how these people are. They want everyone to starve to death first."

"I swear to God. The way my papers are spaced, I thought it was just me. They're definitely doing it on purpose."

August felt himself to be an obtuse object fixed in space. He listened to them talk, their voices rising with excitement, laughter ringing. He was relieved when a taxi pulled up.

"I'll take this one," he said to Segun.

"Oh my God, I'm so sorry. You'll say I ignored you. Sorry."

"It's fine. It's just, you know the exam stress. I'm so sleepy."

It was only as the taxi drove away that August acknowledged his shame. He felt ungainly standing there with them. He kept wondering what people thought seeing the three of them stand there. It was not something he fully understood, this shame, this fear. The way Segun walked, the way he talked, it disconcerted him. Yet when the both of them were together, alone, it all fell away and all that was left was an easy comfort. In that way, Segun reminded August of June, and those memories brought even more guilt and shame. But he couldn't admit such a thing, that Segun embarrassed him.

Because then he would also have to admit how desperately he wanted to be approved of, how much he wanted to be seen as a man, a full man. But Segun made him feel alive, made him anticipate each new day. Thinking of Segun made August smile to himself at random moments in the day.

The taxi stopped at Hilltop and August made his way to his room. He plopped into his unmade bed, fully dressed and lying on his back, and listened to the silence. He thought of home, of his father's illness and the heaviness of the alarm he felt standing there with Segun and his friend, and he felt so alone.

He called Peculiar first. He knew she would be delighted to hear his voice. On WhatsApp, she was always asking how he was, and why he did not call more often. Now she sounded surprised to hear his voice.

"Are you okay?" she asked. "I hope you're fine, exams and all."

"I'm fine," August said. "I just wanted to hear your voice."

"Awww. August, sometimes you say the nicest things. I miss you too."

They talked about their father. Yes, he was taking his medicine. No, there wasn't any problem. She knew how many pills they were in total and ate with him so she could watch him take them. Before August ended the call, she asked again if he was fine, and if there was anything he needed.

When he called Chinyere, she asked the same thing. August sometimes wondered what their lives would be without him, how much more unlabored it would be if he wasn't something they had to constantly think about. It troubled him how the littlest things in his life so greatly worried them.

Perhaps it was their mother's death that made it that way. Her death left him in their charge, a helpless thing no one would worry over and care for, if not for them. There were times August wondered if it was love. Certainly, it appeared that way. They raised him like they loved him, not just as sisters, but the way mothers loved their children. But in his darkest moments, August worried that if he were indestructible, they would not care about him anymore.

And when Uzoamaka asked, "Do you need anything? Are you sure?" it made him think of his own death as a liberation for his sisters, something to set them free. "That isn't true," he said to himself, but sometimes he also asked himself, *Are you sure? How do you know, August? How can you ever know?*

August ran into Segun's friend only a week later, the day his exams ended. Students were loitering outside the classrooms saying their good-byes.

"Last exam of first year. Freedom!" one of his classmates, Ikenna, said. He was the talkative one of the class. He never ran out of words and never did his assignments on his own. One time, he copied August's essay on the French Revolution without changing a single word. They left together, August, Ikenna, and one other guy whose name was also Ikenna but everyone called Kenny. Ikenna was saying how much food he would eat, as soon as he traveled back home.

"You, you don't know what hunger is na," Ikenna said and nudged him.

"Because you buy me food abi?" August replied.

It was then that August saw Segun's friend walking toward them. August couldn't remember his name. Chiemerie or

Chimuanya, something like that. He desperately hoped the boy would not notice him. But he did, and he waved at August enthusiastically. Ikenna and Kenny turned to look at Chiemerie. Chiemerie shook hands with the three of them.

"You guys are done too?" he asked August.

"Yes, yes. I didn't know you were actually in this faculty," August said.

"Theater Arts and Film," Chiemerie replied, pointing in the direction of the Theater Arts department.

They didn't speak for long. After Chiemerie left, Kenny put his hand over his mouth to cover his laughter. Ikenna pushed him. "You're mad o. What you laughing?" but even he was laughing too.

August did not get what was funny but he laughed along, more out of what to say than of mirth.

"But seriously sha, those Theater Arts guys are always like this. There's a spirit that follows that department," Kenny said.

"You are crazy," Ikenna said.

"You people know he actually heard us laughing," August said.

"Ehe? And so? Is he my father?" Kenny said, turning to look back in Chiemerie's direction.

"Father kwa?" Ikenna said, and they burst into laughter again. This time August did not laugh with them.

"I actually know him sha," Ikenna said. "I know his room at Njoku. I heard none of his roommates stay alone with him. They use herd protection."

They laughed again.

"If na you nko? This type of thing eh." He swung his hand over his head and snapped his fingers.

"But I wonder why these guys are like this. That department is cursed. If you go there, their girls are so easy because their guys are so useless," Kenny said.

"You're saying their department. Our own nko? If you look at the set above us, like eh, hmmmm."

August was silent. He wanted to say that they did not even know what they were saying. And that there was no way they could tell something like that just from meeting someone. But his objections sounded like something they would laugh at as well.

"Soon they'll start wearing pampas and leaking everywhere," Ikenna said, squeezing his face.

"Urghh," Kenny said and spat.

August said nothing. Back at his lodge, he would contemplate all the ways he could have defended Chiemerie. He would analyze them and weigh which ones least made him suspect. *You should have said something, August*, he agonized. *Fucking coward.*

When Segun visited later that day, August feared Chiemerie had told Segun how he had been treated. August watched Segun, waiting for him to bring it up.

"What?" Segun asked.

"Nothing," August said.

"You're staring. It's weird."

"It's nothing," August said, and turned away.

He sat on his bed and focused his attention on his fingers instead. Segun was going through his DVDs. When he was through, he picked up August's photo album.

"Who's this?" he asked.

August peered at the picture. "My sister."

"And this must be your father," Segun said, bringing the album to the bed. August nodded. He didn't care very much for pictures. His sisters had put the album together before he left for school. The album reminded him of his mother, and perhaps that was one of the reasons he had not opened it once since moving here.

"Who's this?" Segun asked again.

"My sister, second born."

"They don't look like your father, so I'm guessing they take after your mother."

"They don't look like anybody in our family. They look like themselves," August said.

"Yes, that happens sometimes. My cousin, she does not look like anyone at all, not even a slight resemblance," Segun said, leafing through the album. "This one kwan?"

"My sister," August said again. Segun turned to give him a look.

August smiled. "What? That's my eldest sister when she was in school."

"How many sisters do you have?"

"Just three," August said. August was now leaning close, staring into the album. They went through August's life. When Segun turned to a picture of August's mother, he gasped.

"Oh, my God, you look just like her," he said. "Just looking at her I don't even need to ask. No wonder she spoils you rotten with fridge and everything." Segun chuckled. August made a chuckling sound. Segun turned to another picture.

"She died," August said.

Segun turned to him, his mouth open. "I'm so so sorry. I didn't know."

August nodded. "It's fine. I never knew her sef. She died the day I was born."

Segun closed the album. "I'm sure she was a wonderful woman," he said.

"Not a very smart one though," August said, shrugging.

Segun was taken aback. "How can you say something like that about your own mother?" He sounded like one of his sisters.

"Dude, it's true. She actually wasn't supposed to have me."

Segun shook his head. "I can't believe you right now. Are you being serious?" he said to August.

"Look, it makes no sense dying to give birth to a child you won't even be alive to raise."

"You are here judging her. You don't know what her life was like. She probably didn't know she'd die."

"They literally told her," August said, and then realized that he had raised his voice.

"You're angry at her," Segun said, shaking his head slowly.

"What?"

"You're angry at her. You don't know the pressures that were at play in her life. We live in a patriarchal society that hates women, August."

August tilted his head in thought and then shook his head. "Let's just talk about something else because you don't know what the fuck you're talking about," he said.

August had bought two Claude Ake books that Segun complained he couldn't find. But now he was too upset. Segun had ruined the moment and August would have to wait for some other time to present the books. Segun had tried to find the books for weeks.

"It's sick how we're denied revolutionary literature. Because letting these titles go out of print is definitely deliberate."

"Just order it online," August had told Segun.

"You think I haven't looked online?"

And so August set himself the goal of finding Segun those books. Knowing how touched Segun would be by a gesture like that, August scoured the internet. He bought a VPN and switched countries so he could see different result selections. He called so many bookstores that he tired of talking. But he found both books. He had *Revolutionary Pressures in Africa* shipped all the way from London and he ordered *A Political Economy of Nigeria* from a bookstore at the University of Port Harcourt.

"You people should have a website with all your books so people looking online can see the books you have without having to call," he told the bookseller in Port Harcourt.

"Sure, sure," the man on the other end of the line said.

August thought and thought of what to write in them. He googled "quotes by communists" and skimmed through quotes by Che Guevara and Amílcar Cabral and Stalin and Alexandra Kollontai. But nothing seemed right. Eventually he wrote his own words in them.

In *A Political Economy of Nigeria*, he wrote, "May this book light your world the way you light mine."

And in *Revolutionary Pressures in Africa*, he wrote, "To a comrade dear to my heart. *Vitoria é certa*, as certain as the sun."

CHAPTER FIFTEEN

The holiday did not last very long. The previous semester had ended very late, to offset time lost during the strikes. August's new course modules were all over the place. He was doing a course on East and Central Africa, and one on South Africa, and another Russia and China. He breezed through these courses as he did with his module on Nigeria's Diplomatic History. And always, seeing Segun, hearing his voice, listening to him speak with thick hatred about this or that Western country, would be the highlight of his day. August would feed him the bait, always impressed by how much history Segun knew. "Did you know the British bought some parts of Ghana from Denmark and the Netherlands?" Or, "Did you know the International Criminal Court ruled that America violated international law in Nicaragua, and ordered them to pay Nicaragua reparations, and they just refused?"

Then, without warning, Segun stopped coming to the cybercafé. He called Segun's phone many times, but Segun rarely ever took calls, or made them, unless to apologize for not taking his calls. Each time he went to the cybercafé, he would find a girl sitting behind the desk where Segun used to sit. At first, August wondered if it was *him*, if he had done something wrong. But the more he thought about it, the more unlikely it seemed. Segun was not the type to miss his work for a thing like that. And so on a Monday afternoon, when he was sure Segun would have lectures, August went to Segun's department to look for him. It took him awhile to find Segun's class, but eventually he found Segun sitting at the back, his head buried in a book. August adjusted his bag and walked stealthily to where Segun was sitting. He wanted to cover Segun's eyes with his hands and have him guess who it was but there was no way August could go around without Segun noticing, and so decided against it.

"Hello, Mr. Typist," August said, and Segun looked up.

August froze in his tracks. At first, he wasn't sure what he was looking at, but as he went closer to Segun's seat, it seemed to grow larger. It began just at the edge of Segun's left eye and swept all the way back to his temple. August had never seen a bruise that big.

"What is this? What happened?" Instinctively, he reached out to touch it.

Segun recoiled. "It's nothing. I'm fine."

"It's not nothing. Were you in an accident?"

"Lower your voice, please," Segun said, and turned his face to the side.

August didn't know what else to say. He thought Segun would volunteer an explanation. He did not. Instead, Segun returned his attention to his book, a finger tracing a line on the page. August just sat with him silently. He thought of what to do, what to say, but his mind was empty. And so he just sat there watching Segun read. And then, both slowly and all at once, August saw Segun's eyes soften until they were brimming with tears. Segun looked skyward and blinked furiously. August looked around. There were a handful of students in the class. Segun wiped away the tears that had escaped with his palm and then shut the book he was reading, William Blake's *Songs of Innocence*.

"Are you okay?" August said, longing to take Segun's beautiful hand in his.

Segun shook his head. He looked up again and blinked again, put the book in his schoolbag, and slung it onto his shoulder. August stood and followed.

"What happened?" he asked again, this time his voice low, almost a whisper. They were walking down the stairs now.

"I had issues with my roommate," he said. "Obum."

"Who's Obum?"

"My roommate. I'm staying in Njoku now," he said, and continued walking.

August quickened his steps to keep up. They took the path through the stadium, walking in silence until Segun stopped.

"I'm sorry," August said. "I'm sorry for whatever happened to you."

Segun nodded. He walked up to the concrete seats and sat down. He let his bag drop to the ground and buried his face in his hands.

"I hate cishet people so fucking much," he sobbed. "I don't know how much of it I can take."

"Was it a fight?"

"Not really. He hit my head against the door."

"Jesus Christ. Just like that?" August asked.

"So, they ganged up on me and were just popping off and were calling me homo and asking me why I like putting things up my ass and so on. And I was saying my mind and Obum just attacked me. Like, literally attacked me."

August thought even the guy's name—Obum—sounded cruel.

"So I was standing near the door leading out to the veranda, and I was facing away. When he slapped me, it pushed my head into the door. Then he started smashing my head into the door until I began to bleed. I thought he was going to crush my skull or something," Segun said, as he sniffed and touched the bruise, gently.

August wanted to hug him, but they were in public. He didn't know what else to do, or even say.

"Did you report him? You can report him, right?"

"Report to who? You think they give a fuck? Do you know how many times porter himself has stopped me and asked if I let men fuck me in the ass? Those guys are demented."

"We have to do something about this," August said.

"I just don't know what to do. I mean, it was a fight," he replied, wiping his face.

August wanted to offer his lodge to Segun, to ask him to move in, but how would that even work? His phone began to ring. Instinctively, August looked around. He suddenly felt like Dike was a few feet away, watching. They were supposed to go to the market together and buy a mirror for Dike's room.

"I was held up with some stuff. What's up?" August said into the phone.

"What do you mean what's up? You're supposed to be here." Dike sounded exasperated. "I'll just go by myself. If you knew you didn't want to go with me, man, you should have just told me."

"Chill. I'll be there soon."

Segun stood up and straightened invisible creases in his trousers. "Sorry about this. I really didn't want to disturb you with this."

"Are you kidding? Of course I want to know. We have to do something. Look at your face!"

On the way to Ogige market, August kept thinking of the bruise on Segun's face, how helpless he felt, how worthless.

"You know they could be taking us to trials for Scotland, Commonwealth Games. Just a rumor I heard," Dike said.

"I wonder where you heard such a thing," August scoffed. He wanted Dike to shut up but didn't know how to tell him. There was a painful tightness in his stomach, and when Dike spoke, it rang in his ears. Even the girls talking next to them in the shuttle annoyed him.

"No for real. There were scouts for the SUG games."

Later that evening, as they ran laps in the stadium, Dike brought it up again. "I heard Betty has been picked sef. That girl . . ." He shook his head.

"Just stop. Fucking stop. I'm tired of this bullshit."

"What did I say?"

"What do you mean *that girl*?"

"Look, I'm not saying anything but think about it for a second. She—"

August threw his hands up and turned to walk away. Realizing he should have said more, he stopped and turned back.

"You know, I think your problem is jealousy. Will you ever dominate like she does?"

"Man, jeez. I'm sorry. I was just jonesing you," Dike said.

"Fuck your stupid jonesing. I'm going. Run if you want."

"August, come on. I said I'm sorry."

August didn't stop. Dike stood there calling his name. August would not have said these things if his blood was not already boiling. Back at his lodge, he called Segun. The phone rang but Segun didn't pick up, so he called Betty.

"How was your day?" she asked.

"Fine, fine. Did you hear that there were scouts at the SUG games? For the Commonwealth Games?"

"Is that why you called me?" she asked. She sounded annoyed.

"Of . . . of course not. Come on, don't be like that."

"Yes, there were scouts at the SUG games. But if you think they'll take you to an international competition straight, then you're not really smart. Because all the professional athletes have finished, it's students who have not even gone regional they're coming to take, just like that. See, if this is why you called, I'm very tired. I had a hectic day."

August placed his phone on the table and lay back on his bed. He had a headache, a grinding headache that made his temples throb. He closed his eyes and lay there listening to his own breathing until he fell into a dreamless sleep.

CHAPTER SIXTEEN

His relationship with August came by providence. That was what Segun told his friends when they asked. In the beginning, Segun could have sworn August and Betty were dating. They went everywhere together, and everyone in their faculty talked about them and how nice they looked together. Betty was studying Physical Education but everyone in Nsukka knew her already. When August started coming to the cybercafé, each day with a new document to photocopy, Segun wasn't sure that August was interested in him, especially because of how snobbish he had been on the day they met at the games. But more and more it seemed August was coming up with excuses to be there. It was cute, this shy fresher who always wanted to be around him. They started spending time together at night class too.

Night class was something Segun had always done alone because none of his roommates came to class, to read at night. And even if they did, he would never voluntarily be near them, if he did not have to. Julia did her reading early in the mornings, and he didn't get along with many of his other classmates. When he saw August in Social Science under the fluorescent lights, he decided he wouldn't sit with him. But August looked up, and when their eyes met, August smiled at him. And so he walked down to where he was seated. They kept to their books the rest of the night, their bodies close enough that Segun wondered what it would feel like to touch him. They would meet there in the evenings and talk about school and family. He told August that he applied to UNN because the options everywhere else were taken, UI and UNILAG and FUTA were all out of the question. He wanted a new start, somewhere new where he didn't have to see any of his former classmates. He did not tell him about Tanko though. Because he wasn't sure yet if he could trust him. He was, after all, Dike's friend. As they grew closer, he would tell August about everything—about Trevor, about what his classmates did to him after their SSCE exams, about his roommates too. But never about Tanko.

The day his father phoned him repeatedly from Lagos, it was in August's room that he stayed, to clear his mind. He knew why his father was calling him. The privatization bill had passed and President Jonathan had signed it. Segun knew his father was calling to tell him he had lost his job. He needed his own sadness to wash through him first, so that when he picked up, he could be positive. He knew that was what his father needed from that call. Segun telling him it was okay, and that things on his own end were perfect. When he told August that he was certain his father had lost his job, August hugged Segun's shoulder, and even after that, just let his hand linger on his chest.

In his third year, he had to move from Alvan Ikoku to Eni-Njoku Hall. His new roommates were even worse than the last ones, and several times, he clashed with all of them because they always ganged up each time. Tensions in his room eventually came to a head when Emelie threw his exercise book into a bucket of water. He claimed it was an accident, and that the book had fallen out of his hand and into the water. But what sort of accident was that? It was a book Trevor had gifted him, a book with strong spiral binds and an elastic band running horizontally along the edge of it. In it, he wrote his favorite quotes from *Pedagogy of the Oppressed*, a book Trevor had gifted him too, and then, later on, poetry and story concepts he intended to use in class exercises. He was incensed.

"Are you a child? Who even gave you the permission to touch my things?"

"Don't worry. When the book dries, you can still find the contacts you wrote in it. All those guys wey dey fuck your nyash, I know that's what's paining you," Nnamdi said, laughing.

"What is paining me is none of your business. I've told you people that nobody in this room should touch my stuff. Stay on your own, let me stay on my own."

"Who are you that I won't touch your stuff?" Emelie barked. "Who is your father?"

"Emelie, respect your self o. You're not a child."

"Get out joor. Don't insult me because of one stupid book. Is your book gold?"

"Can you imagine! Are you okay at all?"

"You know he writes his homo stuff in that book," Obum laughed.

"And how would you even know when you don't even know how to read? It's not written in Homophobese," Segun retorted.

He was facing the door, on his way out, when Obum rushed up behind him and slapped him so hard his face slammed into the door and left a dent. Segun felt a sharp pain where his face had made an impact, but Obum did not stop. It was clear he had wanted to do this for a while. Segun was disoriented but he gathered his wits fast enough to punch Obum in the throat. Obum doubled over and Segun pushed him with all his strength. They came crashing into the bunk beds in the room. It was then that the rest of the room intervened, flogging them with belts until they separated. Because he was on top of Obum, most of the lashes landed on his back. He dusted his shirt off and went outside to spread the book. After air drying, he should be able to find everything he had written, intact, still legible.

To everyone who asked about the big bruise on his face, he simply told them that he fell. But something about how shocked August was and how tenderly he touched Segun's face, brought him to tears. He blinked them away, but they returned just as fast, welling up in his eyes. When August asked if he was okay, he shook his head no, and put the book he was trying to read back in his bag. They left the class and walked to his hostel together. At the stadium, Segun sat on the bench, and for the first time, he cried about it. Loud, ugly tears.

"I don't know what to do," he said. August sat with him until he collected himself and then they walked the rest of the way to Njoku.

Asking Segun to come stay in his lodge was the first time August declared his feelings for Segun. In the blink of an eye, the turn of a lip, the warmth of August's hand on his, Segun's heart could just as well have stopped beating for the few minutes it took August to bare his chest. Segun was only half surprised. Each time he saw August, it was as though August were studying him for signs that another fight had occurred. It was such a tender thing, to be worried over, to be cared for in this manner. And so, Segun was not totally surprised when August asked the question. They were in August's room, just after school, and Segun was watching a movie on August's laptop.

"I just want to know you're safe," August said.

Segun was not ready to invest that level of trust in anyone outside of himself. Agreeing to live with August would have solved so many of Segun's problems, but it would have also put him in a position of vulnerability he promised himself he would never be in again.

"Oh don't worry," he said to August, waving the offer away, "I think I can handle a few bigots. I mean, I went to an all boys' school. Homophobe Training Institute."

"Segun, please. I worry about you," August said.

"I'm fine," Segun said, closing the laptop. "Really. Look, I'm sorry if I scared you. I'm extra like that sometimes but I think I'd rather not, August."

August stared at him.

Segun moved closer, leaned on August's shoulder. "You don't have to worry about me," he said. He cupped August's face with both hands, feeling the warmth of August's breath rest on his cheeks. At first, their lips brushed against each other. Then they merged slowly. It was August who broke it off. He wiped his lips with the back of his palm. Segun studied his face and was not sure what he saw there, was not sure if it was shame or if it was all in his head. A wave of humiliation swept over him.

"I'm sorry," he said to August. "I didn't . . . Sorry," he said again, awkwardly. He made to climb off the bed, but August held him and pulled him back. And against his better judgment, Segun let himself be drawn back into August's arms. August's reluctance was visible, it weighed down his every movement, made the most basic movements of making out into something burdensome and heavy. They were awkward, arms flailing, elbows knocking into each other. It made Segun feel so horrible, all the mushiness he had felt earlier turning into smoke and dissipating into air. He pressed a hand to August's chest and broke their kiss. He lay on his back and August lay beside him.

"I'm sorry," August said.

"It's fine. Don't apologize," Segun said. He was suddenly tired, drained. He wanted to go back to his hostel.

August turned on his side so that he was facing him. "I don't know how to live this life," August said.

"I know, August. I know."

August lay on his back again. They both lay there in silence listening to the sound of each other's breathing. Segun thought it was unfair that August was so forward in how he felt toward him, only to then do this. But he did not say that. *We are socialized to despise ourselves, it's not his fault*, Segun reminded himself. But still, he was upset. What did August want him to do? Where did this leave them?

"I have a lot going on," Segun eventually said. He was afraid of loving August, afraid of loving someone who was not ready to love him back. "I can't take uncertainty too. I can't risk this. I know how it's going to end."

"Segun," August began.

But Segun did not want to hear what he had to say. He simply wanted to be out of this room.

"No, August. I . . . it's not easy for me. And I can't handle more. If you've not made peace with yourself, I can't get in the middle of that. I can't help you carry that burden, August. I can't. You have to bear it on your own. You have to work through it because with me it's all or nothing. I'm not ashamed. I refuse to be ashamed. And if you still are, I can't deal with that."

He sat up and turned to look at August. "I can't," he said again.

August nodded. Segun stood from the bed and picked his shirt from his floor, put it on and began to button it. He was facing the door, but he heard August stand from the bed. Still facing the door, Segun put on the rest of his clothes before turning around to take his schoolbag.

"Bye," he said, opening the door and letting himself out.

"Bye," August said. For a moment, August looked like he would say something, but he did not. Segun closed the door behind him. He walked to the end of the hallway before stopping to steady his nerves. Then, with the shakiness in his breath gone, he began to descend the stairs.

CHAPTER SEVENTEEN

In the days that followed, August and Segun barely spoke. August went to night class because he knew Segun read there every night. He sat a few seats away and just watched. Waiting and waiting for something to happen. He was ready to do anything to mend what they had. It felt like they had gotten in a joyride that rose slowly up a rail, and now that they had reached its peak, now that they were supposed to zoom down with the wind blowing in their face, the machines broke down. What Segun was asking of him made sense, August had no doubt of that. But acceptance was not something he could simply give himself. It was not a switch in him he could simply turn on if he wished. It was one of the reasons he admired Segun so much, because he wished he loved himself the way Segun loved himself. August wished his heart did not twist in on itself at the mere thought that someone out there suspected he was gay. It was being with Segun that showed him he could overcome some of that fear, even if slowly. Before Segun, August had come to accept certain things about himself, certain walls he was not allowed to look over, and now Segun demanded August take a bulldozer and bring it all down.

August tried. He went to more meetings of the Socialist Students' Forum. If for nothing else, because it meant he could see more of Segun, hear Segun's voice.

Once Segun facilitated a discussion on the electricity privatization package. Segun kept forgetting to cover the whiteboard marker.

Electricity Sector Liberalization and the Nigerian Working Class, he wrote on the board, but then didn't cover the marker. By the time he tried to write on the board again, the marker had dried out.

"Comrades, I keep forgetting to close this thing," he smiled. "Sorry. Can I get another one? We'll just discuss our role as revolutionary students in continuing to oppose Jonathan's neoliberal agenda, and then we'll call it a day."

August wished he had come to the meeting with a marker in his bag. On subsequent days, he would come with two in his bag, and week after week, he would be disappointed that Segun did not facilitate the class. After a same-sex marriage prohibition bill was introduced in the National Assembly, Segun facilitated the class but did not use a marker at all. He stood in front of the class and asked question after question, his legs shaking ever so slightly, like he was afraid of the answers he would get.

"Comrades, how many of us support this bill? Show of hands," Segun said.

August was surprised that only four hands in the whole class went up. Everyone was looking around. Someone hissed and said, "Socialist but you be bigot," and a muffled laughter swept through the class. But Segun's face looked pained, like somehow even those few hands were too strong a betrayal.

"Okay, a few of us raised our hands. Who wants to explain their position? Let this be a free space. Remember, comrades, contradiction is not our enemy. It is reality and we must study it to get to a closer approximation of the truth, whether it's comfortable or not. I want us to ask ourselves, this bill, this moral panic our society is being whipped into, how does this better our struggle against oppression? Who really benefits from this?"

August raised his hand. "I think this is just a ploy to rally support from the churches and mosques. As we know, many of them have been endorsing this and encouraging the National Assembly to pass it."

Previously, August never spoke in the discussions except when prompted, but he wanted Segun to notice his presence, so that Segun would look at him. And talk to him in a way that did not consist of just pleasantries and small talk.

"That a good answer. But comrades, religion is a super-structure. *Why* are the churches and mosques being mobilized, and for whom? What are the interests of the people doing this mobilization?"

Several hands went up. They took turns giving their answers and Segun nodded and nodded and nodded.

"We must always ask ourselves, regardless of our personal prejudices, what the political objectives of the governing elites are and where that leaves us as revolutionaries," he said eventually. "The question of *Why?* The question of *For whom? In whose interests?* These are crucial questions."

And it made August realize just how little he has lived for himself. How rarely he had made decisions solely because they made him happy.

"How are you?" he asked Segun after the meeting. Segun looked tired and distracted. Like he had exhausted all his strength facilitating the class.

"I'm okay," Segun said.

"Nice class. I still can't believe with everything happening in this country, this is what the people we elect to lead this country are focusing on," he said.

"Honestly at this point that whole building should be set ablaze, let all of us rest," Segun said. He slung his bag over his shoulder and turned toward the door. August followed.

"I miss you," August said downstairs, as they stepped outside and into the open. He said it softly, because he did not want anyone else to hear. But it came out sounding desperate.

"But I didn't go anywhere," Segun said, chuckling.

"Come on, you know what I mean."

"August, we can be just friends," Segun said. "That's what you need, more queer friends."

But August did not want to be just friends. He wanted more. *Just friends* felt like punishment, felt like the potentially best thing that would ever happen to him was right in front of him but he was not allowed to explore, to see how far it could go.

"I want to be more than friends," he said.

"Let's not go through this again. You know—" Segun began, but August cut him off.

"I know," he said, "and I'm trying. I am. I know it's me. It's all me but I care so much for you."

He had thought about this very carefully, what to say. And in doing so, he had wondered if this feeling in his heart wasn't love. He didn't know what that type of love felt like, so there was no way of knowing for sure. And could it really be love if he wasn't sure of it? They sat on the bench outside the faculty, surrounded by trimmed ixoras, a flame tree blazing red above them.

"I don't know if I can give you what you want," August began. "But I won't be giving you my burden. You, it's you that helps me escape it."

"August, that's not healthy. I'm sorry but this is something you have to deal with on your own."

"I don't know how," August said. "I admire you so much, so fucking much. The way you own it."

He said a lot of things. He prepared an entire speech in his head. And somewhere in the middle of it, he saw Segun's eyes soften. In the cab back to his lodge, he was ecstatic. He had an erection straining painfully against his trousers. He tried to hide it, and he'd spent the whole distance home wondering if people could see it. If they could tell. They ended up in his room, their bodies entangled in glorious light. It was the first time August had been with someone and came out of it feeling an ephemeral glow to his skin, like he had experienced light in its purest form. It felt like knowing himself for the first time. Somehow he found himself in the slender contours of Segun's body in a way that was completely untethered to this world, two men sharing something beautiful, something almost heavenly. Because August was not prepared and did not have any lube, the sex was not penetrative. Instead, they found many other ways to explore each other's bodies. The next day, Segun would give him a tube a K-Y Jelly. Each afternoon after school, they would rush back to his lodge, giggling to each other as soon as they stepped into the room and August locked the door. Sometimes he just about tore Segun's clothes off, the impatience that had built up in him seeking immediate release. And other times he went slowly, enjoying the feel of Segun's body against him, enjoying the scent of Segun's body, the musk beneath Segun's underwear, the feel of Segun's lips dragging over his body, the warmth of Segun's mouth.

Afterward, August would hold Segun to himself, their naked sweaty bodies sticking together as the fan did its best to cool the room. And they whispered sweet things to each other. Those were the best days. And now that they had finally found their way to each other, Segun rarely stayed in his hostel.

After school, August would train with Dike and the others. Now they were training for the NUGA games. When he got home, Segun would be waking up from his afternoon nap and they'd spend the evening together, until Segun had to leave for night class. Their schedules merged so effortlessly.

Christmas break that year was the longest Christmas August had ever had. Ever. He called Segun so often his sisters began to whisper amongst themselves.

"I'm sure it's that girl that came for Uzoamaka's wedding." Chinyere and Peculiar giggled at each other.

August would have to lock himself in his room for hours to speak with Segun.

"How is Lagos?" he would ask.

"How is Enugu?" Segun would ask, both of them trying to say it first. For some reason, it made Segun laugh so much, and Segun's laughter made August laugh.

He would end those calls so giddy with happiness.

"Who is she?" his sisters teased.

"Leave me alone. Sis, gosh. It's just someone I know from school."

"Wow. So that's what we're calling it these days?" Chinyere said. August could tell that they were delighted for him and he didn't like that. They would not be so pleased if they knew it was Segun. They had each asked him who Segun was when he made Segun's picture his WhatsApp profile picture.

"A guy I run with," he told them.

When Dike asked, August's heart skipped a bit. He began to type a response and then erased his words, several times.

Eventually, he said, "I just like the picture nau. Nawa for you o."

"You pick the weirdest friends. I mean, this guy? I can't even be friends with someone like that. Dude be careful sha."

"Thanks for your concern. You're actually my weirdest friend. You would know."

As the days of the holiday ran out and heralded a new year, August prepared for their reunion with so much anticipation that he counted down the days.

"I can't wait to see you again," he said on the phone.

"You can't imagine how much I've missed you," Segun said. "Literally it's unimaginable."

August knew that this happiness, this absolute joy he felt could not last. He just knew. It seemed so unlike his life to have this much contentment in it. He thought of it like an airplane, or a ship, a majestic ship. Sailing effortlessly through the water with pride, but for only so long. Soon, he feared, he would be sinking. He relished his happiness with his fear skirting the edges of his joy.

He returned to school a day before Segun. When he heard Segun's knock on his door, he leapt up from his bed. He swung the door open and the wooden frame pushed against the air with a swoosh sound. And there Segun stood, with that smile like two glorious hills standing above a valley of streams and flowers and grass as lush as lush could be. They hugged each other tightly. Holding him, August was sure, as sure as he had ever been in his life, that he loved Segun.

CHAPTER EIGHTEEN

When it came to keeping August out of his life, Segun was, at first, steadfast in his conviction. He was only now getting over all the baggage he brought with him from Lagos. And so, no matter how much he liked August, no matter how much he loved August, he was not going to date someone who would make him doubt himself, not *ever*. But August was relentless. There was something exciting, something comforting about being wooed. Segun did not totally hate it. In fact, he enjoyed it very much, but he knew that if he took August back, August would hurt him again and again and again. But still . . . something about August's persistence weakened his resolve. Then, on a mid-October evening, August prepared a speech. An entire speech. Segun could see him trying to remember his words.

"I admire you so much," August said. "I admire the way you own who you are. It's you who helps me escape this cage that is my mind. It's you who helps me live. I don't know when I'll become at peace with myself, but I promise you, I'm trying."

No one had ever put so much effort into trying to win him over. It softened him. "Trying is a good start," he said, smiling. On their way back to August's lodge, Segun felt a pride he had never felt before. He felt valued. Seen. Happy.

He would begin to spend most of his time in the lodge, even when August was out. In the evenings, while August slept, Segun lay next to him and read, his skin comforted by the warmth of August's body, his mind calmed by August's steady quiet breathing. August looked so innocent, so boyish when he slept. When Segun slept in his hostel, he did not say a single word to his roommates. When he came back and learnt they had used his soap, and the water in his gallon, and all his detergent, he would simply take calming deep breaths while he went down to fetch more water or to buy detergent. He no longer let them dampen his mood, not now that he was so happy, so content, so at ease for the first time in a long long while.

His mother noticed it in his voice. She pointed out how chirpy he was, how his voice was no longer labored by sighs.

"Is there anything you're not telling your mother? Any lovey lovey that is making you this happy?"

"Am I supposed to be sad before? Mummy, please."

"Hmmm," she said. "Okay o. I know you will not tell me. Is it not you, Abe? Be keeping it to yourself o? When you call your other mother, you give her the gist."

"Mummy, it's nothing. Ohhh," he said, laughing.

She was laughing too.

"Well, just be careful," she said.

It was so easy with August because, despite his shyness, he was eager to please. In the darkness, they explored each other. Sometimes tenderly, slowly, softly, as though time did not exist, as though their bodies were flower seedlings that demanded only gentle touch. And other times, it was rough and high paced, so that they had to turn up the sound of August's boom box to drown out the steady sound of skin slapping against skin, the both of them moaning, their sweat creating a wet patch on August's light-blue bedsheet. Afterward, they showered together, washed each other's back, kissed as the showers of water washed the soap off their bodies.

And then the Same-Sex Marriage (Prohibition) Act passed the Senate. It completely took Segun by surprise. He saw it on Facebook while he was scrolling through his timeline. His hands trembled as he downloaded the bill and read it in open-mouthed shock.

"Who was talking about gay marriage in Nigeria? Who was even thinking about it? Absolutely no one. We're just here trying to not get killed and the Senate is here working to make sure millions of Nigerians are in more fear. President Jonathan, veto this bill," the Facebook post read.

August said the same thing. "Is there any day the Senate or the House isn't doing one stupid rubbish? Jonathan won't sign it. He's already under so much pressure now, from within and without."

"That's exactly why he'd sign it," Segun said sadly.

"What?"

"Yes. Do you think he cares about anything but his own political prospects?"

"Well, you, you hate him because he's a bourgeois politician normal normal so of course you'll think the worst," August said, chuckling to himself.

"Oh, you don't? You don't expect the worst? Such bliss," Segun retorted.

"Okay, look at it like this. Jonathan needs to improve things, yeah? He's looking for aid from all this America and Europe, and they've been hammering on human rights and so he'll use this to make a stance. He knows how bad signing it will be. I'm sure people like Okonjo-Iweala who are in his administration will kick against it. He has very open-minded people."

Segun almost laughed. He had never heard something so simplistic, so naïve, and so wrong. It annoyed him, made him think that August was not as conscientized as he had previously imagined him to be.

"Or," Segun said, "you could look at it like this. Jonathan has, in just a few years, managed to end fuel subsidy, privatize electricity distribution and generation as well as other key industries, incur even more job losses, increase poverty, while all the people in his cabinet grow fat on our national cake. He needs to sign this bill to help ingratiate himself to people, by appealing to their bigotry and their religion and their nationalism. Now he'll be the strong man who stood up to David Cameron and Obama. And it'll be quite easy because America has never cared about things like human rights."

"Come on. Even you can't believe that," August said. "They are hypocritical, but you can't say they don't care at all."

"The United States is best buddies with countries like Saudi Arabia, where women can't even drive. Believe me, as long as they can get their oil fix and the minerals, and prevent socialism, they're unbothered. They want you to think they care because they need the PR. When Jonathan signs this bill, all these countries will release statements through their embassies and that'll be it. That'll be where it ends."

"You just hate the West," August said.

"For very very good reason," Segun replied. "I'm not supposed to like my oppressors or hope on them to better my life in any way. That's delusional."

He wanted to be hopeful, he wanted to believe the bill would be vetoed, but no matter what angle he looked at this from, it seemed inevitable.

"Well, let's just watch and see," August said. "I don't think you're giving Jonathan due credit. That man is a professor, hope you know?"

"Just go to any department in UNN and ask a random lecturer there what they think of queer people. Just try it one day. That he's a professor means nothing. And he doesn't care. Rich people have no conscience. He privatized electricity this same year, hope you know? Tens of thousands of people lost their jobs. The more than twenty years my father put into NEPA—"

"I feel like that's your main gripe with him."

"Oh, so subsidy removal never happened then?"

"I'm not saying he's a good president. Just that we can't be personal in our analysis."

"That's not the point. It's not about NEPA. The point is that this regime has basically been on a campaign to crush poor people into the dust. This is their chance to finally try to shore up their hold on power, by inciting hatred. I'm not praying for him to sign it sha."

"Seems very much like you are."

"I'm not. It's just that I've come to terms with the fact that my life means nothing to these people. Class war is actual war, with real-life casualties, and the ruling class knows this and they do not give a fuck."

Christmas break was a welcome out. It seemed they were always arguing about Jonathan, and the bill, which Segun was sure August still hadn't read. Being apart gave him space and the time to miss August. They spoke on the phone like lovers, not adversaries always confronting political realities. It also helped that he was home again, with his parents. As he suspected, they were not impressed by the bill. "If PDP wants my vote in 2015, the least they can do is pay me my gratuity. Because all this gragra is not what will get my vote," he said. Segun's father was a driver now. Each morning, he left early for the car park. The bus he drove wasn't even his, it belonged to Chief Adeyemi, a deacon in the church his parents went to. After each week of work he had to pay Chief Adeyemi, whether or not he worked, regardless of what repairs the cars had required. On Sundays, he wrote application letters to job ads he found in newspapers. No one ever called him back. "I don't blame them," his father would say, as though it did not bother him. "At this age, I should be preparing to retire, not writing job applications."

It was a relief to Segun that his father was by default against this. It wasn't because his father particularly cared for queer people. Segun had heard him speak about them after the UK passed the Marriage Act early the previous year.

"These white people don't hold anything sacred," his father had said.

The three of them were in the living room watching a BBC broadcast.

"How?" Segun asked. His mother glanced at his father, as though she too wanted to find out the how.

"Gay marriage. What exactly will a man get after marrying his fellow man?"

"How is it your concern?" Segun asked.

"My dear o," his mother said. "Ask him. Somebody else's wahala. We won't mind our business. Anything we don't understand, it's bring them out and kill."

"I never said they should be brought out and killed. I just don't understand what the point of them getting married is. I don't support killing anybody but this marriage thing will only normalize it."

"So you don't want them killed, just discriminated against?" Segun asked, and his mother clapped her hand with enthusiasm. His father took his glasses off and wiped them.

"You people are putting words in my mouth," he said and returned his attention to the television.

Segun appreciated that his mother was not homophobic. Growing up, he used to be terrified that she was and that fear lay latent in him still, which was why they never spoke about his sexuality. It was almost an unspoken agreement between them to leave it in the realm of ambiguity. After she learnt of the bill, her hatred for Jonathan only grew.

"All these people know how to do is ban things," she said.

"Literally," Segun replied.

"As if this will change anybody's minds," Segun's father said. "People will celebrate it and still vote for the APC."

They had just had dinner and his parents sat watching the news while Segun cleared the dishes and swept the floor.

"Some people are saying Jonathan will not sign it," Segun said, and his mother made a sound, like the idea was the most ridiculous thing she had ever heard.

"This is everyday business. It is instinctual for the Nigerian state. Their plan, their solution, always, is to ban things, to demonstrate their ability to dominate. It is a shame that this is the target this administration is deciding on this time just to increase public approval. Very shameful. Turning working people against other working people so they can keep enjoying the oil money suffocating this country. It's not even a question of *if* Jonathan will sign this bill, only *when*. There is a rotten mass at the core of his administration. It would not be the first time he would be sacrificing people's lives to keep power."

And she was right. In January, just one week after school resumed from Christmas break, President Jonathan signed the SSMPA into law.

It was after the bill was signed that news of it made it into everyday conversations. And with it came a wave of kitoes in UNN. Each day, there was news of any other gay man set up and beaten. Segun was again seeing firsthand how much violence the weight of the state's power could bring to bear, how heavy the metaphoric boots his mother spoke of were, and how easily it crushed innocent, unsuspecting people. There were stories of people dragged out of their homes and beaten by vigilantes. Many girls in his circle got married as a result, particularly those who were masculine presenting, those already being rumored to be lesbians. Segun felt like the ground was sinking all around him. And each story he heard, the angrier he got. On the UNN Facebook group, he responded to each post celebrating the law with long replies, and then after a while, when he was sure they had read his missives, he blocked them. When other users replied by calling him gay or saying, "You SSF people have been pushing this gay thing since," he blocked them too. It wasn't much but it made him slightly better.

"Easy," August said one evening when he found Segun typing furiously in reply to yet another person on Facebook. "Take it easy. These idiots, they'll exhaust you if you let them."

But Segun's feelings of helplessness would not let him. To know he had been powerless, voiceless, against a law so sweeping . . . it was too much. Sometimes his anger turned to August, because he knew August did not worry. And why would he? Having his beautiful, private living space, being so admired by everyone, he had everything and didn't even know it.

One evening, when August touched him, it made him feel even more anxious. "I'm not really into it," he said, and shrugged August off. He felt like crying but there were no tears.

"Come on," August said, sliding his hand down Segun's shirt.

"August, I'm not in the mood for this rubbish right now."

He could tell how shocked August was.

Later, he apologized. "It's just that I don't know if there's hope."

He thought that if perhaps he could explain this emptiness he felt to August, this unbearable despair, the distance growing between them would collapse. But August said nothing. And with each passing day Segun grew more skeptical that he could deal with August's aloofness. He tried to convince himself that it meant nothing; it was just that August did not fully understand the implications of the bill and did not want to because it was a torturous reality. But the more he tried to convince himself, the more he felt betrayed by August's calm and unconcern, in the face of all this, by the way almost nothing changed for him. And then there was the way August still remained friends with Dike, despite the glee Dike expressed about the law.

"You're his friend on Facebook, right?" he asked August.

"Yes."

"And you see his Facebook post?"

"See that's just the kind of person Dike is. I try not to let it get to me."

"Do you even hear yourself?"

"What do you want me to do?"

"You're buddies with someone who would hate your guts if he knew you, what you were. He is not your friend, August. People like him are why we will never be safe in this country."

August sighed. "Segun, please, leave me alone. I don't want to do this now. I'm tired."

"You're tired?"

"Yes. Do you know how many people I'll have left in my life if I cut off every homophobe I know? My dad, my sisters, my teammates, everybody."

In that moment, Segun pitied August more than he ever had, more than he thought he could. So surrounded by people who only stayed because they did not know who he really was. He imagined how trapped August must have felt. He let it go, but on Facebook he went after Dike, and Dike matched his venom. The tension soon boiled over when they ran into each other outside SUB. They nearly came to blows because Dike also enjoyed his homophobia when he wasn't behind a screen. If August had not been there, a fight would have ensued. It was August who stood between them until Segun, coming to the realization that there would be no fight, stormed off. The fight followed them home. That afternoon August's cowardice became unacceptable, unforgivable. Segun realized, admitted to himself, that homophobia was not a deal breaker for August because *he* did not bear its brunt. His friends could heckle effeminate men, shout *fourteen years!*—the sentence the law proscribed for same-sex relationships—at them in the faculty building or at the TETFund Hall, but they didn't heckle *him*. They could write Facebook posts about how it was good that something was being done to bring back the world where African men were African men instead of copying whites, but August did not see himself in Dike's words.

"In case you forgot, you're also a faggot," Segun said. He felt as though August had chosen Dike over him. As though August would always choose his passing over him. He felt so betrayed, so alone. "You don't care," he said, his voice high and shaky. It embarrassed him how much his voice was laden with accusation and hurt. He stormed out.

Back in his room, he cried silently in his bed. He wished August would try to understand him, stand up for him, stand with him, not take someone else's side. It was times like this that he missed Trevor. Trevor would have understood. Segun knew that because August passed, he did not have to suffer this bill, not the way he, Segun, did. He could never be above the fray like August was; he could never decide not to think about it. People pushed him in the halls now, they raised one finger and then four fingers at him. Eni-Njoku was becoming more and more unbearable, and all Segun wanted was for August to understand and validate his anger. Their relationship was never the same again. It took him many weeks to forgive August for that afternoon.

CHAPTER NINETEEN

Because the thirteenth of January was the worst day of Segun's life, it became the second-worst day of August's life—after the day of his birth. Last December, when the bill sailed through the Senate with overwhelming support, it had sparked such an ugliness across the school, particularly in the Faculty of Arts. Despite the bill's name—The Same-Sex Marriage (Prohibition) Act—everyone simply called it the Anti-Gay Bill. Already August knew how strongly Segun felt about it. The SSF printed fliers and Segun carried them everywhere with him, pinned them on notice boards, handed them out to people who would take them.

Socialism or Barbarism; Homophobia or Revolutionary Consciousness, the fliers read.

August did not feel as urgently as Segun did, though he agreed that it was a horrible bill. And because of this, because August did not feel like it was a collapse of the sky, it tore them apart after President Jonathan signed it into law. For days, Segun walked about with so much anger simmering in him. On Facebook, he called longtime friends devils, and blocked them. August was a bit afraid of all this anger, afraid that it was only a matter of time until it got Segun in trouble, and by extension, only a matter of time until it got *him* in trouble. He wished he could wrest Segun from it, relieve him of it. In the evenings, he watched Segun shouting Yoruba angrily into his phone.

"Look, we've known each other for how many years? Ten? I'm not sure why I am even surprised. Stupid."

He sat down on the bed. When August touched his shoulders, Segun shrugged his hand off.

"You need to calm down," August said, kneeling behind Segun. He held Segun's shoulders and kissed him on the neck.

"I'm not really into it," Segun said, pulling away.

"Come on," August said and slid his hand down Segun's chest.

"August, I'm not in the mood for this rubbish right now," he said, standing abruptly.

August watched him, his hand still suspended in the air.

At night Segun lay in August's arms and sulked. "This is not a working class that can ever win their freedom. If this is all it takes to whip everyone in line," he said to August in the darkness, and August made a sound of assent, trying so hard to fight the sleep that was encroaching on him.

"Are you asleep?" he asked.

"No, no, I'm still here. I'm awake."

"You're not saying anything," Segun said, and August realized he was supposed to dissent, say something to reassure Segun. August did not know what to say. In truth, he still did not fully understand the law, did not understand why Segun was so afraid and angry. Homosexuality was already illegal. What was new? Segun said nothing else, he fell asleep there in August's arms.

In class, August listened to his classmates jest about it.

"Does this mean they'll come and take like all these gay people here, so we can all see road?"

"At least let them do fourteen years."

Just like that, it became something of a slogan: *Fourteen years!*

They threw it about and laughed. "They'll soon come and take you," they'd say, and laugh whenever someone in their class criticized the bill. August never said a word, and for this, he felt even more guilt. Segun sent him a PDF of the bill on WhatsApp, but August got bored after the first few lines and never remembered to finish it. The more he tried to understand Segun, the more he realized that he couldn't. August tried to pretend he could because he wanted Segun to feel like he understood and was there for him. And he was terrified that Segun would figure out he didn't, not really. Segun's rage was a blaze and August was afraid it would burn him. Already Segun was increasingly critical of August's friends. He marked them out and then identified them to August as though signaling to him that he could no longer continuing being friends with them.

"Do you know that Ikenna nigga in your class called me fag right in front of TETFund Hall? Honestly I don't know how you're friends with all these homophobes."

"Which Ikenna?" August asked. "Kenny?"

"Did I say Kenny?" Segun replied, annoyed.

"I'm just making sure nau."

"Well now you're sure."

"Why are you taking it out on me? What did I do?"

"I'm not taking anything out on you."

"No, because it's as if I'm the one that attacked you at TETFund."

"Well, these are literally the friends you keep. People who hate you."

"I and Ikenna are not even close. He's just a guy in my class."

Segun said nothing. He walked into the bathroom, then came out and sat down to read a book. Only a few minutes later, he was up again. August closed his laptop. "What?" he asked.

"I'm going," Segun said.

"I didn't even do anything. You just blame me for things I didn't even do."

"Did I say you did anything?" Segun asked.

"Okay, why do you want to go?"

"I'm tired. I want to sleep."

"What kind of bullshit answer is that? Don't you sleep here anytime you want?"

"August, please, I don't want argument."

After Segun left, August rubbed his forehead with his palm, his frustration gathering into a headache. He was so upset and he wasn't even sure who he was more angry at, Segun or Ikenna. He felt like Segun was being unreasonable, transferring aggression on him, assigning blame by association.

One afternoon Segun called Dike a fool outside SUB. August was not really shocked at it, just at the venom with which he spat the word. They had come to get food and ran into Dike. Normally August and Segun ordered their food in takeaway packs and ate in his room. But because they ran into Dike, they ate there at SUB.

"I've been seeing SSF posters condemning the Anti-Gay Bill," Dike said to Segun, smiling. "You people are trying o but sha know it's a waste of time." Dike's mouth was full of rice and as he spoke a few crumbs fell from the sides of his mouth.

"To you," Segun said.

"To everyone," Dike said.

"Honestly, the SSF is right. Jonathan is just using this to gain support and we all know it," August said, trying to diffuse the situation.

"Doesn't mean it's not a good thing. I've noticed many guys are now doing gay. It's disgusting," and August braced himself for Segun's response.

"Fool. You are a very big fool."

It took Dike aback. He had not expected such a direct confrontation, not from Segun and not in a place as public as SUB.

"See, August, warn your friend. I'm not going to just sit here and be insulted," Dike said. But Segun was already on his feet. He stood so abruptly the plastic seat almost fell over.

"What the fuck are you going to do?" Segun said, waving Dike away. "Get out."

"Segun, calm down," August said.

"Don't fucking tell me to calm down! I'm not the foolish one threatening to beat people up!"

Dike stood and bore down on Segun and Segun squared his shoulders. August wedged himself between the two of them.

"Guy, come on. Chill," he said to Dike.

"This guy think say he get mouth!" Dike shouted, pointing at Segun.

"Are you fucking kidding me?! You stood there and vomited rubbish and now I'm the one with mouth? Isn't your skull empty as you are like this?"

"Segun," August said, trying not to sound too reprimanding.

"Don't fucking Segun me. He stood there and rejoiced at innocent people being incarcerated and somehow he's the one angry? Really? He's the one feeling insulted?"

"Did I call your name? Oh, wait, so you're gay, that why it's paining you like this?"

"Yes, yes that's fucking why. Mumu."

August held Dike tightly. Segun stormed off. August and Dike watched him walk into the distance. Some people had stopped to see what the commotion was about. Dike shrugged August off, straightened his clothes, and left too.

Later that day August and Segun had their own fight in his lodge. It had begun with Segun's complaining again about August's friends but devolved from that so quickly that afterward August was left stunned, wondering what had happened.

"Would you also say this one is not really your friend?" Segun asked.

"Don't even try to make this my fault. You keep doing this," August said. "You have to know when to just ignore."

"I'm not blaming you. But I just . . . to know that someone who has been your friend for as long as I've known you, could just sit there and praise this disgusting inept administration because at least they're doing their bit to keep the gays oppressed, I just lost it. How are you even friends with someone like that?"

August shrugged. "It's not really that hard," he said. "You just need to tone it down."

"Excuse me?"

"I don't mean it like that," August said. "It's just you let this bill thing get to you so much. Since last month you've been so angry. I don't even recognize you."

"Oh . . . Well, I'm sorry I am angry at a bill that would throw me in jail for basically existing," Segun said. "My bad. I mean what was I thinking getting angry at a law that infringes on literally every single one of my civil rights? And yours too, for that matter. In case you forgot you're also a faggot."

"Segun, you know that's not what I meant," August said again, his voice rising.

"No, I don't, August. I really don't. You don't care. You seem to forget that you're gay too. This," Segun said, pointing back and forth between the two of them, "this thing we have is illegal, prohibited. We are criminals, August. And you somehow think surrounding yourself with homophobic friends protects you. It fucking doesn't."

"This is what I was talking about," August said, throwing his hands up.

"Yes, I'm fucking angry. I should be. *You* should be."

"Lower your voice, please. This is not a marketplace."

Segun's eyes widened and he pulled his head back in astonishment. "Wow," he said. "Okay."

When he stormed out, Segun slammed the door so hard, it rattled the windows. August sat on his bed and opened his laptop. He tried to watch a movie but his restlessness wouldn't let him. He closed the laptop and dialed Segun's number. It rang for the first time without an answer, and when he called a second time, the number was unavailable.

"Fucking idiot," August said under his breath, thinking of the myriad ways he could have picked his words better. It was he who suggested they all eat their food there at SUB. He had not wanted Dike to wonder why he and Segun were ordering food and taking it back to his room. But now, the more he thought about it, the more he realized what an irrational suggestion that had been, especially after all the effort he put into keeping Dike and Segun apart. Now, finally, August had given Segun something legitimate to be angry at him for.

Segun knew how to nurse a grudge. For days they did not talk.

"I'm sorry," August said when he ran into Segun at the faculty building. "I shouldn't have said that. I was not thinking."

"I've heard you," Segun said coldly. For weeks, he would hold on to that grudge. When they ran into each other in the faculty again, Segun spoke with August, but his tone was so cordial that August knew all was still not well. Because Segun rarely came over, August began to attend night class. There, they sat next to each other and read their textbooks without talking to each other.

August let some time pass before apologizing again, this time outside Segun's class. Segun's friend, Julia, stood a few feet away staring at them.

"Are you still angry at me?" August asked. "You know I didn't mean it like that. I mean to say one thing and my mouth will be doing another thing."

"It's fine," Segun said dryly.

"Let's get lunch together," August said. "Please. I miss us having lunch together."

They walked to SUB and ordered rice and drinks in takeaway packs. Back at August's lodge, they sat and ate, an awkward silence floating between them.

"Did you hear that the exam timetable would soon be out?" August asked, trying to peel away the silence.

"No," Segun said, without looking up from his food.

"Do you think it's true?"

"Maybe. I don't know," Segun said and glanced at him.

Soon Segun started to visit him at his lodge again. They never talked of the bill again. In fact, they made sure to avoid it. They bemoaned Goodluck Jonathan's administration and sighed as each new corruption scandal unfolded, but they always stopped short of mentioning it.

August's sisters were worried when they heard he'd been chosen for the NUGA games and even more so when they found out the games were at the Obafemi Awolowo University. Nsukka was the farthest he had ever been from them. "Just remember what you're there to do," they said.

But it was *this* that August loved to do. It was the track that energized him. Early each morning, he would sprint around the track, then jog slowly. Most mornings, it was just him and Betty. They would run until their bones ached and then they would sit on the concrete bleachers and talk while they rested. Their relationship had slowly phased into a friendship. After he met Segun, he called Betty less and less, and she called him less. When they ran into each other on the track, they hugged and talked, but the warm intimacy they once shared slowly cooled. August still sometimes thought what if? What if he didn't let what was growing between them fade? What if he asked Betty out again? What if he had not met Segun, what if he had not fallen in love?

And now, as his relationship with Segun rocked and tumbled, and he buried himself in training, he thought about it more and more. August knew that Betty liked him. He could see it in the way she looked at him. A laugh there, a touch of the arm, a smile. The way it felt like the most normal thing when they walked home together after track practice. But she was not the type to go anywhere if she did not fully feel that she was wanted. And now, as he found what he had with Segun strained, he was pulled more and more into the ease of Betty's company.

It was he who kissed her. August never understood why he did it. They were sitting on the bleachers catching their breath, and staring at the small beads of sweat rolling down her face, August felt a tightness in his chest.

"What?" she asked him, smiling, but August did not respond. As he leaned slowly toward her, the smile on her face eased into seriousness. For a brief moment, their lips just stayed locked like that, with August tasting the saltiness of her sweat. Then Betty kissed back. It was a short kiss that made August feel a familiar comfort, and after it ended they awkwardly packed their towels into their bags and stood to go.

"August, we can't," she told him after several moments of walking in silence. "I have to focus. I have so much on my plate right now. I don't want any distractions."

"I understand," August said.

"Yeah. I think us being friends is the best thing for us right now," she said, raising her hand to pluck a leaf from a low-hanging branch.

August would never know how Segun found out. He first tried to deny it.

"Where did you hear something like that?" he asked, trying to act as shocked as he could. This only made Segun angrier.

"Please just answer the simple question," he said.

"I don't know exactly what I'm answering. What nonsense have you been listening to?"

Segun laughed. A mirthless laugh that lasted far too long. Segun raised his hand to his head and grabbed fistfuls of hair. He was still laughing. He wiped away a stray tear as the laughter faded.

"You must think I'm stupid," he said. "Oh, stupid stupid Segun."

"Baby, what are you talking about?"

"Don't fucking *baby* me, August. Don't you fucking dare."

August stared silently, afraid. Afraid that he had done something that Segun would not forgive.

"Who was it?" Segun asked.

August shook his head. Even then he felt the urge to stick to his lie.

"Who the fuck was it?"

"Okay, I'm going to be honest. You were right, but baby, it was nothing, I swear. It was a kiss. It was a mistake, and it would never happen again."

"I just . . . I need you to say her name."

"It was with Betty."

Segun's face steeled. He sniffed and put his hand in his hair again. He sat down on the bed. For a moment, August thought Segun would burst into tears.

"I asked you," Segun said. His voice was calm. "I asked you specifically and you told me there was nothing between the both of you."

"I'm sorry."

Segun laughed again. "What the fuck? You're sorry? What am I supposed to do with your sorry?"

"It was really just a kiss."

"Who kissed who?" Segun asked, looking up at him.

"What?" August asked. He heard Segun but the words took long to form meaning.

"Did you kiss her or did she kiss you?"

"I—"

"Please don't lie to me."

"It was a mistake," August said instead.

"I told you I couldn't do this," Segun said, and the first tears rolled down his cheeks. He wiped them away. "I told you I couldn't deal with this . . . This . . . whatever it is with you. I've suffered enough. I've waged my own war with myself and my shame. I cannot deal with yours. I won't."

Segun bowed his head and wept into his palms. There was silence in the room, save for the sound of Segun's tears. August had the uncanny feeling that someone was listening to them through the walls.

"I thought we were good," Segun said. "Not perfect, but not this bad. Why would you do such a thing to me? Are you so ashamed of yourself, of me?"

"Baby, it wasn't shame."

"Then what was it?"

"Betty and I have history."

"What the fuck is that even supposed to mean?"

"I . . . We were together for a bit during my first year. Before I met you. I swear it wasn't shame. I felt something for her."

"Is that supposed to make me feel better?"

"I love you," August said. "I love you more than anything."

August had never known guilt the way he did that afternoon.

"Why, August, why would you do this?" Segun was saying through his tears.

"It was a mistake," August said again. He realized how often he had said this and how silly he sounded repeating it over and over again, but he didn't know what else to say.

"I don't know what to believe anymore," Segun said. "I just don't. You're so stuck in your bubble, in passing, and you choose that over me every day, over yourself. I've been thinking to myself, perhaps I'm just crazy. Perhaps there's nothing really happening and I'm losing my fucking mind."

Segun paused, and then his tears overcame him again, contorting his face. His shoulders were shaking. August's legs were beginning to ache but it felt out of place for him to sit.

"That's how you make me feel. And I was wondering why you didn't understand."

"I do. I do understand."

"But you don't. You really don't. I can't do this, August. I don't know if you are bi or confused or conflicted. That's for you to figure out, and not at my expense. I'm a human being, not a vessel you can use to explore your sexuality."

He stood up and began to throw some of his books into his bag.

"Segun, Segun . . ." August reached out to touch him and Segun recoiled.

"Please, August. Don't. Just don't."

August watched him leave. And after Segun was gone, he stood leaning against his doorframe staring down the hallway, where Segun had disappeared. That night he dreamt of his mother, but remembered nothing of the dream the following day, only that his mother was in it. He couldn't understand what happened, or perhaps he did, but did not want to accept it. He followed his usual routine, and when he went out with Dike and Kenny, he drank until he could taste the beer rising up his throat each time he burped.

At the faculty building, he searched for Segun with his eyes. Whenever August saw Segun, he planted himself in Segun's path.

"Hey, it's been awhile."

"Yes, it has. How are you doing?"

It irked him, the way Segun treated him like they were simply two people who knew each other. He wanted Segun to shout, to hate him. He wanted something more than this indifference, as though there had never been anything between them.

"Please," August begged. "Please, let's not throw away all that we had."

Segun shook his head, sadly. "I'm not throwing anything away."

When August spoke with his sisters, he swore over and over again, to get some sort of reaction from them. He wanted them to be angry at him. His life was no longer his. Perhaps it never was, and with Segun gone he was plunged into a perpetual restlessness. He went on Grindr and scrolled through countless profiles.

"I can host," he said to one of them, Samson. "Come over."

Samson talked endlessly about August's fridge. He had a prominent forehead that made his eyes look like they were placed too low on his head. But he had large buttocks and a big penis. They had exchanged nude pictures and August couldn't wait for the small talk to be over so he could undress him. They had sex, half clothed, their bodies rushing to find ways to merge and after that, Samson dressed and left. August did not even remember his name or what he looked like. He did not want to remember anything. He felt so raw, like his entire body was an open wound, like his life had been stolen from him, just as he was figuring out what it was about.

"I miss you," he texted Segun. He imagined Segun missed him too. He had to. This wonderful time they had shared surely did not exist just only in his imagination. August went to meetings of the Socialist Students' Forum and talked every chance he got, asked Segun as many questions as he was allowed.

"Comrade August, we have to give other comrades the opportunity to speak too. We all have insights to share," Segun said to him one Thursday and looked around the class, smiling. They were discussing Nkrumah's 1963 speech in Addis Ababa. August had studied that speech, given at the creation of the Organization of African Unity.

"*Unite or Perish*," Segun stressed. "What links do we draw from Osagyefo's words to the present dilemma of neocolonialism in African countries? Someone that has not spoken though. I want all of us to say something."

After the discussions, Segun would hurry off to something, with only abrupt good-byes to say to August. In night class, August made sure to sit somewhere he could watch Segun read, and sleep, then read again. He scrolled through their WhatsApp chats with longing, aching to have Segun back, and when he got to the SSMPA PDF, he downloaded it. He read every word of the bill and then went back to find and read other books Segun had sent him, desperate for something, any remnant of their relationship that he could hold on to.

The night he read the bill, he felt something of an epiphany. He closed his laptop and picked up his phone. He dialed Segun's number and pressed the phone to his ear. His stomach turned each time it buzzed. He wanted to tell Segun that he'd read it, to tell him that he understood now why he should have read it a long time ago. But it was 10:15 p.m. and Segun never picked up his phone. The phone rang and rang and rang, but Segun did not pick.

CHAPTER TWENTY

August was surprised when Dike called to talk to him about Segun. In fact, when Dike said, "It's Segun o," August pressed the phone closer to his ear, almost certain he had misheard. His first suspicion was that there had been another altercation between Dike and Segun.

"What about him?" August asked.

"Guy, I was right about him," Dike said.

August's heart sank and his stomach twisted painfully. A million different meanings those words could have, flashed through his mind. He would later realize that he had been consumed by fear. The fear that Dike had found out about him and Segun.

"What na?" August asked.

"The guy na homo," Dike said.

"What?"

"I know. The things no shock me sha. Guys dey Eni Njoku dey beat am."

It took August time to actually understand the words he'd heard. There was a loud ringing in his ears that grew until the sound was deafening and he could hear nothing at all.

"I don't get," he said, numbly.

"Wetin you no get? Guys dey beat am."

"Dike, be serious."

August dropped his phone and began to pull on his shirt. There was still a faint sound coming from the phone. After putting on his shorts, he picked the phone back up again.

"Are they still there?" he asked.

"I no know o."

"You just left?"

"Ha! Wetin I for do? Make I separate fight? Me I just mind my business o."

August cut the call. Outside the night was dark and silent. August realized there was no way he'd be able to get a vehicle to drive him to Njoku. He started down the road, the urgency rising in him like he was underwater holding his breath and every extra second was more suffocating. He ran, then slowed to a jog, then a fast-paced stroll, and then he broke into a sprint again. As he ran, the Angel of Death returned. A whisper, a nudge, at the back of his mind, asking him if his running was necessary. What did he think he could do? How was he so sure he would get there and not find a corpse? How was he sure he would ever see Segun alive again? August tried to remember when they last saw each other. There was a pain in his abdomen as his body wore out.

At Njoku, he stopped to catch his breath and then he made his way in. His shirt was stuck to his body. He realized he did not know Segun's room number. The students were milling about, chatting excitedly, and there was this rowdy excitement that seemed very uncharacteristic of what a hostel should be like at night. Still, he held on to that tiny shred of faith that there had been a mistake. That it wasn't Segun. That Segun was fine somewhere, unaware of all this, and would shake his head in annoyance when August told him what happened. Dike had played a prank on him and it was all a lie. He would have many epiphanies about these desperate moments in the days that followed. He would see the parallels between that night and the night he was born. The fervency with which he held on to hope, even after it was clear that there was no avoiding reality, the way he continued to reject the knowledge itself, until the very last minute.

He called Segun's number and each time it rang without answer, his fear deepened, grew sharper. In the distance, he heard someone say, "They for kill am." It sounded so very far away, like something carried here by the wind. Those moments were the worst of August's life. He called Dike instead.

"I'm at Njoku. Where is the thing happening?"

"I'm back in my room o."

"You mean you just left him there?"

"Hian! What's my own? You want me to do what? I just minded my business biko."

"I can't find anyone anywhere. And he's not picking up his phone."

"Check his room."

"I don't know his room," August said, flustered. There was pain somewhere at the back of his throat. His body felt terribly heavy as he marched frantically through the hallways of Njoku. He knew Segun might be dead but such a thing was unfathomable. He had worried about Segun many times, but he had never been confronted so forcefully by Segun's mortality or his own.

"Check room two sixty-four," Dike said. "I think that's his room, I'm not sure."

August half ran, half walked, his eyes scanning the doors until he was at 264. He knocked before bending over to gasp for air. There was no response. He knocked again, then again, then yet again. And as the silence greeted him, an ugly sense of loss and grief settled in his chest. He called Segun's phone again, and as before, it rang without answer.

He leaned against the door, watching students mill past. They were all talking about someone that was beaten, and if the guy was okay, and what exactly they caught the guy doing, and it felt so surreal to hear them talk about Segun like that. August blamed himself. For what reason, he had yet to articulate, but his shoulders sagged with guilt. He heard someone say that Segun was at the porter's office and he quickly ran there. He still hoped it was a joke, that it was untrue. Because what would he do if it wasn't? The porter's office was lit by a bulb and even before he arrived, he could see Segun's form slouched on the chair. It stopped him in his tracks. He approached the office, slower now. Segun was a sunken, bloodied mass, and there was a huge bulge over his left eye. He did not look like himself and this terrified August more than the bloody mess of him.

"Do you know this boy?" the man asked.

August nodded slowly, almost uncertain that this was indeed Segun. He looked so mangled, so deformed. There was something almost foreign about his body now. August was surprised by how calmly he spoke to the man, as though there was nothing strange about Segun's broken body heaped on the bench.

"They went to get a cab. Take him to Shonahan so he doesn't die here."

"Okay," August said, nodding.

"You know, una school clinic dey opposite side of school. I no know why e far like that. Dem for put another one close."

Again, August nodded.

"Four hostels. Alvan here and Eni-Njoku. Plus Nkrumah and PG Hall." There the man's voice rose as he raised four fingers in front of his face. "Four hostels, not even one school clinic close. This boy here, his life, na god hand im dey. Pray for am, na your friend. They go tell una to live upright, una no go hear. Today him cup don full."

August sat next to the heap on the chair. He could make out the labored rise and fall of Segun's chest now.

"Segun," he said, almost to himself. "Segun," he called again, this time more loudly. He realized he wasn't even sure Segun could hear him. August wanted to be frantic but the panic he felt was utterly paralyzing. There seemed no other option but to sit and watch Segun, to do an accounting of all the ways his body had been broken. This changed when the shuttle arrived and August sprang into action. He and the man hurriedly carried Segun into the back. August sat next to Segun, holding him. August's hands and shirt were bloodied, too, now. Only then did he begin to cry. His own tears surprised him. They welled in his eyes as he watched Segun's head nestled on his lap, then they poured slowly down, as he watched his own bloodied hands. The threat of Segun's death hung so strongly in the breeze that wafted past as the shuttle maneuvered in the night, bumping this way and that. And the benevolent Angel of Death whispered in his ears. *Steel yourself, August. Steel your heart.* August's nose was running now. He noticed the driver staring at him in the rearview mirror. The man said nothing, and for that, August was grateful. The blood was clammy on his fingers, and cold too. The air, too, was cold. He could tell Segun was still breathing but he wasn't sure for how long. How far away was this hospital? The Angel of Death spoke again, this time so loudly and firmly, it was all August could hear.

He thought back to the night of his birth, covered in his mother's blood. August knew, he had been told, that he was separated from his mother immediately after he was born but he could almost see it, like a vague memory. His mother on the bed, bleeding, her face covered in sweat and tears, the doctors and nurses running around as life drained slowly out of her. The helplessness. The resistance with which he faced the looming eventuality that was Segun's mortality, their mortality. He imagined she asked for that, to hold him, even if just this once, even if only briefly. He imagined that she held him in her arms as she died, and that this, this utter sense of helplessness and loss that he felt now, was what he felt, crying in her dying arms.

All around August, the voices of strange people echoed. The lights of Shonahan blinded him. There were harsh, long fluorescent bulbs beaming from above. A nurse edged her way through the lobby saying, "Come. Come. Come," as though August and Segun and the driver weren't moving fast enough. They laid Segun onto a bed in a less brightly lit room. For a moment, August couldn't fathom why the driver was still there, looking at him. Then he remembered he hadn't paid the man.

The nurse seemed relaxed, too relaxed, as she cut Segun's bloodstained clothes away. August willed her to move faster. To make him whole again.

"What happened?" she asked.

"Fight," August said.

"Ah! What kind of fight could result in this kind of beating? What did he do? Did he steal?"

Because it did not occur to August that she expected him to answer that question, he simply moved back, until his back was resting against the wall. The nurse was pressing Segun's abdomen now. She stopped and looked at him.

"Did he steal?" she asked again, this time more forcefully. August shook his head.

"What did he do?" she asked. "Ah, the person was really angry."

August again did not reply. He had disconnected from his own body and was looking down now at his own bloodied clothes. The nurse turned to look at him again.

"I don't know," August said.

The doctor appeared out of nowhere. August did not remember when he entered the room, only that his presence slowly breached the borders of his consciousness. The doctor was an old, frail man, with leathery skin the colour of almonds. August thought how fair he must have been in his youth. The doctor danced about the room, occasionally pressing his stethoscope to Segun's bare chest. Then he paused, and turned, as though beset by a sudden realization.

"Young man, you're not supposed to be here. Wait at reception."

August shut his eyes so tightly his eyeballs began to ache. He leaned away from the wall.

"We will do what we can for your friend," the doctor said.

August wasn't sure if those words reassured him or intensified the fear spreading through his body. Walking to the reception, he could hear his mother's voice. He wasn't sure what she was saying but she was there with him. If he concentrated, it felt like she would materialize right in front of him. August tried to remember if there had been signs. If there was something that should have warned him of this. He should have foreseen this but he didn't, and now, he had to live with that.

Sitting there, a wave of self-loathing overcame him. He knew he would never be able to forgive himself if anything happened to Segun. There on that seat, in that hospital, he understood for the very first time the danger of his own existence, the fragility of his freedom—he understood it wholly and truly. He was afraid, not of the consequences of disappointing his sisters or not living up to his mother's sacrifice, but of the consequences of being himself. Gay. Even the danger of being here with Segun was not lost on him. Walking through the quadrangles of Njoku, it had not occurred to him how dangerous even that was. He had not had time to think of things like that. He needed to get to Segun, that was all that mattered in those moments.

He imagined how his sisters would have received the news of him lying in a hospital, unsure of his own life, unable to help himself. He thought of Segun's family, his parents in Lagos. It was there in that hospital that August Akasike decided he was going to tell his sisters he was gay. It was there, that he articulated it to himself, for the first time. *August, you are a homosexual.* It was, he understood, the least he could do and the most at the same time.

When the nurse reemerged in the lobby, she showed him how to register Segun's admission. And then she began to list the things they had already used on Segun. The prices overwhelmed him. He heard them but they didn't stick. They were like water, those words, poured on a rock only for it to roll off, onto the ground. He heard her, but her words meant nothing to him. At the desk, he told them he didn't have enough money on him.

"Call his people," the man at the desk said. But August didn't have any of Segun's parents' numbers and Segun's phone wasn't on him when August had found him.

"I can't. They stay in Lagos."

"Well, you have to find the money somehow, and immediately. His condition is very serious. He's lost a lot of blood. We need to transfuse. We have been treating him, but as you know, we need money to run this place."

August went outside. The darkness welcomed him. He called Uzoamaka because that's who he always called when he was most in need. She was alarmed, as August knew she would be.

"Where are you? What happened?"

"Sis, I'm fine. It's my friend. It's Segun."

"Ah, August, I'm not comfortable giving you that amount of money. Why not call his parents?"

"They don't stay in Enugu."

"August . . . that's a lot of money."

"He's going to die," August said, and with that, his voice broke. The tears were warm on his cheeks. "Please. I'll pay you back, I promise."

Uzoamaka was silent on the other end of the line.

"I'm begging you, please," August said.

Uzoamaka sighed. August heard Chime's voice in the background, then his sister said, "It's August." She returned her attention to the call. "August, are you sure you're not in trouble?"

"I'm fine. I'm not in trouble," he said, sniffing back his tears. "But Segun is."

"Okay . . . I'll see what I can do," she said.

The transfer came from Chime's account. And almost immediately, Peculiar called him. He let it ring. Then he sent her a text.

The man at the desk was brisker when August returned, swiping August's debit card through the POS effortlessly and ushering him into the doctor's office. The doctor listed the tests they'd carried out and other ones they needed.

"What did you say happened to him?"

"He was beaten in the hostel."

"What would someone do to deserve that kind of beating. They broke his ribs."

August shook his head. "I don't know what happened," he said.

"He lost a lot of blood. That's the most pressing issue. He needs a transfusion."

"I'm O positive," August said.

"His blood is undergoing lab tests. It'll be back soon. Hopefully, his rhesus is positive too, but even if not, we've notified our contact. Don't worry. He'll be fine."

It sounded like a consolation, the way the doctor said it. The nurse came back to take samples of August's blood. The hospital was near empty now and reeked with the sharp stench of disinfectants. The voice of death never left August, even as he was led into an inner room and his shirtsleeve was rolled up. A frighteningly large needle was guided gently into his vein, and he watched his blood flow slowly down into the blood bag.

"It's like you both are very close," the nurse said. She was simply trying to make idle conversation, August knew that, but he wanted her to shut up.

"Yes," he said.

"You're a good friend. Some friends won't even do all this you're doing," she said.

August nodded. The nurse brought him a can of malt and some biscuits. August sat there, forcing it down his throat.

When he stood to leave she told him, "Nothing will happen to your friend." And it brought fresh tears to his eyes.

CHAPTER TWENTY-ONE

When Segun eventually opened his eyes, August was glad to be there. He wanted to be the first person Segun saw. Each afternoon, he rushed to Shonahan from school. The nurses would look at him with abject pity and he would know, even before asking that Segun was still unconscious.

No matter how many times the doctor repeated "He just needs rest," August still feared for him. Each afternoon, he brought food and ate it silently, sitting next to Segun's bed. Some days he cried silently as he ate. Dike reprimanded him for this waste of time. "You're not his mother," Dike said. But Segun's mother still wasn't here. He had to venture all the way back to Njoku, to Segun's room, to find his phone. August was taken aback by the repulsion he felt when the door to Segun's room swung open. It was these same people that did this to Segun, August thought. They didn't seem to like August very much either and did not offer him any help finding the phone. It was the porter who eventually gave him Segun's mother's number. Segun's mother screamed into the phone when August told her what happened. It was such a loud scream. August imagined her holding the phone to her lips as she tested the capacity of her lungs. She was shouting in a language August did not understand. August let her lament before saying, "Sorry, I don't understand."

"They want to kill that boy! They've been trying, his whole life! They've been trying! They don't want to leave him alone! Hei God."

She was in Nsukka the next day. August took her to Shona-han. She fell on her knees next to Segun and August couldn't tell if she was praying or crying. She stayed for a few days and then went back to Lagos to prepare for a much longer stay.

The afternoon Segun awoke for the first time, August was settled into the chair next to the bed, eating rice, when the movement in Segun's fingers caught his eye. When he looked up the length of Segun's body, Segun's eyes were open. The swelling in his left eye had all but disappeared. For seconds, August just stared, unsure what to do.

"Segun?" he said, and it was when Segun started choking that August rose from his seat and rushed to the lobby to scream for the nurse. All at once, the room was full and some-one gently nudged August out. He stood outside the room, listening as attentively as he could, resisting the urge not to open the door and barge into the room. When he was eventu-ally allowed to see Segun, August struggled to breathe evenly.

"Hi. How are you?" he whispered, softly tiptoeing to Segun's bed to sit next to him. Segun smiled but said nothing else. "You're going to be okay," August said, tears forming in his eyes.

That night, when August got home, he wept with relief, a relief so overpowering it flooded his veins and warmed his fingertips. But it brought fear with it too, in anticipation of the police questioning Segun, now that he was awake. He knew how easily Segun's rage got the better of him. He knew how defiant his pride was, and he knew especially now, how dangerous that was.

He tried to tuck his fears away, to enjoy the relief. That night, when he saw his mother in his dreams, August did not, as usual, break into tiny pieces of need and validation. He simply stared into her disappointed eyes and made peace with the knowledge that there was no overcoming her shadow. He would always be the son unworthy of his mother's foolish sacrifice. And he could learn to live with that.

The day the police questioned Segun, August left class even earlier than usual, before his professor for International Systems had completed his lecture. He rarely attended track practice anymore.

"You're losing form, August. You are. This Segun guy, I don't understand again," Dike said. "Imagine me, I put in more practice than you."

But August could not have abandoned Segun, not now when Segun needed him the most. Running seemed like such a minor, almost insignificant part of his life, compared to caring for Segun. The police questioning was supposed to be a simple conversation. Routine. Protocol. They just want to ask some very simple questions. But August wanted to be there. Segun's mother had returned to Lagos and she wouldn't be back until the following week. She called the day before to apologize and tried to send August money.

"I know we can never repay you but let us just give you the small we have. Please," she said. But August refused to let her do that.

When he got to the hospital, the first thing he noticed was the big police Jeep parked outside. He quickened his pace until he was at the door of Segun's room. He stood there and listened, almost afraid to interrupt with his presence. They were still introducing themselves. He stepped tentatively into the room, greeting the officers one by one as he made his way to the edge of Segun's bed.

"And who is this?" one of the men asked. He was looking at August with an expressionless face.

"Friend," August replied.

There was a pause, the slightest of pauses but a pause nonetheless. The policeman stared at August blankly. August looked away. He wasn't listening to their questions, not really. He was listening to Segun's labored replies. And when August did listen, when he heard their questions, he was incensed by their tone.

"How many were they, the people that attacked you?"

"I don't know."

"What do you mean you *don't know*? You don't know how to count?"

"There were so many. I was on the floor covering my face."

"Okay. Can you estimate?"

"I told you, I was covering my face."

August also found it unsettling that they weren't writing anything down. One of the men had a writing pad he held in his hands, unused.

"Like five? Ten?"

"More than."

"More than ten?" the officer asked in shock, and when Segun nodded, the other police officer with the pad wrote something down.

"What did you do to them?"

August's heart froze. Time slowed to a standstill and in the brief moment before Segun replied, August realized what a bad idea it was, his being here. But he couldn't imagine not being here for this. He wanted to hold Segun's hand but he restrained himself.

"Nothing," Segun said.

"Let me remind you, lying to the police is a criminal offense."

"I did nothing to them," Segun said again, his voice suddenly stronger, more defiant.

"So why did they attack you?"

"I don't know."

"Okay, let me put it like this. What were you people quarreling about when they started fighting you?"

"I don't . . . I don't remember."

"You don't remember? Are you sure?"

Segun nodded.

"Okay o. You said your roommates started the altercation? You know their names abi you also don't remember that one?"

Segun listed them one after the other and the officer with the notepad finally scribbled the names down. As Segun spoke, August felt an overwhelming need to exact revenge on them, to crush their bodies until they crumbled into the dust of their bones, to render them unrecognizable, to mark them with scars they would always remember.

★　★　★

August was reading Segun a book. He understood very little of what he was reading but he tried to shape each sentence in a way that made sense. There were many books stacked near the wall, and each day when he visited Segun, he read him one. The day before, the last day of Segun's mother's stay in Enugu, he read Segun *An Introduction to Syntax*. The semester exams were looming over them, and August did not want Segun's grades to suffer too much. He collected the materials from Julia after she and a few of Segun's classmates came to the hospital to visit. They brought Get Well Soon cards. They were all a little bit angry on Segun's behalf and a little bit vengeful, and quite poetic about it. They helped August make photocopies of lecture notes. August was touched by how many people cared about Segun. Some days before, members of the SSF had visited, crowding Segun's room, their voices and laughter so loud a nurse came to tell them to keep it down. After they left, Segun's face seemed brighter, as though all their "comrade, please get well soon" had made him better. And after his friends from class visited, he looked the same.

Now August was reading him a lecture on Akachi Ezimora's *A Companion to the Novel*. Outside, the sun was retreating and the clouds were becoming flush pink balls. August stopped reading.

"They're going to come next week for your official statement," he said. Segun looked away. He was always quiet these days.

"And?" Segun asked. "I'm not going to tell them we fuck if that's what you're so afraid of."

"Segun . . ."

"What? They're coming next week. What do you want me to tell them?"

"You know this is the only way to get those bastards punished. I'm not saying you should say anything, or not say anything, but it'll be so much easier. If we say you're gay, they'll let those demons go free and face us."

Segun said nothing. Each time August brought up anything about it, Segun became very distant, his face turned solemn, like someone in mourning.

"Barrister Iheme was telling me . . ." August continued.

"I've heard you," Segun interjected.

August looked at the door, before taking Segun's hand in his; it was cold. Before his roommates were released on bail, Segun was always running a fever. August would hold his hand to take some of that heat. Now Segun's hand was just cold, and so was everything else about him. It was as if on that terrible night, as the blood seeped from the cuts in his skin, something else seeped out with it too, leaving nothing but a distant, tired, hollowed-out body. Some mornings, August would come to see Segun before class and his eyes would be swollen and the area around it crimson. There was no appropriate way of asking him about it. August imagined those sorrowful moments were deeply private ones, certainly not ones to be prodded at, or asked about. And so he pretended as though he did not notice.

"Soon," August said, "soon, you'll be out of here and we'll put this behind us."

But Segun did not seem at all like someone who believed those things. August knew looking at him that this hospital, and the night that led to it, would always hang over them. On his WhatsApp status, August wrote about it, how demoralizing it was and how scared he had been. And then he deleted it. He felt guilty about the way it sounded like he was claiming Segun's pain. Peculiar immediately messaged him.

"I saw your status," she said.

"Yeah?"

"Why did you take it down?"

"I just felt like it was inappropriate. Selfish, kind of. To make it about me."

"You really like this friend of yours," she said.

August decided then that there was no better time to tell her.

"We're not just friends. He is so special to me. What we have is way more special than a friendship."

For a long time, she did not reply, and August wondered if he had made the wrong decision, telling her. Then she called him.

"I don't understand," she said. "What do you mean?"

August was silent. He knew she did understand.

"Are you gay?"

August was again silent, and for a while they just listened to each other breathing through the phone.

"Yes," he finally said.

"August," she began, "are you being serious? You never told me. Does anyone else know?"

August shook his head. Then, realizing she couldn't see him, said, "No. No one else."

It was the first time he said it out loud to another living soul. And it felt good, it felt liberating. He felt as though he had declared himself to the world.

If Peculiar sounded defeated at the news of August's homo-sexuality, Chinyere sounded elated. It was almost as if, for the first time, he was telling her something that really interested her.

"I actually suspected, you know, the way you and Obiajulu were always like, you know . . . you were very close."

"We were just friends, I and Obiajulu," August said.

"Why didn't you tell me? I would not have judged you."

It brought tears to August's eyes. August had called her right after ending the call with Peculiar. He understood that where he was concerned, his sisters had no secrets among themselves. He hadn't been sure how they would react. Some years ago, he heard them discuss Abere, the Yoruba celebrity who wore his hair in curls and walked everywhere in high heels.

"I heard he's his father's only son," Uzoamaka said. Her voice was filled with pity for Abere's father. And as he did tell her, he knew it would devastate her.

"What did you say?" she asked, like she was giving him a chance to take it back, to recant those words. Perhaps if he did so, right there and then, she would have gone on pretending that he'd never said them.

"I'm gay," August said once more.

She cut the call. August dropped the phone on the bed and lay on his back. He felt the onset of a headache. No matter what happened next, his life had changed in ways he could never undo.

When Uzoamaka called back, August knew from her voice that she had been crying.

"You are an only son," she said. "You know this. It's only you."

"I'm sorry," August said. He didn't know what else to say.

"August, please. This thing, we can do something about it. I've heard of miracles. There's nothing God cannot do."

But August did no longer want God's redemption. He felt redeemed, and sure in his newfound redemption.

"You know this path isn't one that can lead you anywhere," Uzoamaka said. August did not reply. It was not a path, it was simply who he was. But he did not want to argue with her.

After that, they spoke even less often. August wondered if his sisters already told his father. He wondered, too, if the news had managed to bring the man to even more sorrow, knowing he lost his wife for nothing.

After Segun's official statement, his roommates were arrested again. The news spread like wildfire. August was surprised when, in his own department's WhatsApp group chat, it popped up. It started with a reposted article. There were so many things in the article that just weren't true. He began to write a response, began to explain why it wasn't an "altercation between a gay guy and his roommates," but his words were inadequate. The police came to question Segun many times and August was with him every time, standing next to him, the warmth of their bodies holding each other up. Barrister Iheme filed a lot of charges, so many that August had to write each one down so as not to forget. Weeks after the charges were filed, Barrister Iheme came to visit Segun at the hospital and told them the defense lawyer had offered money for the charges to be dropped. August rejected the offer immediately, in his mind. But it was not his place to speak that rejection aloud, and so he waited for Segun to do it instead. It threw him off when Segun asked, "How much?"

"We haven't settled anything yet, but upward of five hundred, five hundred and fifty."

"Thousand?"

"Yes. Yes. Five hundred or five hundred and fifty thousand. Or more. It could be higher than that."

"You're not considering taking the money, are you?" August asked Segun back at the lodge. "They have to pay for what they did to you."

"August, I'm tired."

August wasn't sure if Segun meant he was tired at that moment or if he meant that he simply did not have the strength to take the case through court.

August dreamt of Segun's roommates, their happy, smiling faces, free, unpunished. And for weeks he held that against Segun. After they paid Segun six hundred and fifty thousand, and he said he wanted to move into his own room, even if in the same lodge, August did not protest. Some nights they slept in Segun's room, ate there, and studied there. A week before their exams, August saw a magazine in the faculty with Segun's face on it. *The Gist* was written in a small script below it. That day, August went to SUB and bought chicken suya and fried rice, and when he arrived, they ate in silence. August wasn't sure if Segun had seen the magazine.

He didn't want to bring it up, if Segun hadn't seen it. And so he said nothing.

"Did anything happen?" Segun asked.

"Huh?" August asked, realizing he had been staring.

"You're acting weird," Segun said dryly.

"Sorry," August said, unsure if Segun was upset. His moods were so unpredictable now, and the last thing August wanted was to upset him. August felt like he was always on eggshells now. A careless comment could be all it took for Segun to shut him out again, the way he did after he found out about Betty. August wondered if Segun still thought about it. And if so, if Segun had forgiven him, if Segun would take him back. Of course, there was no way August could bring it up. Segun needed to recover first, recover fully.

After they finished eating, Segun crawled into bed while August took the plastic plates into the kitchen and threw them into the refuse bin. The bin was already filled to the brim, and one of the plates fell to the ground. August packed it all up and tied the refuse bag. He leaned the filled trash against the door and made a mental note to take it with him when he left, and then he got another refuse bag and placed it in the refuse bin the way the last one had been, before washing his hands in the sink. When August went back into the room, Segun was already asleep. August got in bed and lay next to Segun for a while before he stood back up and let himself out.

The exams started. August expected to be behind. He had ignored so much. Segun's hospitalization had swallowed so much of his time. He was surprised when he wasn't, when he wrote the answers to the questions easily, remembering every date and the correct spelling for every name. On his way home, someone called him. He stopped. Behind him, Julia was running toward him.

"What happened?" she asked when she was within earshot. She was breathless.

"How? I don't understand," August said, but his heart had already missed a beat.

"Why didn't Segun write?"

"What?" August's heart sank. His first fear was that Segun's roommates had attacked him again. He half ran, half walked, as soon as the shuttle dropped him outside Hilltop. He flew up the stairs. When he knocked over and over and Segun did not answer the door, his heart shattered in his chest. He tried the door handle and the door creaked open. August swung it ajar. Segun was lying in his bed and for a minute August thought he was dead. Only as he got closer did it become obvious to him that Segun was alive, awake even. When Segun turned to look at him, what August saw in the depths of those eyes frightened him.

"What happened?" August asked.

Segun wiped his eyes. "I couldn't do it," he said.

"What do you mean you couldn't do it?"

"I couldn't get myself to climb out of the bed. I couldn't." He was crying now. "I just couldn't. August, I don't know what is wrong with me."

August climbed into the bed and shushed him, hugging Segun's head to his chest.

"There's nothing wrong with you," he said, rocking Segun gently as he cried. August's heart was breaking, he could feel the sting of tears in his own eyes, but he knew he could not let them fall. He had to be strong for Segun, for both of them. For so long Segun had been the rock August trusted to keep him grounded. Now Segun needed him to be the same for him.

"There is nothing wrong with you," August said again.

Months later, August would find the magazine buried under a heap of Segun's books. He would look back at that moment, at the fear that he felt reverberating through Segun's words, and his body, and sob.

CHAPTER TWENTY-TWO

After Segun's attack, his life broke into two. A before, when he knew what he wanted, the type of world he wanted to see, or at least try to help build, and the certainty of self with which to sustain himself no matter how alone he ever became. And then, an after.

After the semester ended, his family's flat in Iyana-Ipaja provided a needed change of scenery. With its constant background noise of traffic, it helped Segun clear his mind, so that for the first time he was forced to truly confront what had happened to him. For the rest of that semester, he had counted down the days in anticipation for the holiday, in anticipation of home. The Friday he came back, his mother held him in a tight hug, her hands tightened around his back as though she had not seen him in forever. She stood out of the way and Segun picked his bags back up, feeling tears in his eyes. The comfort of his room, that stuffy nostalgia of being waited for, soothed his frayed nerves. His room was spotlessly clean, even the window net that was always dust brown was its original black, and when he lay on the bed, still fully dressed, his sheets smelled freshly washed.

His mother knocked on the door and then opened it without waiting for an answer.

"You will eat nau?" she asked.

Segun shook his head. "I ate when we stopped at Ore," he said.

"Ehe? This one is night food nau. It's spaghetti o," she added, knowing that would convince him.

"Okay," he said, "I'm coming."

They ate together in the living room, and as they ate, Segun realized that she must spend all her evenings alone. His father drove till 9:00 p.m. before closing for each day, and until he came home, she was all by herself.

"How were your exams?" she asked him, twisting her fork into her plate and scooping the spaghetti into her mouth.

"It was good," Segun said.

"I hope they gave you people enough time to prepare?"

"Yeah, yeah. But it was still a lot sha. I'm so exhausted. But thank God now I have just one year left."

"Don't worry. You're home now. You can rest."

But Segun's body did not just rest, it broke down completely the very next day. He got a fever so high his mother left a cold damp towel on his forehead at all times. He would wake up with the towel on the bed next to his face, a damp spot beneath it.

For a long time after Segun was attacked, he tried to live as though what happened had not happened. After being discharged from the hospital, he avoided speaking about it as though that was in itself a reenactment. In the morning when he lotioned up after taking his bath, he made sure not to hover over the scars on his legs and the sides of his stomach. They could just as easily have been bruises sustained from knocking over a table. He tried to train his mind to forget, to forget the fear he had felt lying on that ground, the humiliation. To forget the exhausted panting of his attackers' tiredness as they kicked and kicked with all their might. He refused to entertain questions from anyone regarding what happened. Why the fight ensued, how it burgeoned into something that almost killed him. Whose face he could remember and whose he couldn't. Only weeks after he was discharged from the hospital, the SSF Coordinating Committee asked if he wanted to facilitate a discussion on mob violence, and Segun did not have to think about it before saying no. The committee was having its monthly meeting. Segun had missed the previous two.

"You don't have to make it about *just* mob violence. It can be about lateral violence as a more expanded concept," Ngozi said. She was in her last semester and had been elected the chair the previous year.

"No," Segun said again.

There was silence and Ngozi flipped through the sheets of paper in her hand. It seemed like she would move on to something else but another person butted in.

"Why, comrade?" It was Osinachi, a 300-level student of Combined Biological Sciences. He was supposed to be away on his internship, and Segun wanted to ask him why he was here anyway. *Why the fuck are you not on your IT?*

But he did not. Instead, he said, "I don't know why you'd think I'm the best person to facilitate such a class. Is there any particular reason?" and his voice shook a little, as though it would break.

"Comrade, let me start by apologizing," Ngozi said. "We were just thinking that with the wave of mob violence sweeping the country, as revolutionary students we have to discuss its dimensions and purpose. And I thought you would like to facilitate it. I'm very sorry if I crossed a line or it was insensitive."

"I'm not upset," Segun said abruptly.

"Okay," Ngozi said. "Maybe I'll ask Comrade Stellamaris if she would like to facilitate. I'll take Color Revolutions and you can take Occupy Nigeria. What do you think?"

"It's fine," Segun said.

"It's good?"

"Yes."

But he was indeed upset. He felt like the only reason she would ask him was because he had been attacked. He could not say that because he could not justify his emotions logically. He was supposed to want to share. To bequeath his experiences to building the collective, to building revolution in any capacity in which he could. It was the right thing to do, the revolutionary thing to do. But Segun simply wanted to go back to a place before that day, with his memories completely erased. He put so much effort into doing this, into not letting his body take account of what had happened to it. He went to class and bought lunch with August and said, "I'm fine" as many times as he was asked. When the opportunity to settle the case emerged, Segun jumped on it. August did not like this. August wanted Obum and Ifeanyi and everybody that had

joined in beating him to pay for their crimes and he wanted
Segun to give him that. It infuriated Segun, this expectation. The same August who would not even question his
friendships, wanted him, Segun, to give him the satisfaction
of punishing his attackers.

"I'm tired," Segun said the first time August brought it
up. But when August brought it up again, Segun said, "I'm
not your slave."

He was still in the hospital and August had brought him
food and some books. August had found him Kwame Ture's
Ready for Revolution.

"Comrade, if I tell you what I had to do to find this book
eh," August said, his eyes widening with his smile. "Nigerian
bookstores will never have radical books, only motivational
books. Tufiakwa."

Segun laughed. "They really stressed you."

"See eh . . . And they'll never have a website with their
books listed. Na 2014 we dey o, not 1950. Somebody needs
to notify them."

August glanced at the door before sitting next to Segun
on the bed and taking Segun's hand. He brought it up to his
cheek, kissed it, and pressed it to his cheek. "How far?" he
asked. And it lifted Segun's spirits just how much like the
old times that moment was.

"I'm better now that I have Kwame Ture's biography,"
Segun said.

"Oh, so you're not even better now that I'm here. It's
Kwame Ture? Wow. Wow!"

Segun laughed. And then August ruined it by bringing
up the settlement again.

"I don't get it, honestly. Don't we want them to pay for what they did to you? Is it because of the money?" August asked.

He was taken aback by Segun's response. Segun saw his face contort with hurt.

"What is that supposed to mean?" he asked Segun.

"It means I'm not going to change my mind so you can have the satisfaction of seeing them 'pay' for what they did," Segun said, making air quotes. "I don't care if they go to prison or not. It will add literally nothing to my life. It will not stop them from being homophobic. Who the fuck goes to prison and comes out less violent? It won't repeal all our queerphobic laws either. So why exactly are you so stuck on wanting me to want it because that's what you want? Did they attack you?"

As Segun said those words, he wondered if what he was feeling was not resentment. Resentment because August wanted to eat his cake and have it, resentment because August was the type of person who ate his cake and still had a whole bakery left. Could he really resent someone he loved so much, someone who made his chest tingle? Or was he feeling something else? He knew for sure it wasn't envy. He did not want to be August, definitely not. He did not want to be someone who was afraid of himself, who did not have an identity outside of being liked, outside of other people's approval. But he did feel bitter that even now, August was centering himself, centering his own need for revenge. Even after behaving for the comfort of the type of people he now wanted revenge against.

"I didn' . . . I didn't mean it like that. Baby, where is all this coming from?" August said.

"You weren't there," Segun shouted. They both glanced at the door, and then, in a lowered voice, Segun said, "You weren't there. It didn't happen to you. You don't get to tell me what to want. There is no *we*. It was *me*. *I* was the one who was attacked. *I* almost died. Not us. *Me*."

Tears were welling in his eyes and he looked up at the ceiling and blinked them away.

"I'm sorry," August said.

"Jesus Christ! I don't need your sorry," Segun said between clenched teeth.

August stood there staring at him with what Segun thought was pity, and it took Segun all the strength in him to continue to hold himself together. August brought out the food and placed it on the bedside table. It was coconut rice and smoked fish. Beside it, August placed a bottle of Sprite and then he left. He did not say good-bye, and Segun knew that he had really hurt August. But it was necessary because he wanted to forget. He had read somewhere that the brains of people who suffered really traumatic experiences sometimes suppressed memories of the event so well that they forgot what happened to them. And that was exactly what Segun wanted.

But his avoidance worked for only so long. After he came back to Lagos, his body decided that it did not want to forget, that it wanted reckoning, that it wanted to take stock, that it wanted to be acknowledged as broken.

"What kind of sickness is this one? Eh Abe?" his mother would ask as she gave him a sponge bath. "You're scaring me. Since when do you get this type of sick?"

Some days Segun said, "I don't even understand what kind of sickness this is." And other times he was too weak to voice his words.

On the phone, Segun told August it was just malaria and typhoid.

"I get it once a year or so. I'm even shocked it didn't come earlier. I'll be fine."

But there were nights that Segun cried himself to sleep in unbearable pain, nights that he doubted he would live through the night, nights that he doubted he even wanted to live through the night.

To take him to the hospital, Segun's mother had to miss an entire day of sales. He heard her on the phone with the man she bought her vegetables from. Six days a week she woke up in the small hours of the morning so she could get to the market and select the freshest bundles of vegetables before they were all snatched up by other market women. Some days he reserved some bundles for her even when she was late, and so on whatever day she would be absent, she made sure to inform him.

The day she took Segun to the hospital, she woke up very early too, so that they could get to the Federal Medical Center at Ebute Metta before it became crowded. They took a direct bus to Yaba from the Iyana-Ipaja market. On the almost hour-long drive, Segun sat with his face pressed to the window, staring at the road, at the occasional tree saplings struggling to grow on the road demarcation, roadside sweep-ers in their amber vests, the APC banners at almost every junction, sometimes with General Buhari's face embellishing them.

"Hmmmm. They're really trying to get this man into Aso Rock," Segun said weakly. He was even surprised his mother heard him.

"My dear o," his mother said, peering out the window. "Everybody is now on the Sai Baba train o."

The woman sitting in front of them turned to glare at them.

"What?" Segun's mother asked sharply. "Did I call your name?"

"So you like how things are going now?" the woman asked.

"Did I tell you that? Is Goodluck Ebele Jonathan written on my forehead?" Segun's mother asked, clapping her hands.

"Madam, it's not fight," the woman said and turned to face her front.

"Better o," Segun's mother said. Segun smiled.

At the hospital, the doctor asked him several questions and then administered some tests. But there was nothing wrong with him.

"I'll prescribe you pain medication. Just rest and eat enough food. Your body is only recovering from what it went through. It is not a machine."

Eventually, Segun's fever broke but the weakness in his bones remained. He woke up every day exhausted. In the begin-ning, it was an exhaustion that did not seem total, that did not seem permanent. And so Segun held on to hope that it would pass. He read books and slept and spoke with August on the phone.

"You should go out," August said. "Attend a party or go to the cinema. Anything."

And Segun did. First he went to the cinema to see some movies. *Transformers*, and then *The Fault in Our Stars*. And it made him feel better, took his mind off his sadness. But only temporarily, only while he was watching. After he went home, the clouds descended again, and it was so total, so choking that it scared him. Because the longer it lasted, the less sure he became that it would pass. For so long, Segun had held on firmly to the fire that was his own resistance. A fire that warmed him, and assured him that he would always have that warmth. And now he woke up every day feeling a chilling cold, feeling like the only thing that would satisfy him, that the only thing he truly needed was to sleep and sleep forever. He went to a queer party in Ikeja. He did not enjoy it. The music was too loud, he did not drink alcohol or smoke, he hated the flashing red and green party lights, and he did not feel like dancing. Still, he stayed till very late into the evening. His mother did not protest. She too was worried about him.

"Talk to me nau? You always keep to yourself. I cannot remember the last time a friend came here to look for you. This boy, you're scaring me o. You're scaring me," she told him days later when his mood had still not improved.

"Mummy, I'm fine. I'm recovering from sickness," he said, but she was not satisfied. She made them both stay up till almost 10:00 p.m. so she could tell his father.

"This boy is depressed. I'm scared. I'm scared o. Please he doesn't talk to me. I've tried my best, maybe he'll talk to you."

She left the two of them there in the living room. Segun stared at his father and the man stared back at him.

"Oluwasegun," his father called.

"Sir?" Segun replied.

"What's this I'm hearing? What's going on? Is it because of the incident?" Segun's father looked guilty, as though his wife had laid the blame at his feet.

"Daddy, I'm fine," Segun said, a little annoyed that his mother would do this.

"You're not fine. Are you saying your mother doesn't know what she's saying?"

Segun said nothing. He made a mental note to stop brooding around the house, he did not need his mother on his back. The holiday would be over in less than two weeks and maybe that was for the best.

"You know we love you? We don't have another child. It's only you. You're our one sun. And when you're not happy, how do you expect us to be happy?"

"I will cheer up," Segun said, unsure of what else to say. His father smiled.

"Well . . . it's a good start. But if something is bothering you, share with your mother. Or even with me. Don't carry it alone or thought will age you o. I'm telling you."

Segun thanked him. But it was precisely that, because he was all they had, that he was afraid of truly considering rest. An end to everything, a reprieve from this tiredness. If he killed himself, what would they do? How would his mother ever recover? And August, what would he do? What would his life become, how would he learn to live for himself? Because apart from those, apart from love, apart from fear of how those he loved would be devastated by his death, what other reason did Segun have not to choose rest, not to choose himself? He spent the whole day thinking about it, thinking about the possibility of not feeling anything at all, the possibility of not having to fight any minute longer. It beckoned to him. The next day, he plastered a wide smile on his face, a smile he would wear all the way back to school. A smile he would take off only when he was alone with himself, only when no one else could see and worry.

His mother was cautiously relieved. But still, after dinner that night, after he washed the plates while his mother swept the living room, when he retired to the darkness of his room, he opened his browser and searched, *Is sniper poison painful?* The first reply was an article from Tribune Online titled, *Experts warn suicidal Lagosians: Sniper won't kill you instantly.*

But even then, Segun was not fully dissuaded. Maybe the half an hour it would take the poison to work was a justified price to pay for peace.

CHAPTER TWENTY-THREE

August did not like that he would be separated from Segun for so long during the holidays.

"Promise me you would pick up your calls," he said to Segun, just before they parted for the holidays. "Promise me."

"I promise," Segun said dully. It was a hollow promise, a resigned caving in, as though he was only doing so because he was too tired to argue. He seemed always to be tired these days. He simply stayed indoors and slept and slept and slept. Sometimes he dozed off with August lying right next to him. August would stay in the silence, listening only to the sound of Segun's heavy breathing. Then he would let himself out. Segun sounded the same way on the phone, like he was about to sleep, or he'd just woken up.

"Lagos is big," he was always saying. "There is so much going on. Just go out. Buy yourself some ice cream at Cold Stone or see a movie. For me, please."

"Maybe tomorrow," Segun said.

The house closed in on him sometimes, so August tried to go out by himself. His own room felt foreign now. It had the musty scent of old, abandoned places. Every morning, he ran, along his street, through New Heaven and up past Chime Avenue. On his walk home, the shops would be opening. Boutiques, furniture stores, convenient stores, wine and spirits outlets, the city unfurling to the morning light. He redownloaded Tinder. Then Grindr. He would start conversations and then not follow up with them, exchange pictures with people only to never make concrete plans to meet. He had been pushing back his desires, giving Segun time to heal. He just did not know how to bring up sex. He was not even sure where their relationship was, if they were back together by default, if they would ever get back to that place of easy happiness where they had been content.

August met the first man from Grindr in a family house. There were people in the living room as they undressed each other in the man's bedroom. August wondered who he was turning into. He felt like he was doing something horrible, but all he wanted was to feel something other than this sense of perpetual waiting. The second one was in his room. His sisters were out and he was home alone and so he went on Grindr, where there was no shortage of people seeking no-strings-attached rendezvous. The man, Emeka, kissed with too much spit. August found this repulsive.

"What's wrong?" the man asked.

"I don't do kissing," August lied.

The man went on shedding the rest of his clothes and pulled August to him. After he left, August felt horrible.

"Segun and I are not even together," he told himself. It did not assuage his guilt. He called Segun. "I miss you," he said. "I miss you terribly."

"I know," Segun said, and after a pause, "I miss you too."

"Maybe I should come to Lagos. For a weekend or something."

Segun made a sound. August fiddled with the idea. Mentioned it to Peculiar even. He could always count on her as a gauge for how Uzoamaka might accommodate his suggestions. Of course, Uzoamaka was not pleased.

"Who do you even know in Lagos? Nobody."

"It's to see Segun," August said.

"Segun kwa? For what? The same Segun you go to school with, or is it another Segun?"

August wasn't sure what else to say.

"Look, August, money doesn't grow on trees. And let this be the last time you tell me anything about this thing you've decided to do with your life. Just imagine. You want to travel to Lagos? You can't hold the thing again? You can't wait for school to resume so you can both continue whatever it is you do with yourselves?"

Their previous phone call had not ended in a resolution, and now she was venting her frustrations. August had outright rejected all her pleas to seek deliverance.

"It will help," she begged. "We will tackle it together. August, please."

But he refused. And so now, August removed the phone from his ear and let her unburden herself.

"Our mother would be turning in her grave, August. This is not who you are supposed to be. This is not what well-raised men are supposed to be."

After she cut the call, he sat on the bed and tried to gather himself. His nose tingled, almost painfully, the sign of impending tears. But the tears never came. Instead, he dreamt of them. Himself, alone, weeping on his mother's grave. He wasn't sure if those qualified as nightmares. He woke with a soreness in his throat and all morning it weighed on him. Uzoamaka called him two days later to apologize.

"You know I love you. I love you so much and all I do, I do from the love I have for you."

"Sis, it's fine."

"Understand it from my perspective, August, maybe because you're not thinking into the future. This is not something you can be forever. Eventually, you will have to settle down. My name is no longer Akasike. I am no longer an Akasike. And soon too Chinyere and Peculiar. No one will carry this name, if not you."

But August wanted his life to be his. He did not want to simply be a vessel to carry on the Akasike name, and to burden his children too, with this duty to a name.

"It won't be easy then. You have to start now to fight this," she said.

But August was tired of fighting himself, of the constant struggle to live up to something he knew now he would never, could never, did not want to be.

When school resumed, what shocked August the most was how thin Segun had become. His shoulder blades strained against his skin. Segun was naturally a thin man. His body didn't seem like one that could ever not be thin. But now he seemed to be a mass of bones held tightly together by skin. His Afro looked extra thick and extra unkempt, like he didn't once comb it while he was in Lagos. It made his head appear even bigger, too big for his body. August was perplexed. As they hugged, he held onto Segun, taking stock of Segun's body with his own. They ate together every afternoon. August goading and goading till Segun ate his entire plate of food.

After his performance at the NUGA games, August had been drafted for the National Sports Festival coming up in November. He knew how out of form he was now; training regularly in the afternoons was simply not something he did anymore. He ran in the mornings though, and each morning he tried to convince Segun to run with him. Occasionally, he would wear Segun down, and they would run together. Segun walking for the most part, his hands huddled to his chest as the cold Nsukka breeze whipped around them.

There were times things seemed fine and other times it seemed like in the darkness of that balcony, those attackers had managed to break more than Segun's bones. August worried constantly about Segun's disconsolation, worried it might never lift. Whenever anyone spoke about any gossip, August immediately feared they were talking about Segun. The *Gist* frenzy that whipped up after the settlement was paid had died down, and now in its place was a sort of quiet resentment. More than once, August opened his WhatsApp group chat to see posts that began with FAGS HAVE TAKEN OVER NSUKKA or PAYING GAYS ISNT RESTORING THE DIGNITY OF MAN.

Each time a post like that circulated, August would watch Segun more closely, ever more afraid. One Friday, near Kwame Nkrumah Road, August saw Segun's face on a poster in black and white. They must have gotten it from Facebook. **GAYS REPENT OR PERISH!!!!!!!!** it said.

August stopped and stared at it. Segun's smiling face, the script, the sheer number of exclamation marks. He tore it off, all four of them, side by side to each other. It frightened him, because in place of Segun's passion there was now something unrecognizable, something that terrified him and made him ache in ways he didn't know were possible.

That same day, Segun had a fit. August immediately knew something was wrong because Segun almost never called his phone. When August arrived, Segun was crying.

"It hurts," he said. "My bones."

August sat next to him on the bed and looked Segun over as though trying to locate the source of his hurt. "Where?"

Segun touched the parts of his limbs that were once swollen, where skin covered freshly healed bones. "August, I can't do this. I can't. I don't know what's happening to me."

"It'll be fine," August said. "Do you have Robb? I can try to massage it. If that doesn't work, we can go to the hospital."

"I don't have," Segun cried.

August used Vaseline instead. As he rubbed Segun's legs, he thought back to the growing pains of his childhood. Segun's eyes were closed now and his breathing had calmed.

"Is it better now?" August asked.

Segun nodded but did not open his eyes. There were dried tearstains on his face.

"*Ndo*," August said.

The next time Segun said those words, August got a sinking feeling from the way Segun clutched his shirt like he was holding on for dear life. August likened it to a man at sea, a man who had struggled against the waves for so long but who had now resigned himself to their power and was ready to sink beneath the surface of the turbulent waters.

There were, sometimes, bursts of laughter in between, short periods of respite, when August could recognize Segun, when he saw Segun come back to himself. The sun was bright in the sky, and Segun's laughter rang with a trueness that made August conscious of his own heartbeat. In these moments, Segun seemed to be a recovered man. Sometimes it could be a simple test that went well or a novel that brought him comfort. The day he read *And the Mountains Echoed* by Khaled Hosseini, it lit him up from the inside. In those rare times when Segun smiled, August was struck by how rarely Segun smiled, now. After Segun finished the novel, August cradled Segun's head in his lap and listened to him describe the characters, mesmerized by their stories. Suddenly, he stopped and sat up, turning to face August. "It was so beautiful," he said. He kissed August, leaning heavily into him as he did this. There was something aggressive about it, the abruptness with which it happened.

Days later, when August began to read the book, he was captivated by the story about the father and his son and the jinn. By the father's long journey into the mountains to rescue his son from the fortress of the jinn only to realize that his son was happy, thriving, and that leaving him there was the greatest act of love, not saving him. August wondered if perhaps the beauty Segun spoke about wasn't a tragic one. It made more sense, seeing how that evening ended with both of them separated by the immense, pitch-black void between them, one August had no idea how to breach. When Segun finished telling August about the story, he had pulled August's face toward his, and kissed him, softly at first, and then not so softly. Soon Segun was pulling August's shirt over his head, pulling on the strap of August's belt, their clothes falling all around them, flung in the fit of passion. Segun's nails marked him, drawing blood on his back and his shoulders. The bed squeaked. They had never had sex that passionate, so heightened that it felt like everything around them was shaking, formless, like all that remained were their pumping hearts and their panting. Afterward, they collapsed on the now bare bed, with Segun's back turned to him. And as August watched Segun's bare shoulders, he realized that what he thought was the rise and fall of heavy breathing, was actually the shaking of tears. Segun sniffed. When August tried to look into his face, Segun covered it with his hands. His shoulders were shaking even harder now.

"I'm . . . I'm so sorry," August said. "Baby, what's wrong?" He tried to hold Segun once more, but Segun pushed him away. August sat up and watched Segun cry. He tried again to hug him and this time there was a bit of struggle, until finally, August won. He put his arms around Segun's chest and held him tightly. The sobs escaped Segun's mouth then. Loud painful sobs that found their way to August's heart and broke it even more.

"It's okay," August said, fighting his own tears. "It's okay."

On the fifteenth of July, on a Tuesday, just a week before the second-semester exams, August Akasike told Dike he was bisexual. Dike was looking at him strangely, and at the last moment, August said that word, bisexual, instead of the truth. He was ashamed of it, ashamed of cowering. But it was something, at least some of the truth. "I have a slight preference for boys over girls though," he added, softly, but that admission did nothing to lessen his shame.

After that, when he spoke to Dike, it became increasingly clear to him that Dike had always known. They started training in the afternoons again. The National Sports Festival was a few months away and August wanted to be ready. His teammates wanted to know why he just dropped off the track like that.

"I was busy with stuff," he told them.

And even then, he wasn't consistent. Some afternoons he would stay in Segun's room and read one of Segun's books while lying next to a sleeping Segun.

The Tuesday he came out to Dike, Dike pulled him to the edge of the bleachers. "Man, what's going on with you and this Segun guy, for real? He's really messing with your form."

August knew Dike must have expected the answer. Or at least suspected it.

"It's just between us, though. I'm telling you because of how close we are. I think you deserve to at least know what's up," he told Dike.

"So, you and Betty, what was that all about?"

"I do both. That's what it means," August said. They sat down and August tried to explain himself. Saying he did both, seemed like something Dike could swallow. August wanted to be proud, to own his truth. But try as he may, that pride petered out in front of Dike.

Segun would have said, "Stop. Stop. Stop. Stop. You do not apologize, August. There is nothing to be apologetic for." The old Segun at least. The new Segun would simply turn his head away, quietly disappointed.

"How does that even work?" Dike asked. August was looking down at his feet. "You fuck his ass or he fucks you? I know he's very girly."

August wanted to tell him that it didn't matter, that it could go either way, that they had some of their best sex without. The first day he had let Segun top him, months ago now, he had felt humiliation, the type he felt with Timothy. But with time, he stopped feeling that way. It was Segun who taught him that his body was a canvas to be explored, to be scaled and kneaded into marvelous, magical shapes.

"I always do the fucking but you know it's more than that. Much more," August said.

Dike made a sound, an incredulous sound, and for a moment it seemed like he would simply stand up and walk away.

"Well, you know me, I don't like gays, because . . . man, the thing is just disgusting. But not like I have a problem with you. You're still my nigga. Just sad that I almost never see you run and I know how much you love running."

"I know. It's just, we're struggling. You know, since the hospital."

Dike made a sound. He stood up and dusted off the back of his shorts even though the seats were clean. August watched him walk back to the track and felt like he had betrayed himself. He was grateful that Dike's words had been kind, even if only to him. *You're still my friend.* August realized how selfish he was to be pleased with this. Segun words echoed in his head. *He is not your friend, August. People like him are why we will never be safe in this country.*

Segun had come back from the long holidays acting more adjusted, like he had balled all his pain together and thrown it into the Atlantic Ocean. When they were out, he smiled. He laughed. And he spoke as though nothing had ever happened, as though life was just the way it always had been, and the only inconvenience was how stressful everything about school was.

"Sometimes I think they purposely make even the simplest of things unnecessarily long and hard to suffer us."

"Wow. That pun is on fire," August said, laughing.

Segun laughed too. But at home, the happiness fell away, like a robe. The smile faded, his face crumbled into a distant and empty look. Sometimes he performed happiness for August too. He cracked a joke, laughed, nibbled on August's neck. And in those moments, August let himself enjoy it; he let himself believe the lie that Segun was himself again so he could lose himself in the pleasure of that. Before he left for his own room each day, he wondered if there was another dimension even he couldn't see, an extra layer of desolation Segun hid, even from him.

On Segun's birthday, they went into town to Polo Park Mall to see a movie and eat chocolate Cold Stone ice cream. Segun smiled and shut his eyes blissfully when he put the ice cream in his mouth. He sighed so contentedly August knew it was a show for his benefit. August smiled at Segun, though his smile did not quite reach his eyes. He took a bite of his ice cream and tried to believe they would get through all this.

"You know I'm here," he told Segun later that day. They were back in Segun's room. Segun was kicking off his shoes and August was standing next to the wardrobe.

"I'm right here. You don't have to carry it alone. Talk to me. Let me carry all this with you."

"I don't know what you're talking about," Segun said lightly. "I'm fine."

August could tell Segun was trying to avoid looking at him. He walked over and leaned his chin on Segun's shoulder.

"Just in case, you know. You've been down, I noticed. I don't know if it's because of . . . you know, what happened."

"I'm fine," Segun said again.

"I'm just saying," August continued, turning Segun to face him. "I'm here. I'm always here. You can talk to me, no matter what it is or is not, no matter when."

He pressed his forehead against Segun's. In many ways, he still felt guilty for what had happened, and Segun's resignation only sharpened that guilt.

Segun sighed. "I'm sorry," he said. "I'm trying, I swear. I am. But I don't . . ." He paused.

August wiped the tears from his cheeks; they were warm against his palm.

"I don't recognize myself, August. I can't talk about it because I don't even know what it is."

"This is what they wanted," August said. "To break you."

It sounded like a warning, like he was begging Segun to fight, like he was baring his fears for the first time.

"Maybe they got what they wanted. Maybe I'm broken. I know I don't feel whole."

"Don't say that," August said.

"You don't understand," Segun said. "And I don't know how I can explain it."

It was then that Segun's knees buckled. Perhaps they decided they were done holding him up. August only knew that his arms became the only thing keeping Segun from falling to the floor. Segun's hands clung to August's shirt. It surprised him, how fast it happened. How Segun's legs sprawled on the floor. He sat Segun on the bed and lay with him until he was done crying.

"I'm sorry," he kept saying to August. "I'm so sorry."

"Shhh. You don't have to be sorry for anything."

August lay with him till he fell asleep.

CHAPTER TWENTY-FOUR

The day Segun died, the rains had come in light showers that lasted all night and raised the petrichor to such a rich thick scent that for days, August could almost taste the dust in his mouth. The skies had held signs of rain—gray, drowsy, and tired. It was in early October. October the fifth. August would forever remember that day, for how much his life had come apart, in one single day, how much all the meaning he thought he had begun to make of his life, seemed to fade into the harmattan drizzle. Many moments after discovering Segun's body, August simply stared blankly, waiting for what he was seeing to make sense. And when it eventually did, August couldn't breathe. He wanted to scream for help, but the screams were stuck somewhere in his throat, choking him.

Standing at the door knocking, it had crossed his mind, a fleeting thought that Segun had finally surrendered to the darkness that had burdened him since the attack. In the early days after Segun was discharged from the hospital, such thoughts weren't so fleeting. He used to be relieved just to see Segun and know he was okay. But on the day he died, when Segun did not answer the door, August assumed he was out. He tried to use his own key but the door was unlocked, and there Segun was. On the bed, with such a peaceful expression on his face that before August tried to wake him, he watched him sleep. He would think of that Segun so many times, how at peace he was, how relaxed. Segun's face was the only thing August remembered about that day. That, and the way the room was so neat and tidy. The shirts that would have been hanging around or lying on the chair, folded away or strung from a hanger. The shorts tucked away, the shoes lined by the wall, so symmetrically there was almost an art to it. No matter how much he tried, he couldn't remember anything else about Segun himself, other than his face, and how cold his skin felt when August touched him. *Segun must have killed himself the night before, after he was with you in the afternoon,* he thought to himself.

It was only after he touched Segun's cold body that he noticed the unlabeled container of liquid on the reading table. August was not sure if he screamed, or how the events ordered themselves. He only knew he was confused, expecting that there was some sort of mistake somewhere, and that soon it would resolve itself and everything would make sense. He repeated himself so many times as people filed into the room.

I saw him like this.

I came this morning.

His door was unlocked.

There were suddenly so many people in the room. A cab arrived and they put Segun in it and off they went to the hospital, August sitting next to him, refusing to accept his death. In the chaos of those moments, he heard someone shout, "Wetin happen?" and the response, "One final-year guy off himself."

August was holding the unlabeled liquid container, and defying all hope, at the hospital, the doctor told him what he already knew: Segun had died.

August had no recollection of his father's retirement. He only realized how present the man was, and then Peculiar told him.

"Is it today? He retired awhile ago. How don't you know about our own father's retirement?"

August said nothing. The truth was that August and his father almost never talked, but his sisters loved to pretend not to notice. Even now, while they were home alone together, they never spoke. In the morning, they sidestepped each other to get breakfast. August had resigned himself to the knowledge he would never be close with his father. The man regarded him with nothing but complete indifference, and August had unconsciously learnt to regard his father with the same apathy, especially now. He only wanted his peace, to brood and feel sorry for himself.

At school, everyone had overwhelmed him with condolences, and he hated it, hated how they all had something nice to say about Segun, now that he was dead. He hated how they all stared at him, the friend of the guy who killed himself. And so after Segun's mother came for his body, August packed his things and went home. Segun's mother seemed like she too did not understand what had happened and the meaning would form only later on. Her eyes were bloodshot and her voice was broken from crying. She hugged August, hugged him so tightly, the way Uzoamaka used to hug him when he was a child. Seeing her ripped through with grief made Segun's death even more real. As did being questioned by the police and by Student Affairs. He told them he and Segun were close friends. He hated that he said that but he was so exhausted, so tired, of everything.

He thought of his mother, what she would think of him if she could see him now. What she would say were she here, and what he might say back to her. He thought of ending his own life, many times, saving himself from this pain his body was embalmed with. But he wasn't able to bring himself to do it. Many times he would decide to end his life only to once again be confronted by his own lack of resolve. Always, he entertained the plans because it helped to imagine an end to his pain. Segun's mother's broken, scratchy voice still found him in his dreams. Her screaming as she descended to the covered body on the ground, as though still shocked that it was her son's corpse. The man with her, he assumed was Segun's father. Now at home, he spent all his time grieving. There seemed to his grief, a catharsis, one he did not ever want to let go of.

On Saturday, he went to Immaculate Boys' and ran laps there until his limbs ached. At home, he walked past Peculiar reading on her iPad at the dining table. She said something about food and he mumbled back. She had grown weary of nagging him about getting back to school, of giving him speeches about death, and the moving on that the living must do as a duty to the dead.

First, she told their father. "I don't know what is wrong with him. It's true that he's in grief, but this is too much."

His father spoke to him out of mere formality. August listened. When his father began to tell a story about a classmate of his that had died in university, August interrupted him to say, "He wasn't my classmate."

"Your friend?"

"He killed himself. Do you know what that means?"

"So you want to drop out of school?"

"No," August said.

"Your sisters are worried sick," August's father said.

"I know," August said.

Uzoamaka came home the following weekend. She was so angry August had left school. August also knew that part of her anger was because it was Segun he was grieving. He stayed in his room the entire time, away from her passive aggression. Downstairs he could hear her giving Peculiar war stories about sitting her final MBs. Peculiar was about to sit for hers. August thought of going back to school, for her sake, so she did not have to worry about him. He had been to the faculty building only once since Segun's death and it was to answer questions from the dean. And he had gotten so many condolences he almost broke down in the faculty. He couldn't go back to that. Uzoamaka stayed for the entire week. The following Sunday, after they had their lunch of rice and stew with plantains all prepared by Uzoamaka, she called everyone to the living room.

As soon as August saw his father, he knew the meeting was about him.

"August," she said.

"Yes?"

"I don't know, I've been watching. I just said let me understand what it is you have in mind. Is it that you're tired of school, or that you're okay with failing this entire semester, or I don't know, perhaps you're now one of those students who pay master's students to come and write your exams for you. Tell us your mind."

His father was in his seat, his hand tucked between his thighs. Uzoamaka and Peculiar were sitting next to each other on the three-seater. August said nothing, sat silently watching his sisters.

"August," Uzoamaka said, again.

"Yes," August said, again.

"Are you the only person to lose somebody?"

Again, August was silent.

"What is my name?" she asked him.

August looked up from the ground to look at her. "Uzoamaka," he said.

"Uzoamaka who?" she prodded on. August realized then where she was going with her line of questioning. He decided he would not answer this question too.

"I am Uzoamaka Obaji. Peculiar," she turned to put an arm on Peculiar's shoulder, "will soon marry and take her own husband's name. Chinyere, after all her gragra, eventually she too will marry. Forget whatever she says now. And she will take her husband's name too. I have told you that this thing you are doing is not for you. Maybe if our mother had many boys it would be thinkable. But no, you are the only son. The single eye with a debt to the blind."

She turned to their father and continued. "This boy he's mourning now is a boy he told me he was together with. Together, like husband and wife. That is who this boy is now mourning like a destitute widow. He wants to throw his life away for the boy. Because of this boy, August did not go to Cross River for the National Sports Festival. Am I lying?" She turned to August.

"They postponed the festival," August said.

"Postponed?" Uzoamaka asked. "Who postponed it?"

"How should I know?" August said.

"That is still not an excuse for you to want to throw your life away."

"*Biko* the last time I checked, it's *my* life. I am not throwing away your own," August said coldly.

"August!" Peculiar said sternly.

Uzoamaka shook her head and clicked her tongue. "*I machaghi ihe*," she said. "You're not smart at all. A big ingrate is what you are. Do I blame you?"

"Do you even know how he died?" August asked.

"*Biko* how did he die that no one has died like before? So he killed himself and you want to throw your own life away?"

August had never been so angry at Uzoamaka, never despised her like he did in those moments.

"Are you done?" he asked.

"I'm going to slap you o, August. Don't test me."

"Only slap?" August asked.

"August, that's enough. You don't talk to her that way," his father said.

"Maybe it was me who should have died. I mean, who knows? If I had died, maybe you would not have changed your name. This precious name you want to preserve so much."

Peculiar stood from her seat and put her hand over August's mouth.

"It's enough. Ahn-Ahn. What has come over you?"

But August was not done.

"I know his life meant nothing but you see this name, this Akasike you are so bent on preserving, better tell Chime that you people will give your children Akasike o, because it's not me."

"It is you," Uzoamaka said. She was a little rattled. August had never spoken to any of his sisters like that.

"No. It is not me." And as he said this, he shook his head and clicked his tongue.

"August, I said it is you."

"Uzoamaka, I said it's not me. I know that's all you see me as, something to keep a name alive. But I am a human being. I am a human being. Do you hear? I am a fucking human being."

And as he said this, he tried to keep the tears in his eyes from falling.

Still, the next day, he went back to school. He did not know what type of pain this was, how so badly he did not want to be in his own skin, how he felt like if he did not bury his legs into the ground he would drift away and lose himself somewhere in the darkness of the night. He went back to the track because he was afraid now of being by himself, of waiting for the devastation that washed over him in waves. Sometimes, it seemed to him like he still did not understand Segun's death, that its reality was yet to dawn on him. He had opted not to go to the burial because he did not want to be confronted by Segun's mother's grief, by his father's pained silence. And because Segun was gone anyway, all that was left was a body, a corpse, not the man he loved. He regretted it. He wished he had gone, if only to see Segun's face one last time.

Running gave him a clear mind and so he decided that was what he would do. Preparations for the next SUG games were underway, anyway. And August wanted to really impress, so he would maintain his invitation to the National Sports Festival, which had been postponed until April.

His coach looked at him. "Are you back back? Or you still need time? What happened to your friend was horrible."

"I'm back," August said.

"Hundred percent?"

"Hundred percent."

He said the same thing to Betty. Yes, he was back. Yes, he was fine. Yes, he was ready to train. Dike made a joke. Something about how he too would lie low for a while if he found a dead body. August did not find it funny and simply pretended he did not hear. It did not take too much to get back in top form. His time was good, and his endurance wasn't bad. For some reason, this embittered him, how his body did not bear witness to what happened, did not bear

AND THEN HE SANG A LULLABY   281

witness to how his life had lost meaning. After the training, Henry, a 300-level law student that exceled in long distance races, said the same thing. That he too would lie low for a while if he found a dead body.

"It's crazy man," he said. "I can't even imagine dealing with something like that."

August did not say anything. He was fuming inside. He wanted to scream at him to shut up. Shut. The. Fuck. Up. Henry.

"The guy sef, why he kill himself? His gay self was too much for him? Me sha, I'd rather kill myself than be a gay, so I guess there we agree."

Something in August snapped. Before he could stop himself, he had knocked Henry to the ground. He punched Henry in the face and saw blood. August's knuckles ached but then Henry punched back, and it set off something automatic in August. He punched and punched and punched till the other athletes pulled him off.

"*Nawa o.* Because of this small thing he said?" someone said. August looked around but he wasn't sure who had said it.

Dike pulled a still enraged August away and to the far end of the track.

"Geez, man. What's up? You need to calm down."

"Fuck off," August said. He could taste blood in his mouth. He spat it out.

"Ah. See it's horrible what happened but it's really no one's fault."

"Dike, I swear to God, if you don't get away from me right now, whatever happens to you, you take it like that."

"As in that you're the only one with hands for punching or what? Because I'm separating you from fight? Oya go and fight nau."

August shoved Dike and Dike shoved him back. Betty arrived just then. She pushed Dike away. "What is wrong with you people? Can't you see he's not fine?"

She turned to August and put an arm to his chest. "You . . . Calm down."

"He was there," August shouted, thrusting his finger at Dike. "This bastard was there the night they killed Segun and he did nothing. Nothing."

She held his face with both hands. "August, listen to me."

"He knew we were dating. He knew."

"August, listen. Listen to me. You are in pain. You are grieving. But you have to calm down. We have an opportunity to go to Cross River next year. He doesn't even have that."

"I don't care," August shouted.

"You do," Betty said. "Listen to me. You've worked so hard."

"Betty, I don't care. I don't fucking care."

The tears came then. Almost all at once, the wave of desolation, one so eternal, so whole. He would never get Segun back, never get another chance to do things differently. He crumbled onto the pavement, his face buried in his knees. His tears were loud and guttural. It was impossible for anyone to make out what he was saying. His grief distorted his words. August could not believe those sounds were coming from him.

"I don't care," he was saying over and over.

"It's okay."

"But it's not. He's gone. They've killed him. They've killed him."

Betty squatted in front of him and put a hand on his shoulder. August could tell that she was trying to shield him from view of the others, from Dike, who was standing a few feet away, looking on as though in remorse. But August didn't care how loud he was being. Those painful sounds found their way out of his chest along with his tears. Betty hugged him, rubbing his back. And hugging her too, he wept into her shoulder.

August's breakdown got around school and with it, rumors that he and Segun had been boyfriends swelled. This brought August some comfort, being known as Segun's boyfriend, an acknowledgment of the wonderful thing they had shared. He was never asked to confirm the rumor, but August fervently wished someone would ask him so he could say yes.

Sometimes, August overheard people speaking about him. At SUB, in the faculty, even at the lodge.

"What? He fought? Actually fought someone?" he once heard someone say at SUB.

"They say he injured Henrico. Knocked his teeth out. Omo, because of his fellow man."

August relished the look of horror on their faces when they turned around and saw him standing behind them. People always quieted and greeted him guiltily when they realized he heard them. Sometimes, August greeted back, a small smile on his face. Other times, he did not acknowledge the greeting. August stopped training again. After classes, he went to Segun's now empty room and lay on the bed, a gnawing desire for vengeance eating away at him. August was angry at everything, angry at the world, angry at the school, angry at God.

"Anger is good, if channeled in the right direction," Segun had told him once, in the early days of the SSMPA. "We can channel it into hate and blame and violence. Or we can fashion it into a fuel that sustains us as we try to make revolution."

Where did Segun's anger go? August wondered. Why did it not sustain him? How did someone so bright burn out so completely? The anger August felt, it did not seem like it could ever exhaust itself. August did not know what making revolution meant. He told Segun this many times.

"Subjective factors," Segun always said. "Revolution is the solution but the people have to first reach that conclusion. They have to overcome false consciousness of religion, tribalism, sexism, all of that. We have to help them question and get to that conclusion by themselves."

"But how? Have you met Nigerians?" August once asked.

"I can't tell you how. There is no map. It's something we have to figure out. If I knew how, the revolution would have happened yesterday."

It seemed unwise then, that Segun was committing himself to a struggle he was not even sure how best to wage. But now all August could think of was that something had been stolen from him and that committing himself to a world where that would not have been possible did not seem farcical.

When Segun's mother came to take the rest of Segun's belongings back to Lagos, she let August keep a lot of Segun's things—his shirts, his comb, his bedding—small things that held the memory of him. They only disagreed about how to share Segun's books. She wanted them too.

"I let you keep so many of his things," she said. "Let me keep these ones. I want to know what he was reading, what he was thinking. He is so secretive. I want to know my son, please." Her voice was twisted with grief.

August looked away for a moment. "I bought many of these books. They were so hard to find but I found them for him," August said softly. "And I want to know him too."

They decided August would keep those books he had given to Segun, and Segun's mother would keep the rest, as well as his notes. As they sorted, August claimed some books he did not buy Segun. It felt like he was cheating a mother out of her dead son's memories, but she had known Segun all his life. She had a lifetime of memories, and he could only mourn the lifetime of memories he and Segun would never be able to make.

He took the books and stacked them next to the cabinet in his room. He liked to think he could smell Segun on every page. Reading through them, he would stop at the lines Segun had underlined, or the notes written in the margin, still almost unsure if he was dreaming or not, unsure if Segun was really dead, gone forever.

In time, August joined the Socialist Students' Forum. Thought he had attended several meetings when Segun was still alive, he never joined. He had never considered himself a comrade, not really. But now, more and more, the SSF made sense. Sometimes things were so unredeemable that only destruction was suitable. That day was the first time he was attending a meeting that Segun was not a part of. August took a breath and looked around the room. These people had been Segun's comrades. They had known Segun too; they were his friends. As always, the meetings started with arranging the seats into a semicircle. Several comrades shook August's hand.

"Comrade, it's been awhile," they said. "Welcome back."

"I want to become a member," August told Ngozi, who managed such things.

"Oh. That's good news," she said. "After the meeting, let's talk."

August nodded and went to find a seat, feeling as though he had done something important, something that would have lit up Segun's face and made him proud.

"Comrades, let's sing 'The Internationale,'" someone said, and the seats groaned against the tiled floor as people stood and began to sing energetically. At the first meeting Segun took him to, August had to read the lyrics of "The Internationale" from his phone, but now, as he sang along, he realized he knew the words by heart.

ACKNOWLEDGMENTS

I would like to thank Favour Orji, for reading my early works, for suggesting and editing, and for encouraging me to keep on writing. I thank him for being such a wonderful friend who was always available to hear my stories and assure me that it was necessary to tell them. His moral support was instrumental in my becoming a writer.

My editor, Roxane Gay, has been so wonderful throughout the process of polishing my manuscript into a novel. I am grateful to her for seeing my vision and being so committed to helping me create the very best version of this book.

Warren Jeremy Rourke did everything he could to make my road less daunting. He fought to make sure this book found the best home it could possibly have. I thank him for caring, and for showing me the way.

My agent, Emma Shercliff, went above and beyond to ensure that my experience publishing my first book was as seamless as possible. She checked up on me, helped with reading and edits, and was a constant voice of encouragement and support throughout the process. Thank you.

I would also like to thank Dr. Idris Ajia, my dear comrade, who has been such a wonderful friend, and who was always ready to help me in whatever way I needed help. Many times, I would have fallen if his kindness was not there to catch me.

And finally, I would also like to thank my comrade, Lea. They were such a rock of support while I finished up this book and sent it into the world. Thank you, thank you, thank you, for the laughter and the joy and the revolutionary love.